THE
GRAVEYARD
BOOK VOLUME 2

THE GRAVEYARD BOOK
Volume 2

Based on the novel by: NEIL GAIMAN
Adapted by: P. CRAIG RUSSELL

Illustrated by: DAVID LAFUENTE SCOTT HAMPTON
P. CRAIG RUSSELL KEVIN NOWLAN GALEN SHOWMAN

Colorist: LOVERN KINDZIERSKI

Letterer: RICK PARKER

HARPER
An Imprint of Harper Collins*Publishers*

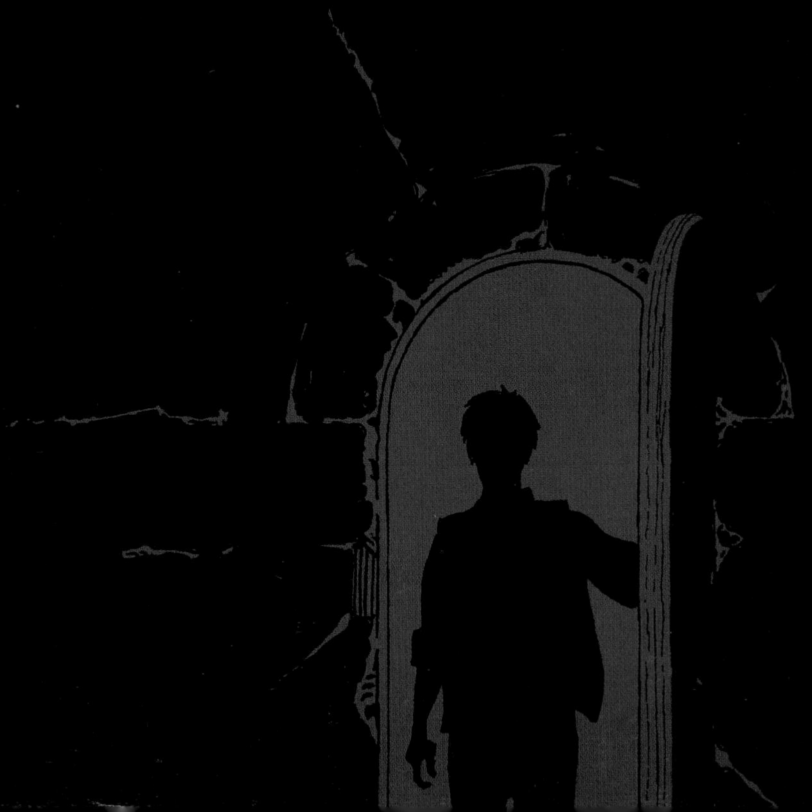

For information address HarperCollins Children's Books, a division of HarperCollins Publishers, 195 Broadway, New York, NY 10007.
www.harpercollinschildrens.com

Library of Congress catalog card number: 2013953799
ISBN 978-0-06-219483-1 (trade bdg.)
ISBN 978-0-06-219484-8 (pbk.)

Typography by Brian Durniak
15 16 17 18 19 SCP 10 9 8 7 6 5 4 3 2
First Edition

To Brooke and Andrew, Jadon and Josiah, and Naomi and Emmeline
(and special thanks to Galen Showman and Scott Hampton for service above and beyond)
—P.C.R.

6
Nobody Owens' School Days

Illustrated by David Lafuente

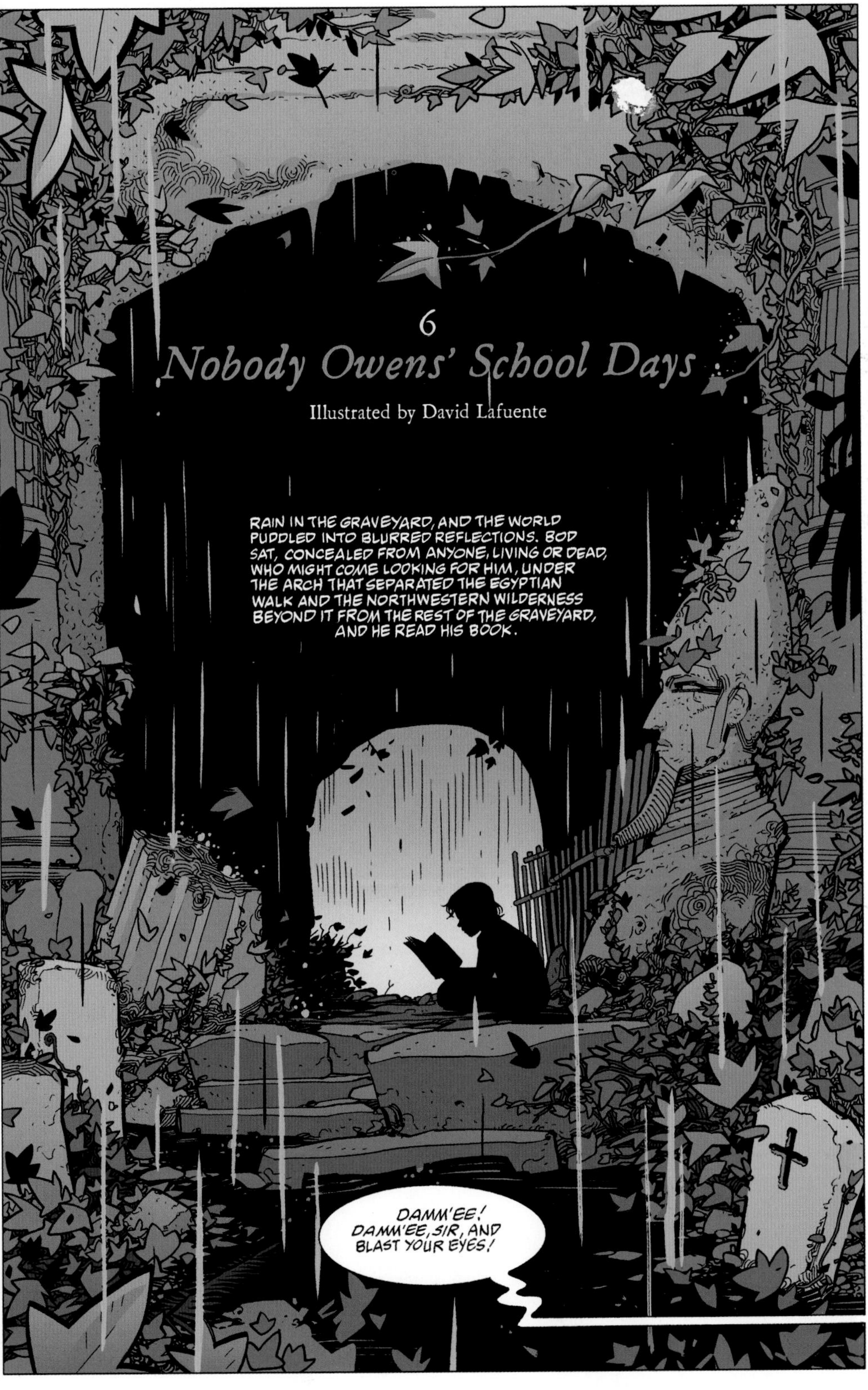
RAIN IN THE GRAVEYARD, AND THE WORLD PUDDLED INTO BLURRED REFLECTIONS. BOD SAT, CONCEALED FROM ANYONE, LIVING OR DEAD, WHO MIGHT COME LOOKING FOR HIM, UNDER THE ARCH THAT SEPARATED THE EGYPTIAN WALK AND THE NORTHWESTERN WILDERNESS BEYOND IT FROM THE REST OF THE GRAVEYARD, AND HE READ HIS BOOK.
DAMM'EE! DAMM'EE, SIR, AND BLAST YOUR EYES!

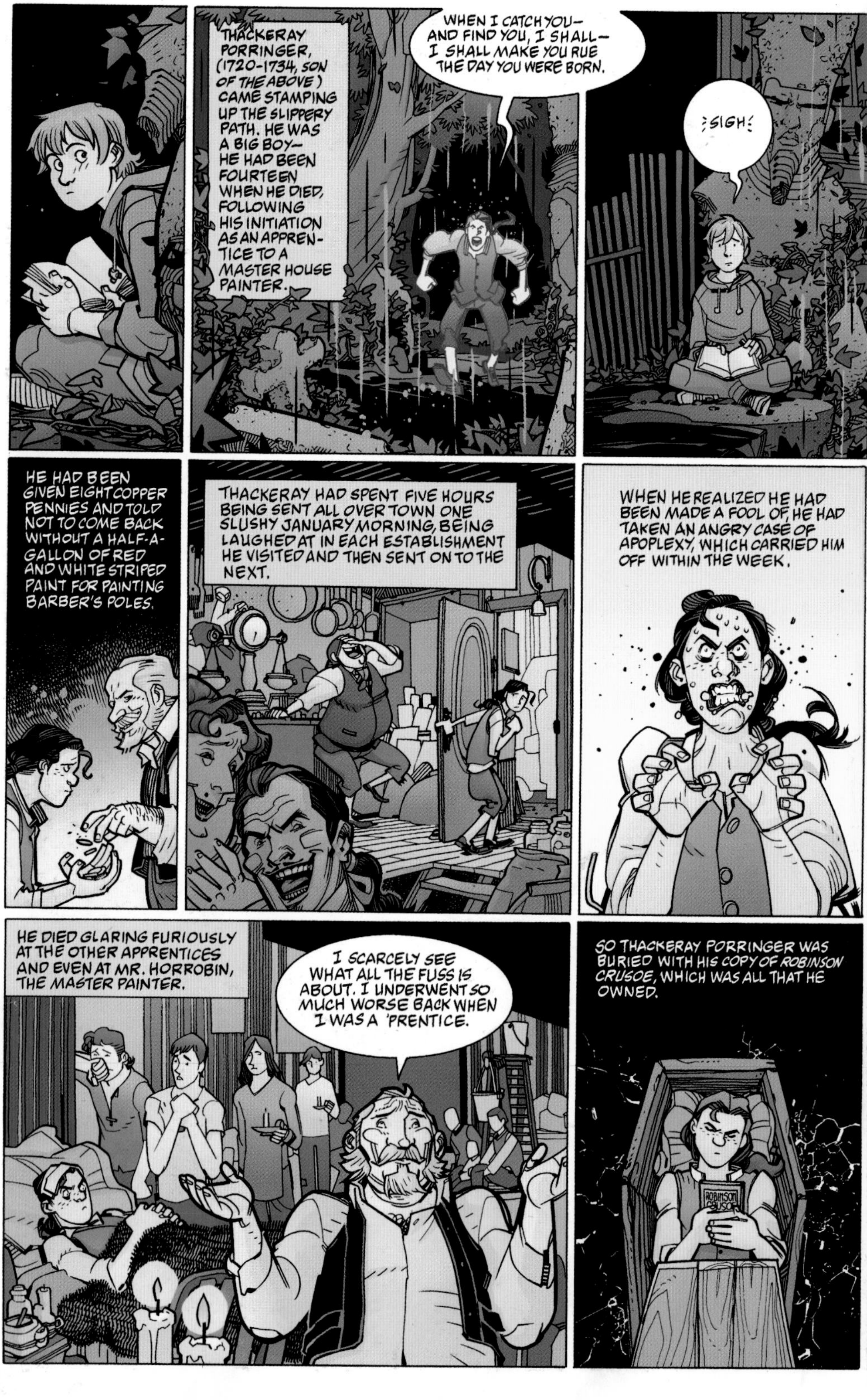
THACKERAY PORRINGER, (1720-1734, SON OF THE ABOVE) CAME STAMPING UP THE SLIPPERY PATH. HE WAS A BIG BOY—HE HAD BEEN FOURTEEN WHEN HE DIED, FOLLOWING HIS INITIATION AS AN APPRENTICE TO A MASTER HOUSE PAINTER.
WHEN I CATCH YOU—AND FIND YOU, I SHALL—I SHALL MAKE YOU RUE THE DAY YOU WERE BORN.
SIGH
HE HAD BEEN GIVEN EIGHT COPPER PENNIES AND TOLD NOT TO COME BACK WITHOUT A HALF-A-GALLON OF RED AND WHITE STRIPED PAINT FOR PAINTING BARBER'S POLES.
THACKERAY HAD SPENT FIVE HOURS BEING SENT ALL OVER TOWN ONE SLUSHY JANUARY MORNING, BEING LAUGHED AT IN EACH ESTABLISHMENT HE VISITED AND THEN SENT ON TO THE NEXT.
WHEN HE REALIZED HE HAD BEEN MADE A FOOL OF, HE HAD TAKEN AN ANGRY CASE OF APOPLEXY, WHICH CARRIED HIM OFF WITHIN THE WEEK.
HE DIED GLARING FURIOUSLY AT THE OTHER APPRENTICES AND EVEN AT MR. HORROBIN, THE MASTER PAINTER.
I SCARCELY SEE WHAT ALL THE FUSS IS ABOUT. I UNDERWENT SO MUCH WORSE BACK WHEN I WAS A 'PRENTICE.
SO THACKERAY PORRINGER WAS BURIED WITH HIS COPY OF ROBINSON CRUSOE, WHICH WAS ALL THAT HE OWNED.
ROBINSON CRUSOE

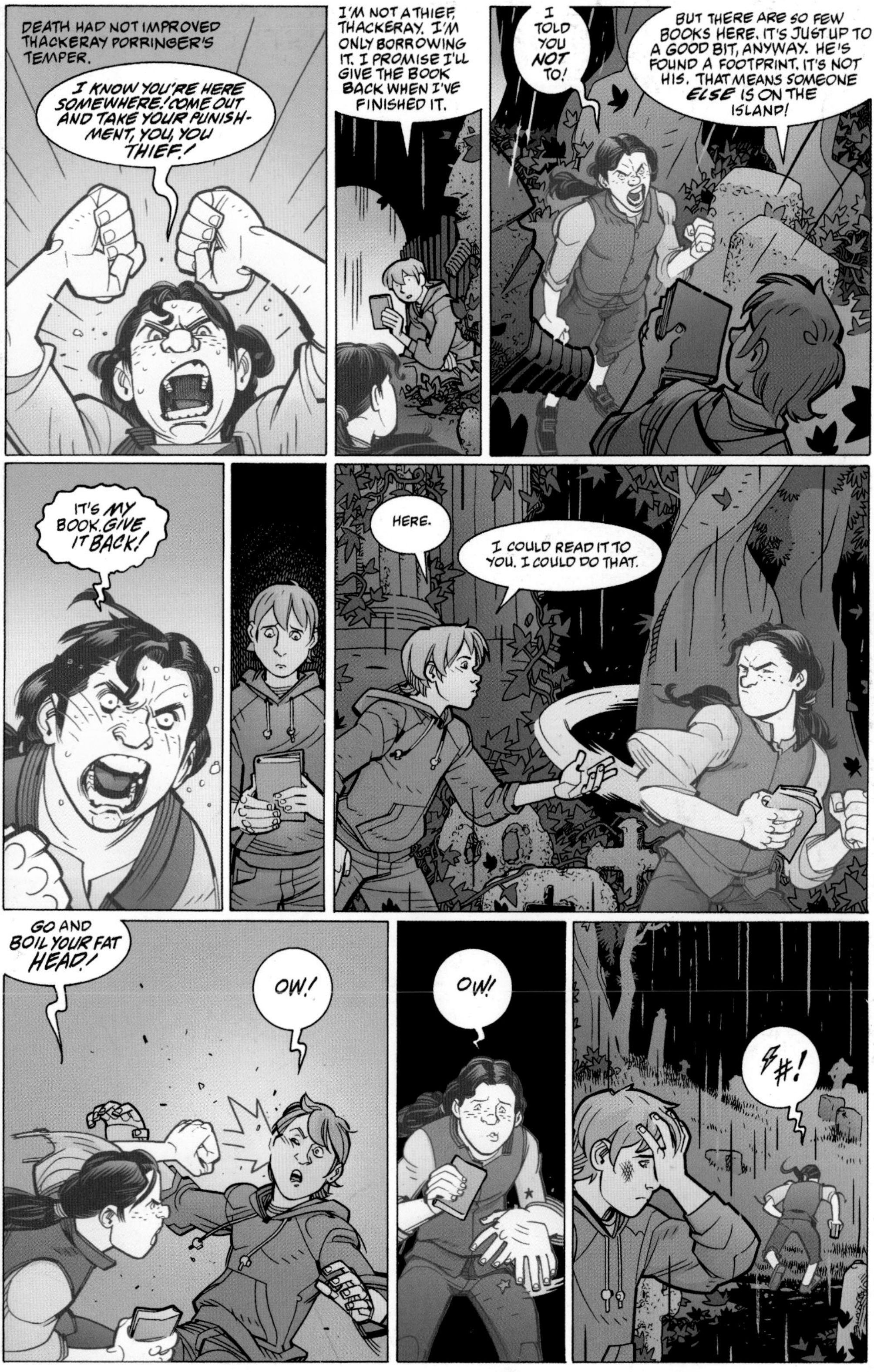
DEATH HAD NOT IMPROVED THACKERAY PORRINGER'S TEMPER.
I KNOW YOU'RE HERE SOMEWHERE! COME OUT AND TAKE YOUR PUNISHMENT, YOU, YOU THIEF!
I'M NOT A THIEF, THACKERAY. I'M ONLY BORROWING IT. I PROMISE I'LL GIVE THE BOOK BACK WHEN I'VE FINISHED IT.
I TOLD YOU NOT TO!
BUT THERE ARE SO FEW BOOKS HERE. IT'S JUST UP TO A GOOD BIT, ANYWAY. HE'S FOUND A FOOTPRINT. IT'S NOT HIS. THAT MEANS SOMEONE ELSE IS ON THE ISLAND!
IT'S MY BOOK. GIVE IT BACK!
HERE.
I COULD READ IT TO YOU. I COULD DO THAT.
GO AND BOIL YOUR FAT HEAD!
OW!
OW!
$#!

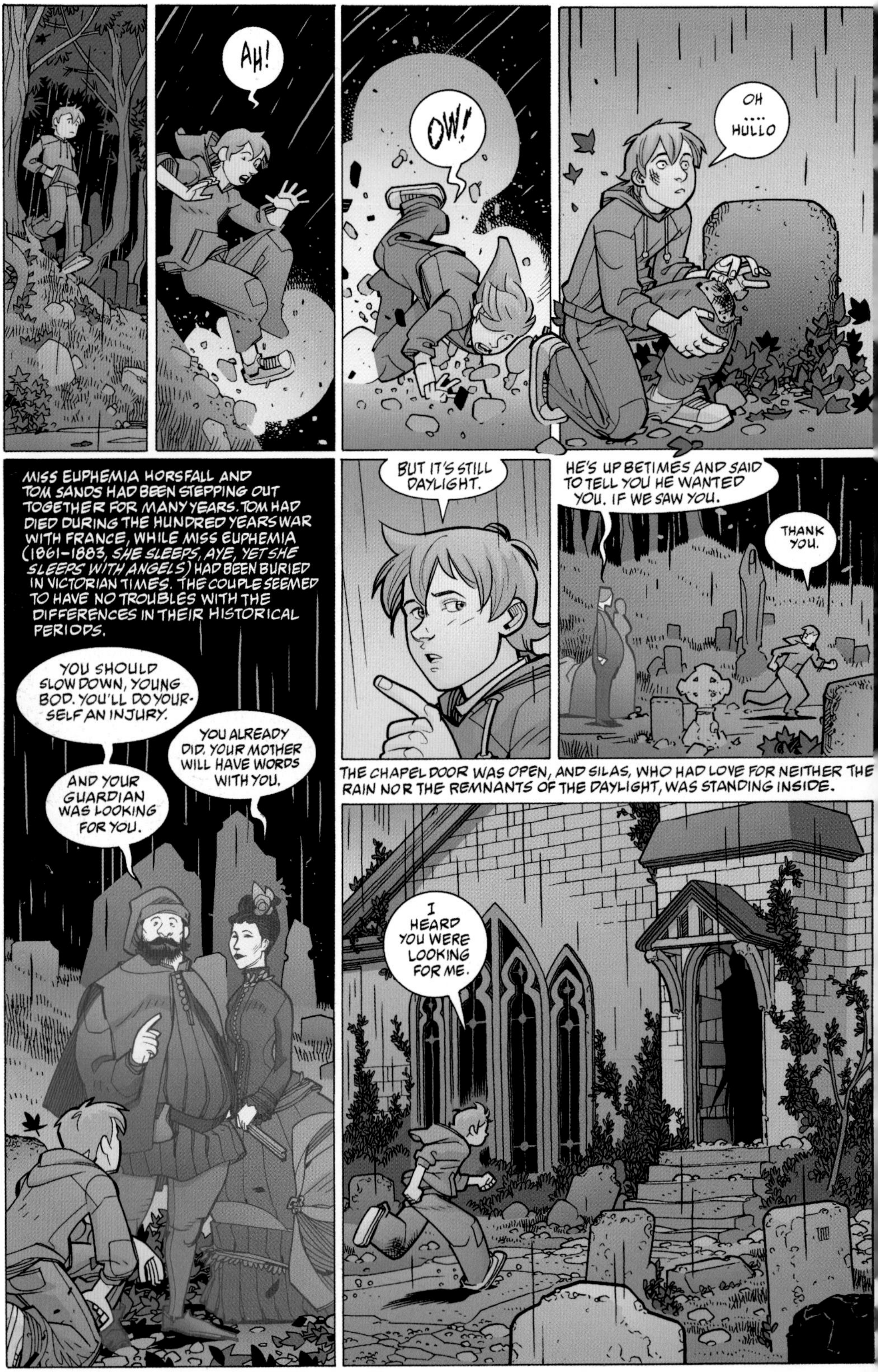
AH!
OW!
OH .... HULLO
MISS EUPHEMIA HORSFALL AND TOM SANDS HAD BEEN STEPPING OUT TOGETHER FOR MANY YEARS. TOM HAD DIED DURING THE HUNDRED YEARS WAR WITH FRANCE, WHILE MISS EUPHEMIA (1861–1883, SHE SLEEPS, AYE, YET SHE SLEEPS WITH ANGELS) HAD BEEN BURIED IN VICTORIAN TIMES. THE COUPLE SEEMED TO HAVE NO TROUBLES WITH THE DIFFERENCES IN THEIR HISTORICAL PERIODS.
YOU SHOULD SLOW DOWN, YOUNG BOD. YOU'LL DO YOURSELF AN INJURY.
YOU ALREADY DID. YOUR MOTHER WILL HAVE WORDS WITH YOU.
AND YOUR GUARDIAN WAS LOOKING FOR YOU.
BUT IT'S STILL DAYLIGHT.
HE'S UP BETIMES AND SAID TO TELL YOU HE WANTED YOU. IF WE SAW YOU.
THANK YOU.
THE CHAPEL DOOR WAS OPEN, AND SILAS, WHO HAD LOVE FOR NEITHER THE RAIN NOR THE REMNANTS OF THE DAYLIGHT, WAS STANDING INSIDE.
I HEARD YOU WERE LOOKING FOR ME.

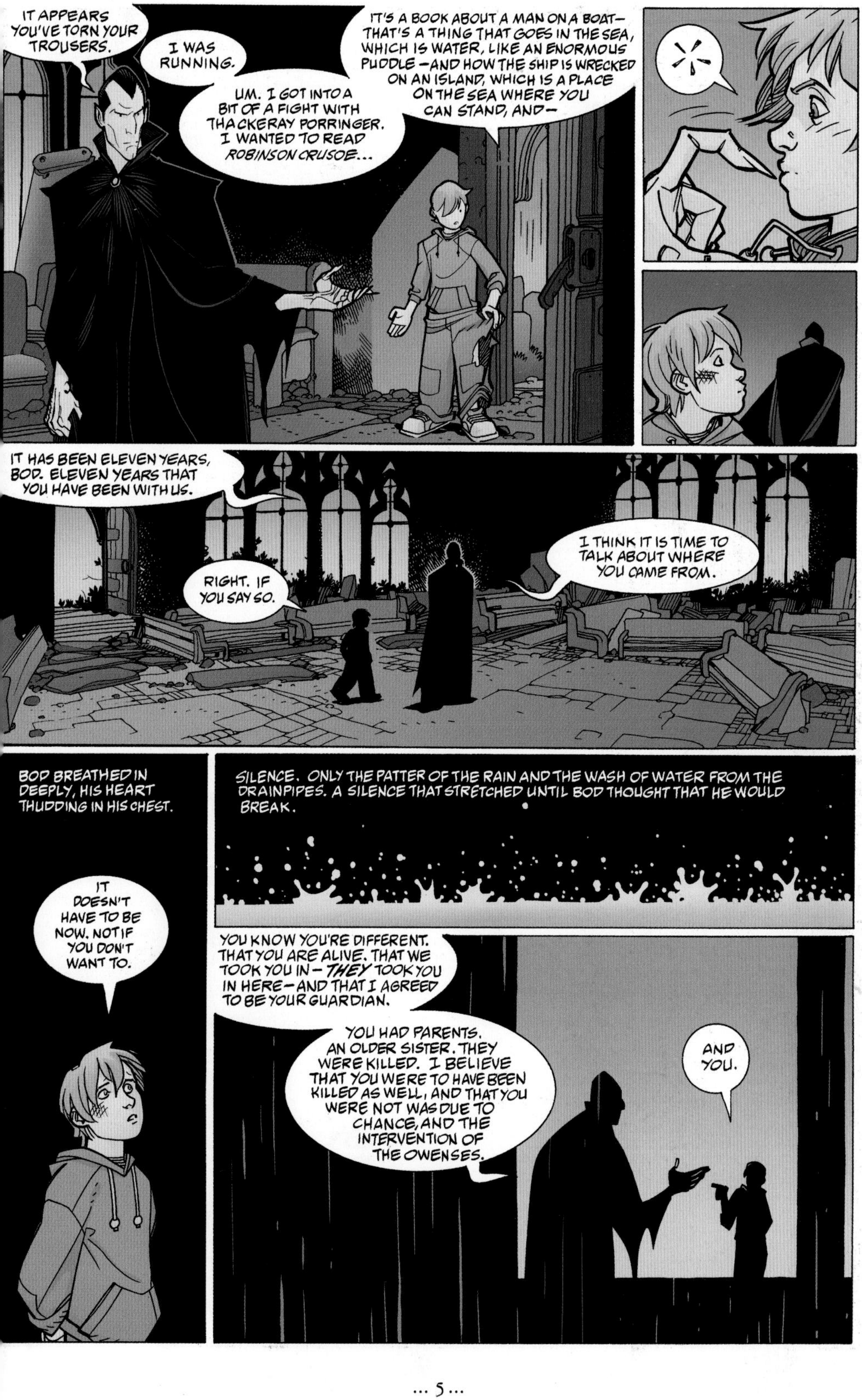

IT APPEARS YOU'VE TORN YOUR TROUSERS.
I WAS RUNNING.
UM. I GOT INTO A BIT OF A FIGHT WITH THACKERAY PORRINGER. I WANTED TO READ *ROBINSON CRUSOE*...
IT'S A BOOK ABOUT A MAN ON A BOAT— THAT'S A THING THAT GOES IN THE SEA, WHICH IS WATER, LIKE AN ENORMOUS PUDDLE —AND HOW THE SHIP IS WRECKED ON AN ISLAND, WHICH IS A PLACE ON THE SEA WHERE YOU CAN STAND, AND—
IT HAS BEEN ELEVEN YEARS, BOD. ELEVEN YEARS THAT YOU HAVE BEEN WITH US.
RIGHT. IF YOU SAY SO.
I THINK IT IS TIME TO TALK ABOUT WHERE YOU CAME FROM.
BOD BREATHED IN DEEPLY, HIS HEART THUDDING IN HIS CHEST.
SILENCE. ONLY THE PATTER OF THE RAIN AND THE WASH OF WATER FROM THE DRAINPIPES. A SILENCE THAT STRETCHED UNTIL BOD THOUGHT THAT HE WOULD BREAK.
IT DOESN'T HAVE TO BE NOW. NOT IF YOU DON'T WANT TO.
YOU KNOW YOU'RE DIFFERENT. THAT YOU ARE ALIVE. THAT WE TOOK YOU IN—*THEY* TOOK YOU IN HERE—AND THAT I AGREED TO BE YOUR GUARDIAN.
YOU HAD PARENTS. AN OLDER SISTER. THEY WERE KILLED. I BELIEVE THAT YOU WERE TO HAVE BEEN KILLED AS WELL, AND THAT YOU WERE NOT WAS DUE TO CHANCE, AND THE INTERVENTION OF THE OWENSES.
AND YOU.

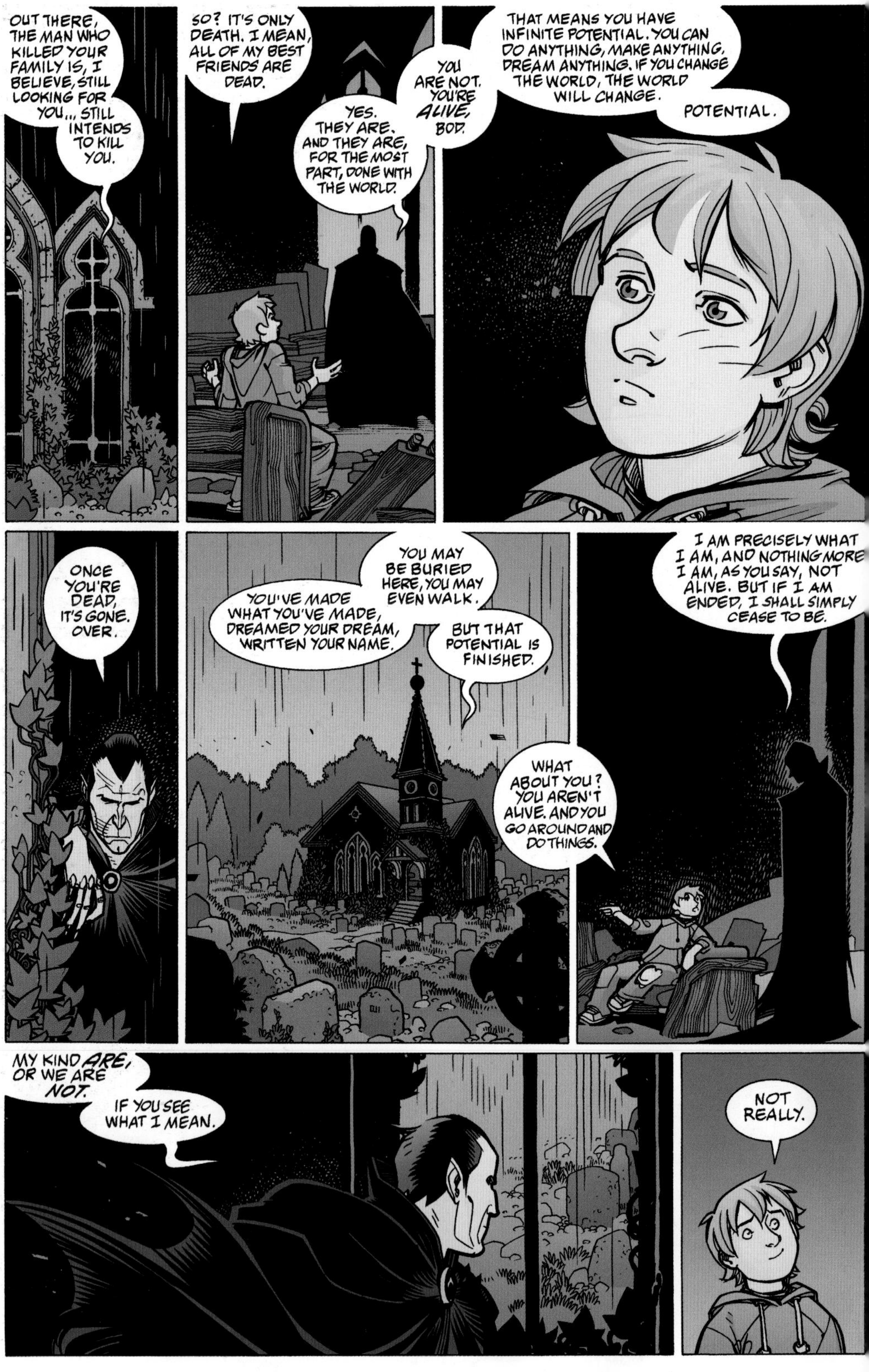
OUT THERE, THE MAN WHO KILLED YOUR FAMILY IS, I BELIEVE, STILL LOOKING FOR YOU... STILL INTENDS TO KILL YOU.
SO? IT'S ONLY DEATH. I MEAN, ALL OF MY BEST FRIENDS ARE DEAD.
YES. THEY ARE. AND THEY ARE, FOR THE MOST PART, DONE WITH THE WORLD.
YOU ARE NOT. YOU'RE ALIVE, BOD.
THAT MEANS YOU HAVE INFINITE POTENTIAL. YOU CAN DO ANYTHING, MAKE ANYTHING, DREAM ANYTHING. IF YOU CHANGE THE WORLD, THE WORLD WILL CHANGE.
POTENTIAL.
ONCE YOU'RE DEAD, IT'S GONE. OVER.
YOU'VE MADE WHAT YOU'VE MADE, DREAMED YOUR DREAM, WRITTEN YOUR NAME.
YOU MAY BE BURIED HERE, YOU MAY EVEN WALK.
BUT THAT POTENTIAL IS FINISHED.
WHAT ABOUT YOU? YOU AREN'T ALIVE. AND YOU GO AROUND AND DO THINGS.
I AM PRECISELY WHAT I AM, AND NOTHING MORE. I AM, AS YOU SAY, NOT ALIVE. BUT IF I AM ENDED, I SHALL SIMPLY CEASE TO BE.
MY KIND ARE, OR WE ARE NOT.
IF YOU SEE WHAT I MEAN.
NOT REALLY.

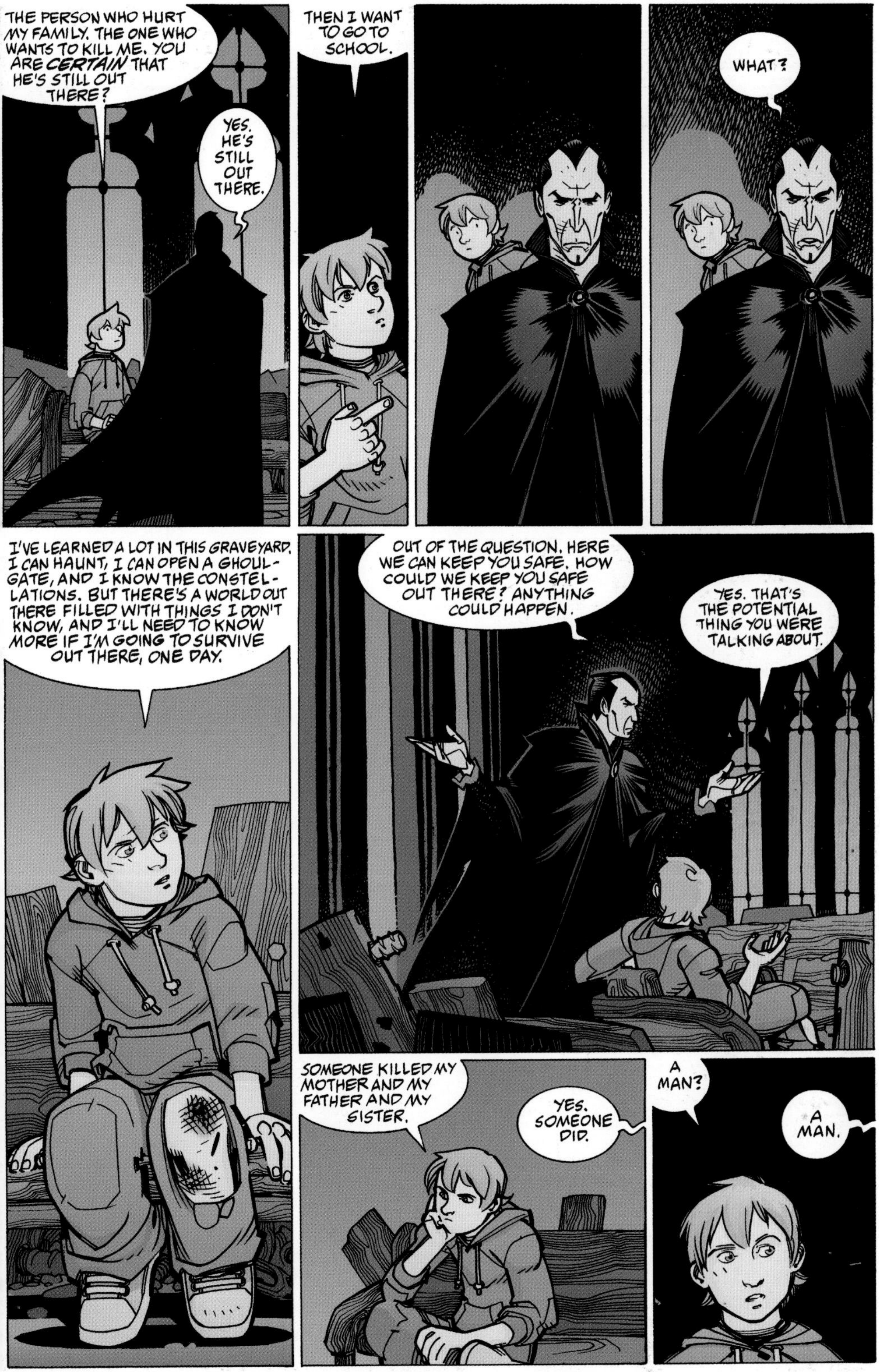
THE PERSON WHO HURT MY FAMILY. THE ONE WHO WANTS TO KILL ME. YOU ARE CERTAIN THAT HE'S STILL OUT THERE?
YES. HE'S STILL OUT THERE.
THEN I WANT TO GO TO SCHOOL.
WHAT?
I'VE LEARNED A LOT IN THIS GRAVEYARD. I CAN HAUNT, I CAN OPEN A GHOUL-GATE, AND I KNOW THE CONSTEL-LATIONS. BUT THERE'S A WORLD OUT THERE FILLED WITH THINGS I DON'T KNOW, AND I'LL NEED TO KNOW MORE IF I'M GOING TO SURVIVE OUT THERE, ONE DAY.
OUT OF THE QUESTION. HERE WE CAN KEEP YOU SAFE. HOW COULD WE KEEP YOU SAFE OUT THERE? ANYTHING COULD HAPPEN.
YES. THAT'S THE POTENTIAL THING YOU WERE TALKING ABOUT.
SOMEONE KILLED MY MOTHER AND MY FATHER AND MY SISTER.
YES. SOMEONE DID.
A MAN?
A MAN.

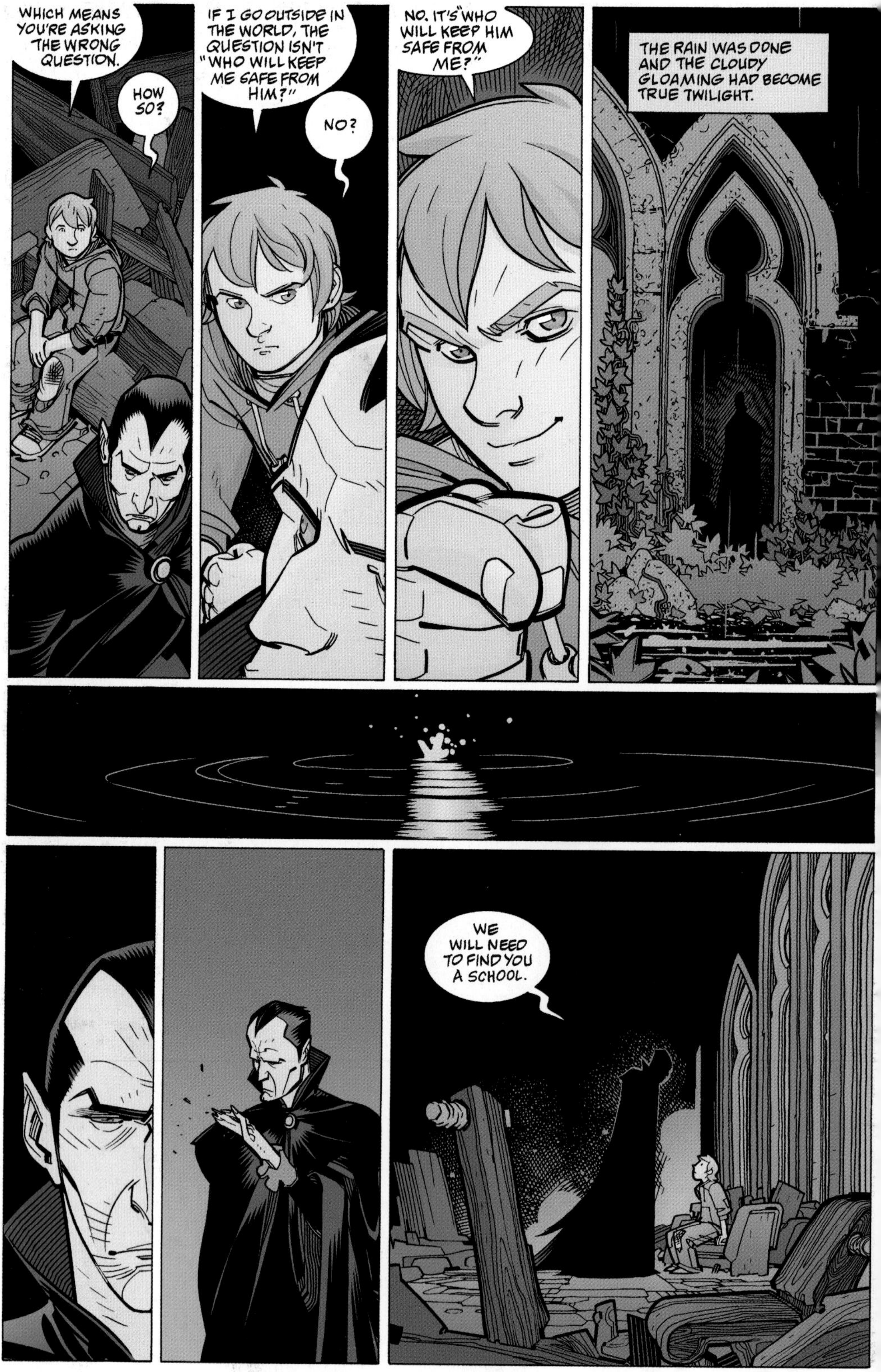
WHICH MEANS YOU'RE ASKING THE WRONG QUESTION.
HOW SO?
IF I GO OUTSIDE IN THE WORLD, THE QUESTION ISN'T "WHO WILL KEEP ME SAFE FROM HIM?"
NO?
NO. IT'S "WHO WILL KEEP HIM SAFE FROM ME?"
THE RAIN WAS DONE AND THE CLOUDY GLOAMING HAD BECOME TRUE TWILIGHT.
WE WILL NEED TO FIND YOU A SCHOOL.

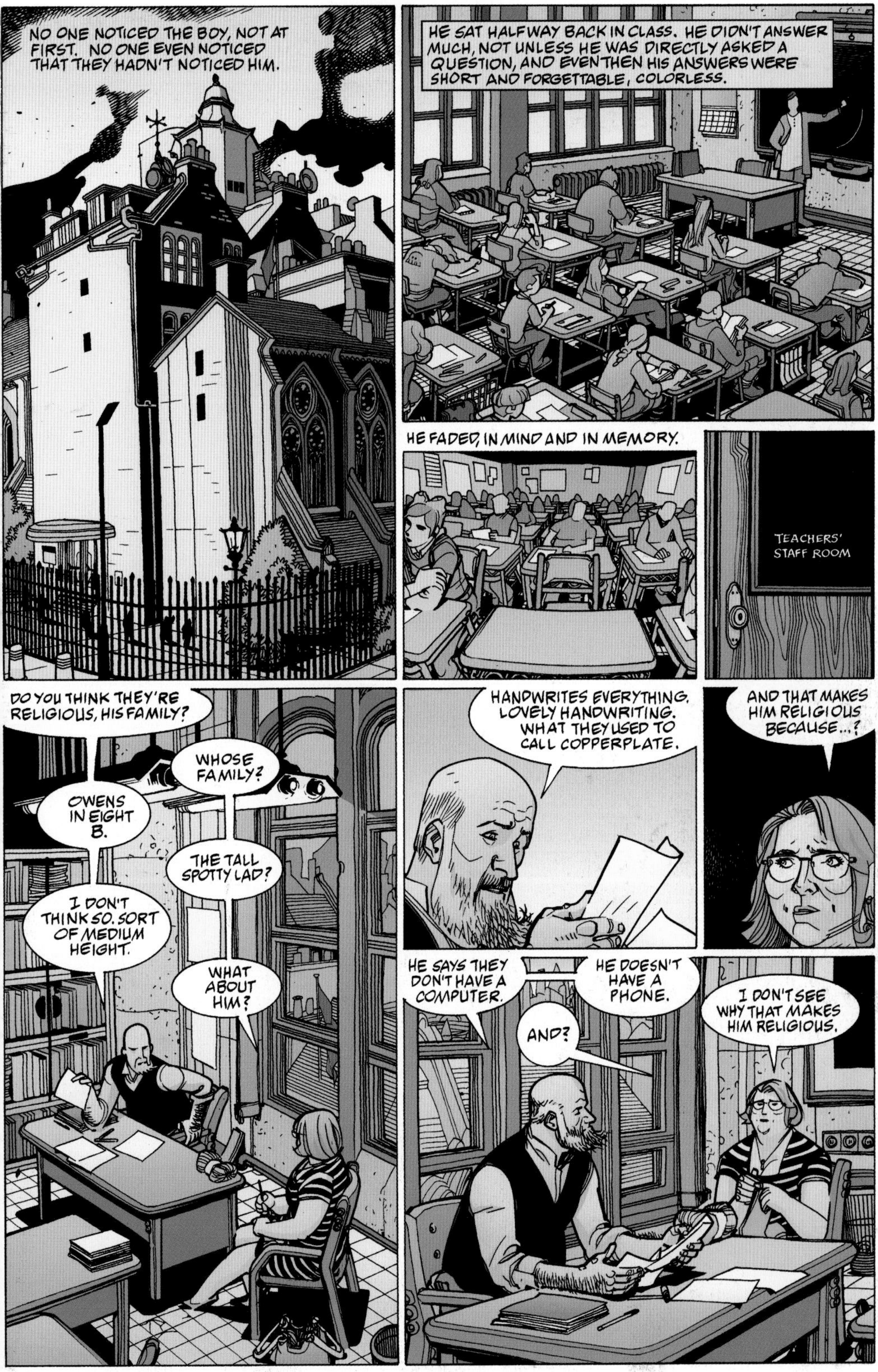
NO ONE NOTICED THE BOY, NOT AT FIRST. NO ONE EVEN NOTICED THAT THEY HADN'T NOTICED HIM.
HE SAT HALFWAY BACK IN CLASS. HE DIDN'T ANSWER MUCH, NOT UNLESS HE WAS DIRECTLY ASKED A QUESTION, AND EVEN THEN HIS ANSWERS WERE SHORT AND FORGETTABLE, COLORLESS.
HE FADED, IN MIND AND IN MEMORY.
TEACHERS' STAFF ROOM
DO YOU THINK THEY'RE RELIGIOUS, HIS FAMILY?
WHOSE FAMILY?
OWENS IN EIGHT B.
THE TALL SPOTTY LAD?
I DON'T THINK SO. SORT OF MEDIUM HEIGHT.
WHAT ABOUT HIM?
HANDWRITES EVERYTHING. LOVELY HANDWRITING. WHAT THEY USED TO CALL COPPERPLATE.
AND THAT MAKES HIM RELIGIOUS BECAUSE...?
HE SAYS THEY DON'T HAVE A COMPUTER.
HE DOESN'T HAVE A PHONE.
AND?
I DON'T SEE WHY THAT MAKES HIM RELIGIOUS.

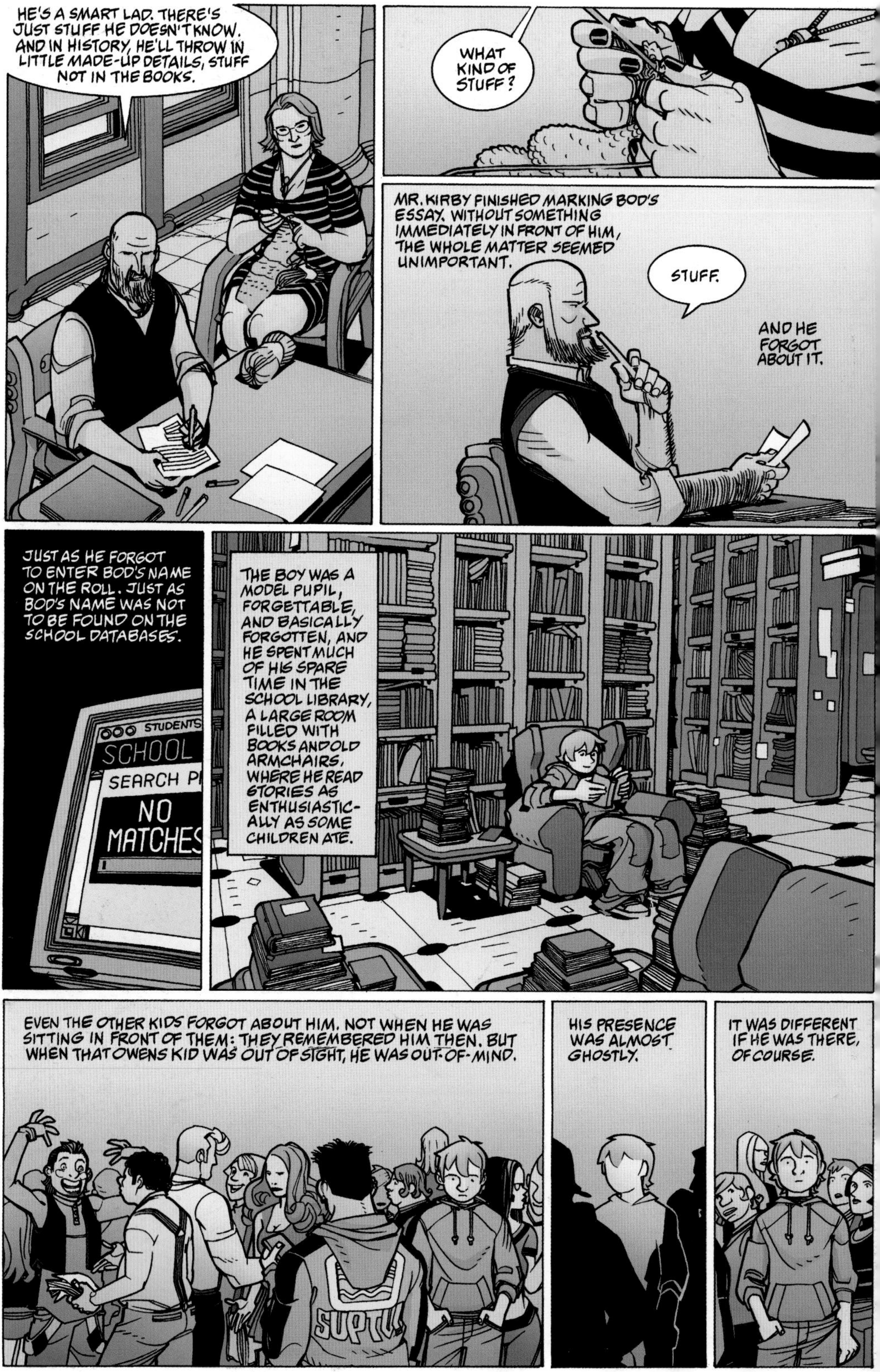
HE'S A SMART LAD. THERE'S JUST STUFF HE DOESN'T KNOW. AND IN HISTORY, HE'LL THROW IN LITTLE MADE-UP DETAILS, STUFF NOT IN THE BOOKS.
WHAT KIND OF STUFF?
MR. KIRBY FINISHED MARKING BOD'S ESSAY. WITHOUT SOMETHING IMMEDIATELY IN FRONT OF HIM, THE WHOLE MATTER SEEMED UNIMPORTANT.
STUFF.
AND HE FORGOT ABOUT IT.
JUST AS HE FORGOT TO ENTER BOD'S NAME ON THE ROLL. JUST AS BOD'S NAME WAS NOT TO BE FOUND ON THE SCHOOL DATABASES.
STUDENTS
SCHOOL
SEARCH P
NO MATCHES
THE BOY WAS A MODEL PUPIL, FORGETTABLE, AND BASICALLY FORGOTTEN, AND HE SPENT MUCH OF HIS SPARE TIME IN THE SCHOOL LIBRARY, A LARGE ROOM FILLED WITH BOOKS AND OLD ARMCHAIRS, WHERE HE READ STORIES AS ENTHUSIASTICALLY AS SOME CHILDREN ATE.
EVEN THE OTHER KIDS FORGOT ABOUT HIM. NOT WHEN HE WAS SITTING IN FRONT OF THEM: THEY REMEMBERED HIM THEN. BUT WHEN THAT OWENS KID WAS OUT OF SIGHT, HE WAS OUT-OF-MIND.
HIS PRESENCE WAS ALMOST GHOSTLY.
IT WAS DIFFERENT IF HE WAS THERE, OF COURSE.

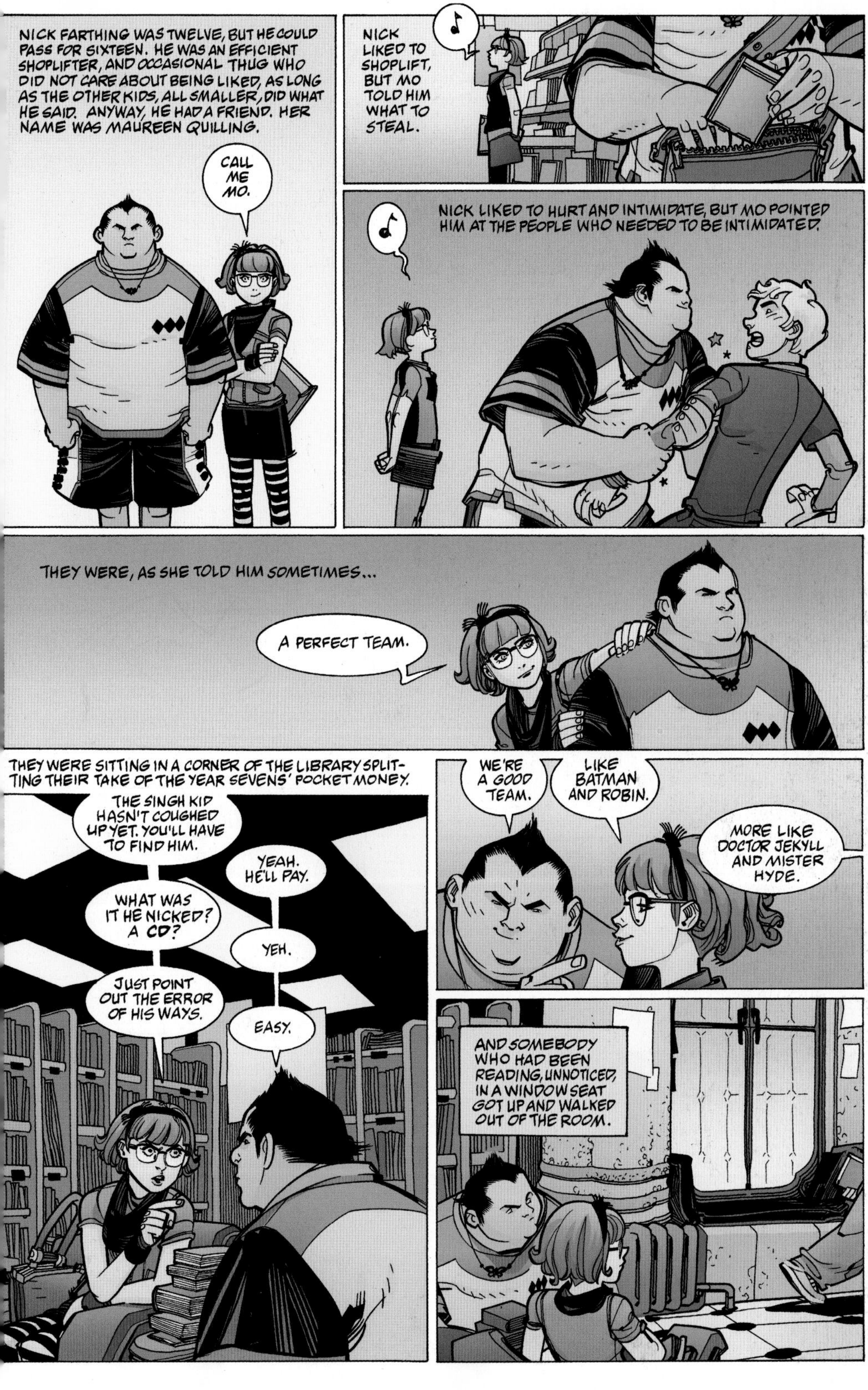
NICK FARTHING WAS TWELVE, BUT HE COULD PASS FOR SIXTEEN. HE WAS AN EFFICIENT SHOPLIFTER, AND OCCASIONAL THUG WHO DID NOT CARE ABOUT BEING LIKED, AS LONG AS THE OTHER KIDS, ALL SMALLER, DID WHAT HE SAID. ANYWAY, HE HAD A FRIEND. HER NAME WAS MAUREEN QUILLING.
CALL ME MO.
NICK LIKED TO SHOPLIFT, BUT MO TOLD HIM WHAT TO STEAL.
♪
NICK LIKED TO HURT AND INTIMIDATE, BUT MO POINTED HIM AT THE PEOPLE WHO NEEDED TO BE INTIMIDATED.
♪
THEY WERE, AS SHE TOLD HIM SOMETIMES...
A PERFECT TEAM.
THEY WERE SITTING IN A CORNER OF THE LIBRARY SPLITTING THEIR TAKE OF THE YEAR SEVENS' POCKET MONEY.
THE SINGH KID HASN'T COUGHED UP YET. YOU'LL HAVE TO FIND HIM.
YEAH. HE'LL PAY.
WHAT WAS IT HE NICKED? A CD?
YEH.
JUST POINT OUT THE ERROR OF HIS WAYS.
EASY.
WE'RE A GOOD TEAM.
LIKE BATMAN AND ROBIN.
MORE LIKE DOCTOR JEKYLL AND MISTER HYDE.
AND SOMEBODY WHO HAD BEEN READING, UNNOTICED, IN A WINDOW SEAT GOT UP AND WALKED OUT OF THE ROOM.

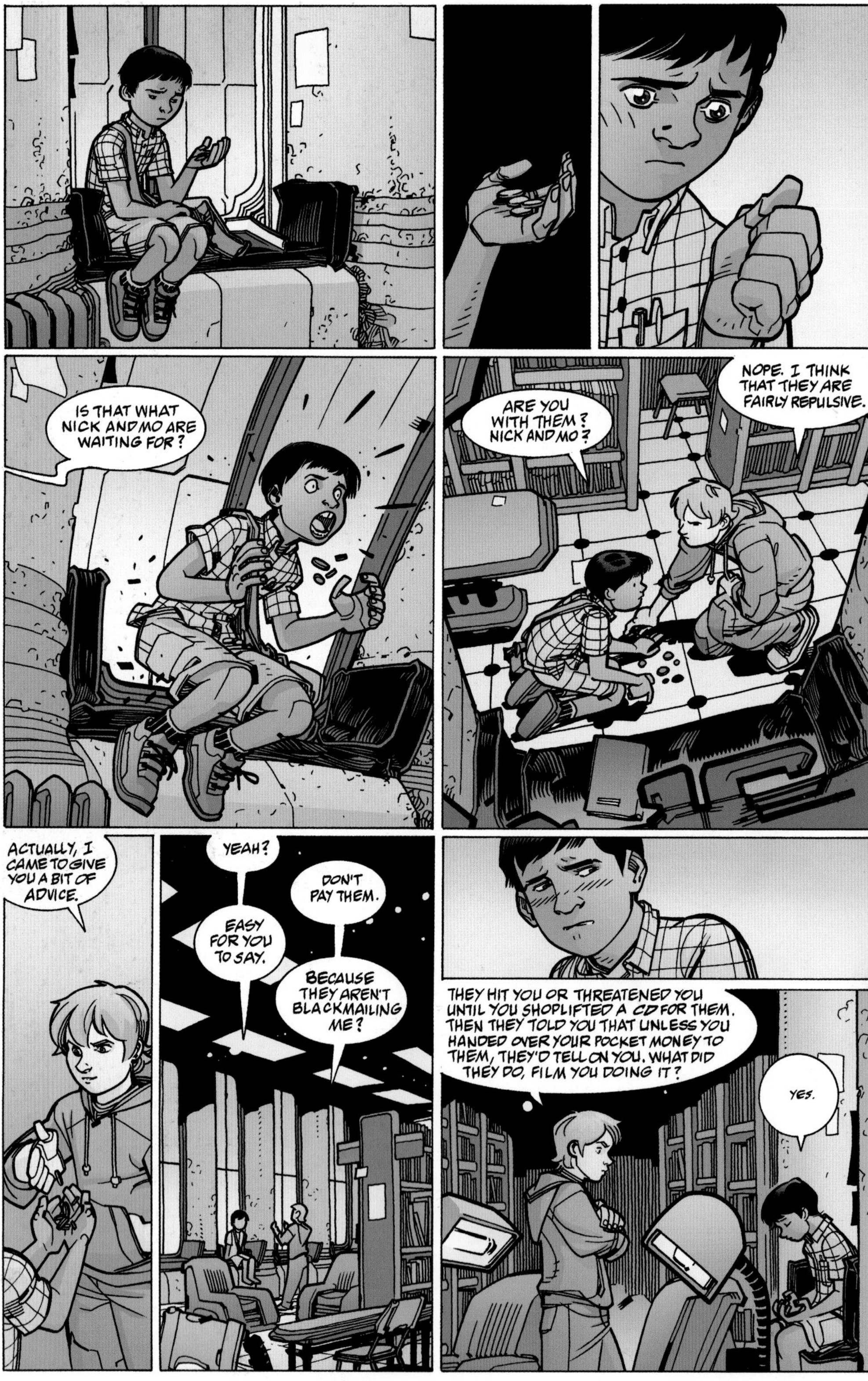
IS THAT WHAT NICK AND MO ARE WAITING FOR?
ARE YOU WITH THEM? NICK AND MO?
NOPE. I THINK THAT THEY ARE FAIRLY REPULSIVE.
ACTUALLY, I CAME TO GIVE YOU A BIT OF ADVICE.
YEAH?
DON'T PAY THEM.
EASY FOR YOU TO SAY.
BECAUSE THEY AREN'T BLACKMAILING ME?
THEY HIT YOU OR THREATENED YOU UNTIL YOU SHOPLIFTED A CD FOR THEM. THEN THEY TOLD YOU THAT UNLESS YOU HANDED OVER YOUR POCKET MONEY TO THEM, THEY'D TELL ON YOU. WHAT DID THEY DO, FILM YOU DOING IT?
YES.

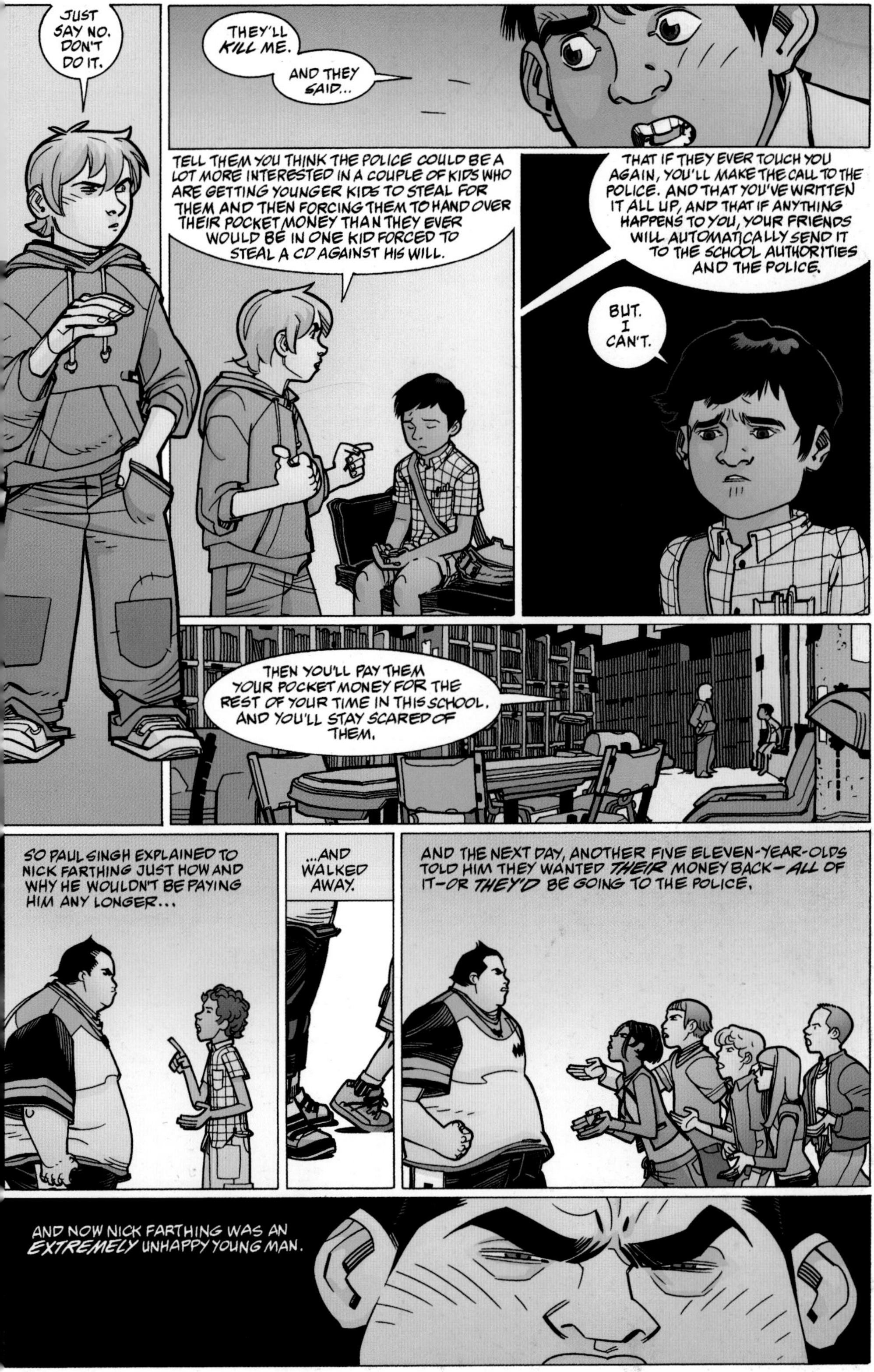

JUST SAY NO. DON'T DO IT.
THEY'LL KILL ME.
AND THEY SAID...
TELL THEM YOU THINK THE POLICE COULD BE A LOT MORE INTERESTED IN A COUPLE OF KIDS WHO ARE GETTING YOUNGER KIDS TO STEAL FOR THEM AND THEN FORCING THEM TO HAND OVER THEIR POCKET MONEY THAN THEY EVER WOULD BE IN ONE KID FORCED TO STEAL A CD AGAINST HIS WILL.
THAT IF THEY EVER TOUCH YOU AGAIN, YOU'LL MAKE THE CALL TO THE POLICE. AND THAT YOU'VE WRITTEN IT ALL UP, AND THAT IF ANYTHING HAPPENS TO YOU, YOUR FRIENDS WILL AUTOMATICALLY SEND IT TO THE SCHOOL AUTHORITIES AND THE POLICE.
BUT. I CAN'T.
THEN YOU'LL PAY THEM YOUR POCKET MONEY FOR THE REST OF YOUR TIME IN THIS SCHOOL, AND YOU'LL STAY SCARED OF THEM.
SO PAUL SINGH EXPLAINED TO NICK FARTHING JUST HOW AND WHY HE WOULDN'T BE PAYING HIM ANY LONGER...
...AND WALKED AWAY.
AND THE NEXT DAY, ANOTHER FIVE ELEVEN-YEAR-OLDS TOLD HIM THEY WANTED THEIR MONEY BACK—ALL OF IT—OR THEY'D BE GOING TO THE POLICE.
AND NOW NICK FARTHING WAS AN EXTREMELY UNHAPPY YOUNG MAN.

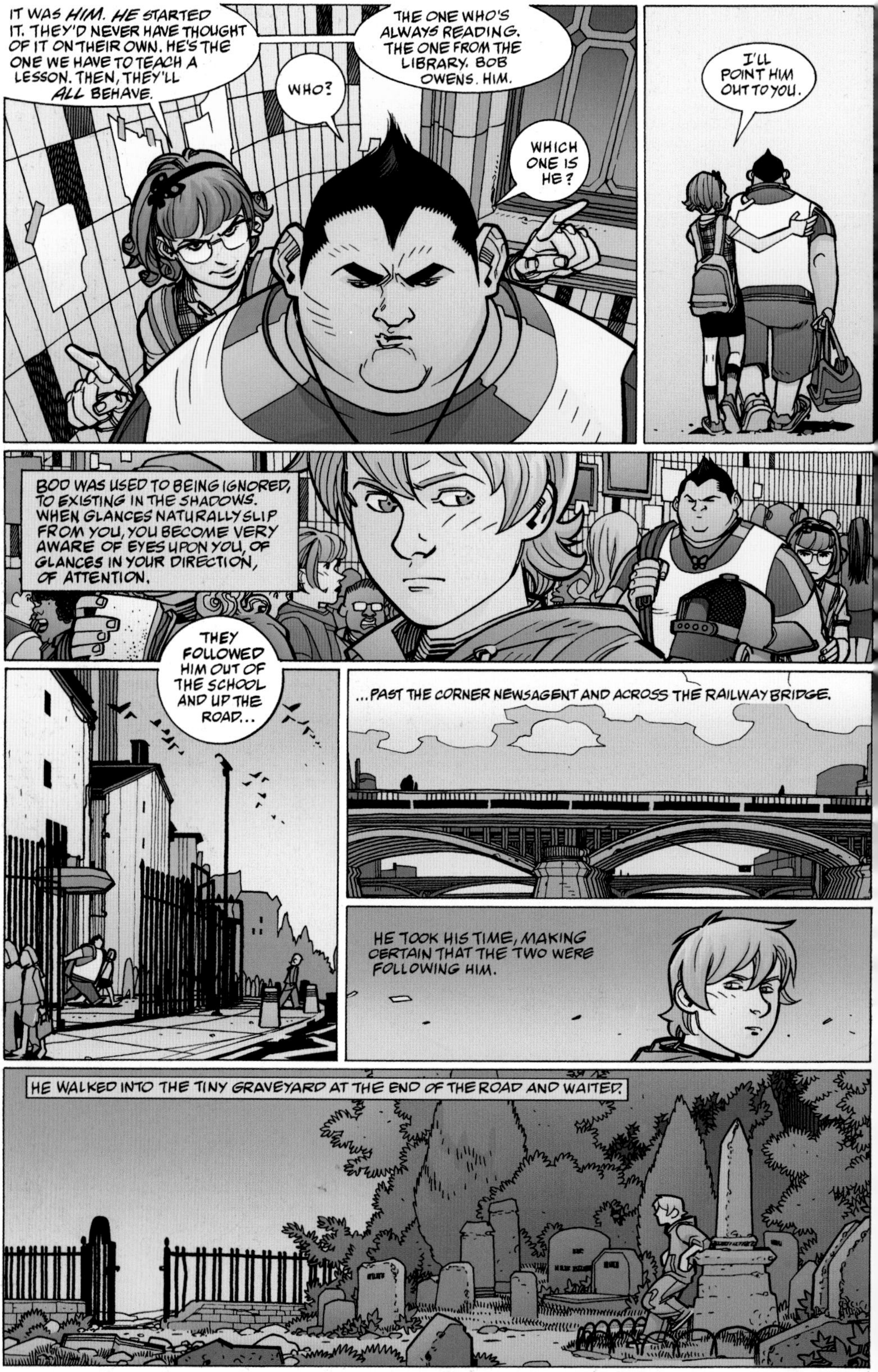
IT WAS HIM. HE STARTED IT. THEY'D NEVER HAVE THOUGHT OF IT ON THEIR OWN. HE'S THE ONE WE HAVE TO TEACH A LESSON. THEN, THEY'LL ALL BEHAVE.
WHO?
THE ONE WHO'S ALWAYS READING. THE ONE FROM THE LIBRARY. BOB OWENS. HIM.
WHICH ONE IS HE?
I'LL POINT HIM OUT TO YOU.
BOD WAS USED TO BEING IGNORED, TO EXISTING IN THE SHADOWS. WHEN GLANCES NATURALLY SLIP FROM YOU, YOU BECOME VERY AWARE OF EYES UPON YOU, OF GLANCES IN YOUR DIRECTION, OF ATTENTION.
THEY FOLLOWED HIM OUT OF THE SCHOOL AND UP THE ROAD...
...PAST THE CORNER NEWSAGENT AND ACROSS THE RAILWAY BRIDGE.
HE TOOK HIS TIME, MAKING CERTAIN THAT THE TWO WERE FOLLOWING HIM.
HE WALKED INTO THE TINY GRAVEYARD AT THE END OF THE ROAD AND WAITED.

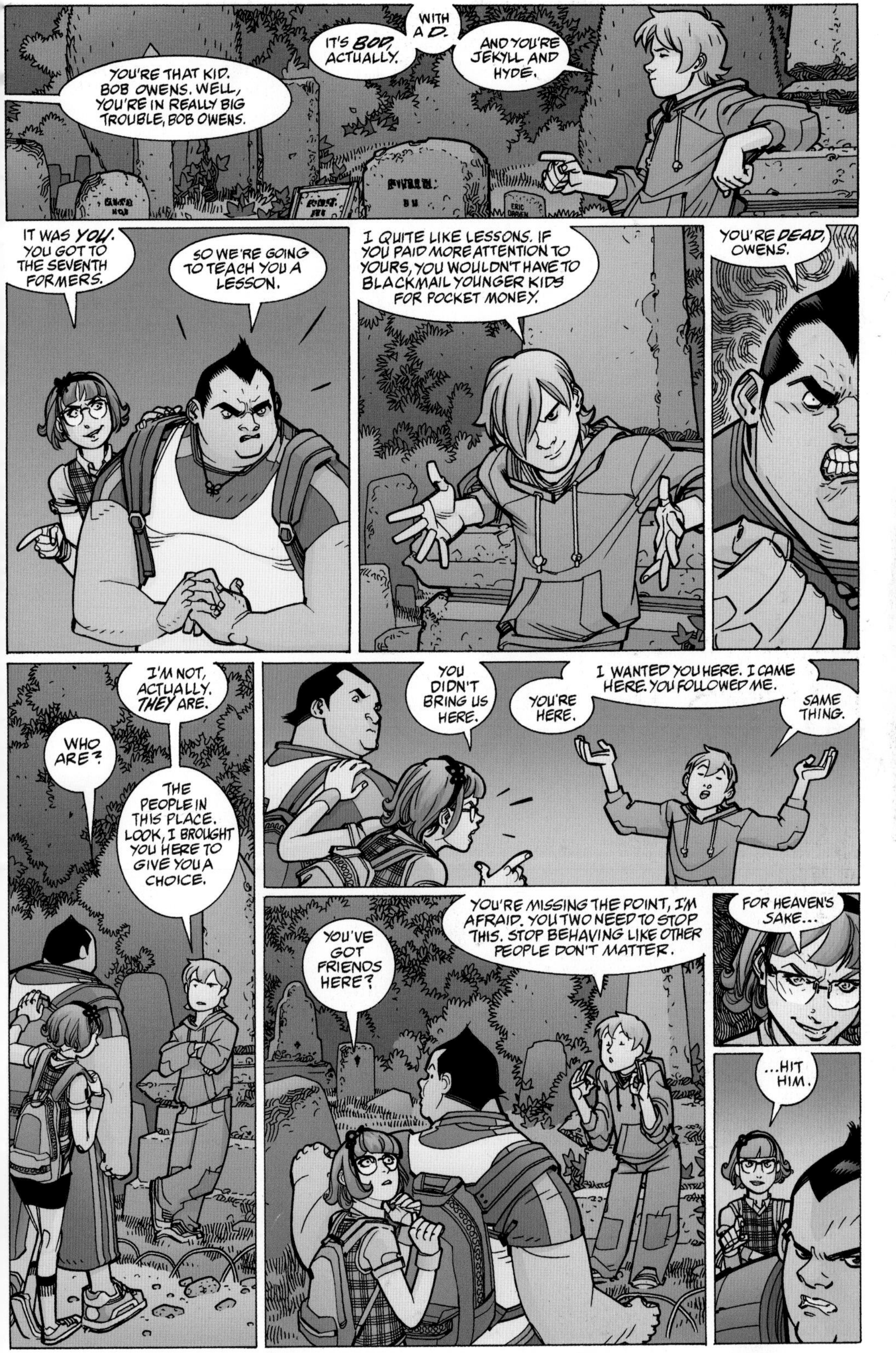
YOU'RE THAT KID. BOB OWENS. WELL, YOU'RE IN REALLY BIG TROUBLE, BOB OWENS.
IT'S BOD, ACTUALLY.
WITH A D.
AND YOU'RE JEKYLL AND HYDE.
ERIC DRAVEN
IT WAS YOU. YOU GOT TO THE SEVENTH FORMERS.
SO WE'RE GOING TO TEACH YOU A LESSON.
I QUITE LIKE LESSONS. IF YOU PAID MORE ATTENTION TO YOURS, YOU WOULDN'T HAVE TO BLACKMAIL YOUNGER KIDS FOR POCKET MONEY.
YOU'RE DEAD, OWENS.
I'M NOT, ACTUALLY. THEY ARE.
WHO ARE?
THE PEOPLE IN THIS PLACE. LOOK, I BROUGHT YOU HERE TO GIVE YOU A CHOICE.
YOU DIDN'T BRING US HERE.
YOU'RE HERE.
I WANTED YOU HERE. I CAME HERE. YOU FOLLOWED ME.
SAME THING.
YOU'VE GOT FRIENDS HERE?
YOU'RE MISSING THE POINT, I'M AFRAID. YOU TWO NEED TO STOP THIS. STOP BEHAVING LIKE OTHER PEOPLE DON'T MATTER.
FOR HEAVEN'S SAKE...
...HIT HIM.

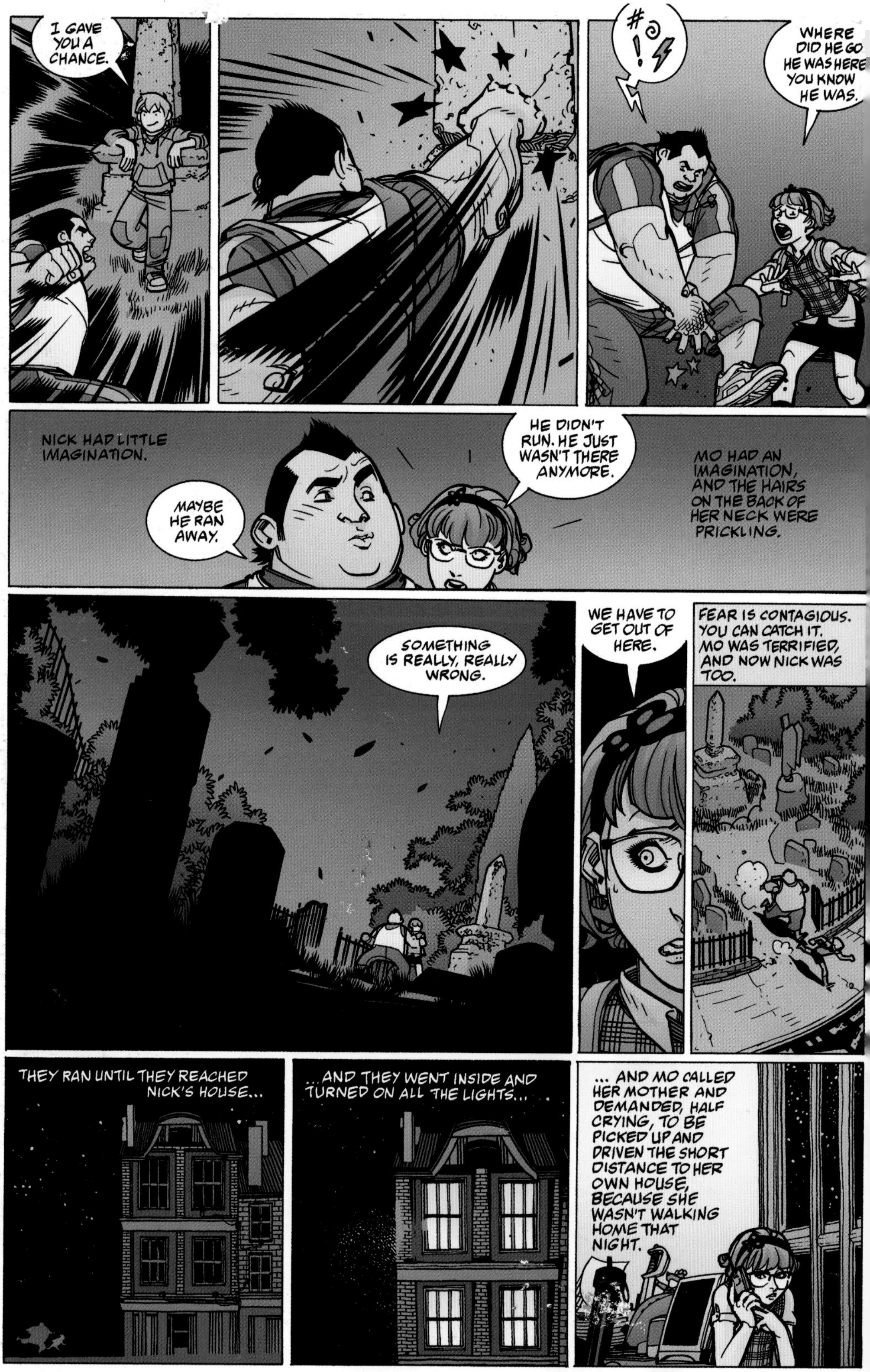
I GAVE YOU A CHANCE.
#@!
WHERE DID HE GO HE WAS HERE YOU KNOW HE WAS.
NICK HAD LITTLE IMAGINATION.
MAYBE HE RAN AWAY.
HE DIDN'T RUN. HE JUST WASN'T THERE ANYMORE.
MO HAD AN IMAGINATION, AND THE HAIRS ON THE BACK OF HER NECK WERE PRICKLING.
SOMETHING IS REALLY, REALLY WRONG.
WE HAVE TO GET OUT OF HERE.
FEAR IS CONTAGIOUS. YOU CAN CATCH IT. MO WAS TERRIFIED, AND NOW NICK WAS TOO.
THEY RAN UNTIL THEY REACHED NICK'S HOUSE...
...AND THEY WENT INSIDE AND TURNED ON ALL THE LIGHTS...
... AND MO CALLED HER MOTHER AND DEMANDED, HALF CRYING, TO BE PICKED UP AND DRIVEN THE SHORT DISTANCE TO HER OWN HOUSE, BECAUSE SHE WASN'T WALKING HOME THAT NIGHT.

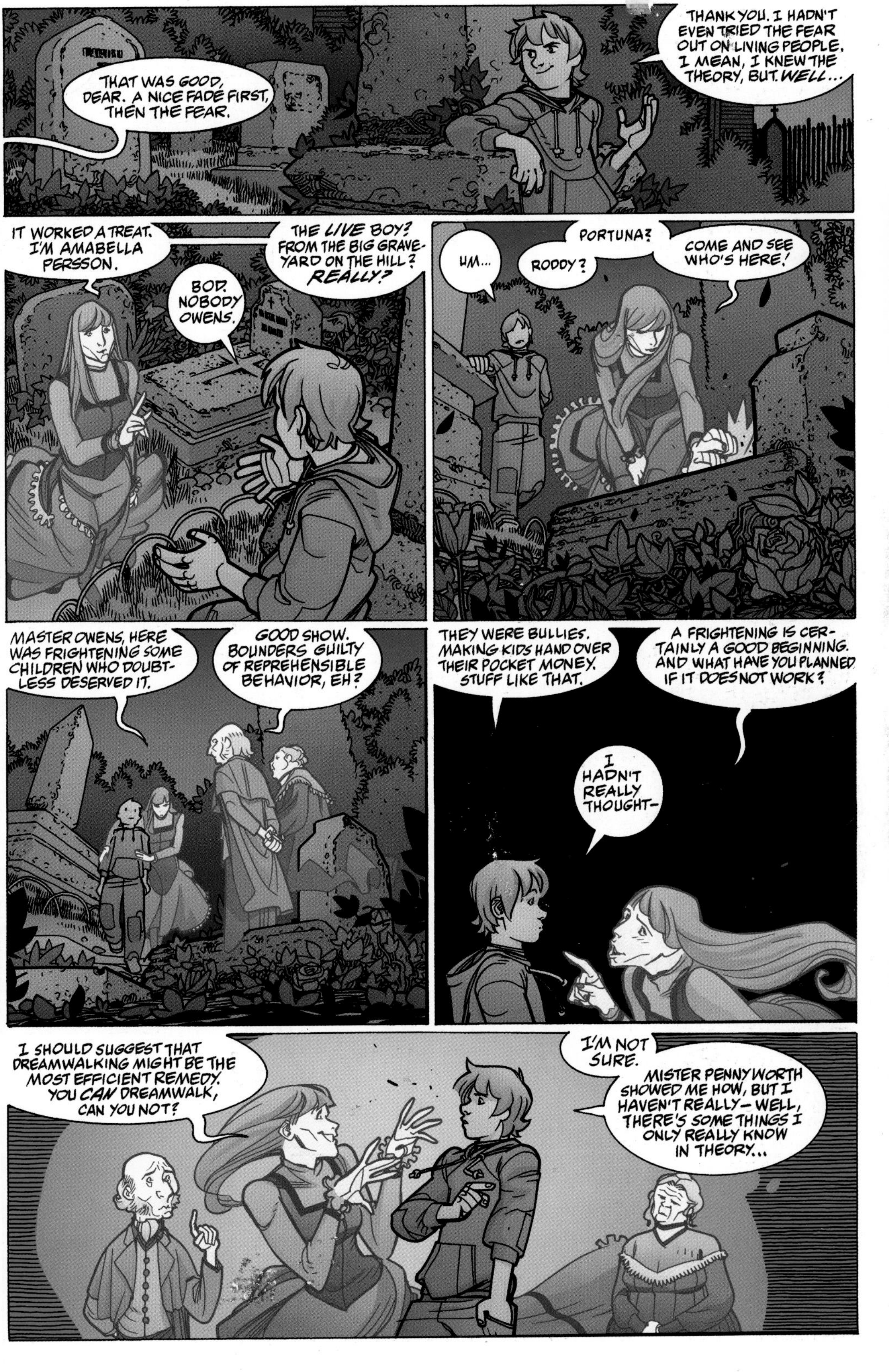
THAT WAS GOOD, DEAR. A NICE FADE FIRST, THEN THE FEAR.
THANK YOU. I HADN'T EVEN TRIED THE FEAR OUT ON LIVING PEOPLE. I MEAN, I KNEW THE THEORY, BUT. WELL...
IT WORKED A TREAT. I'M AMABELLA PERSSON.
BOD. NOBODY OWENS.
THE LIVE BOY? FROM THE BIG GRAVEYARD ON THE HILL? REALLY?
UM...
PORTUNA?
RODDY?
COME AND SEE WHO'S HERE!
MASTER OWENS, HERE WAS FRIGHTENING SOME CHILDREN WHO DOUBTLESS DESERVED IT.
GOOD SHOW. BOUNDERS GUILTY OF REPREHENSIBLE BEHAVIOR, EH?
THEY WERE BULLIES. MAKING KIDS HAND OVER THEIR POCKET MONEY. STUFF LIKE THAT.
A FRIGHTENING IS CERTAINLY A GOOD BEGINNING. AND WHAT HAVE YOU PLANNED IF IT DOES NOT WORK?
I HADN'T REALLY THOUGHT-
I SHOULD SUGGEST THAT DREAMWALKING MIGHT BE THE MOST EFFICIENT REMEDY. YOU CAN DREAMWALK, CAN YOU NOT?
I'M NOT SURE.
MISTER PENNYWORTH SHOWED ME HOW, BUT I HAVEN'T REALLY- WELL, THERE'S SOME THINGS I ONLY REALLY KNOW IN THEORY...

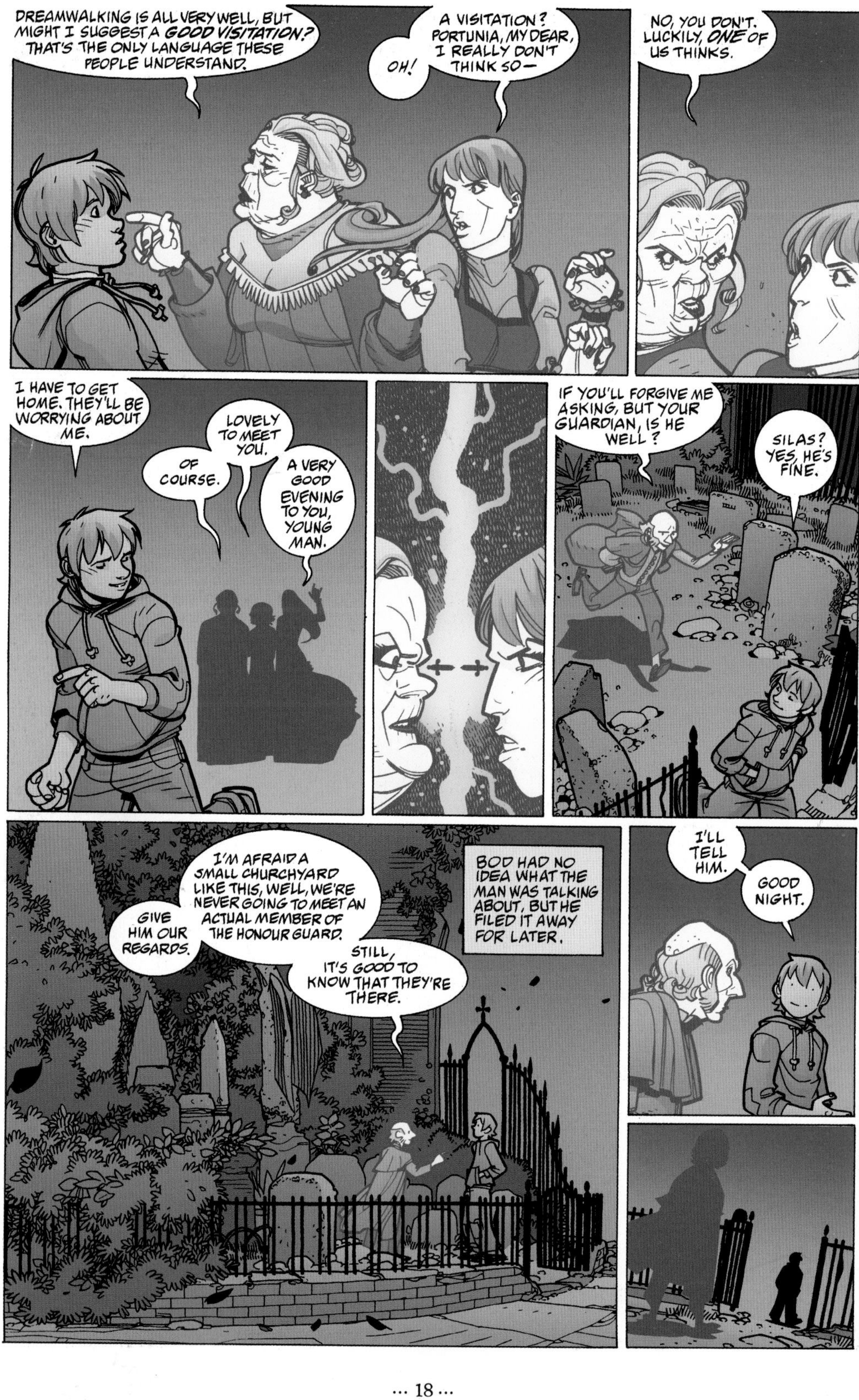
DREAMWALKING IS ALL VERY WELL, BUT MIGHT I SUGGEST A **GOOD VISITATION?** THAT'S THE ONLY LANGUAGE THESE PEOPLE UNDERSTAND.
OH!
A VISITATION? PORTUNIA, MY DEAR, I REALLY DON'T THINK SO—
NO, YOU DON'T. LUCKILY, **ONE** OF US THINKS.
I HAVE TO GET HOME. THEY'LL BE WORRYING ABOUT ME.
OF COURSE.
LOVELY TO MEET YOU.
A VERY GOOD EVENING TO YOU, YOUNG MAN.
IF YOU'LL FORGIVE ME ASKING, BUT YOUR GUARDIAN, IS HE WELL?
SILAS? YES, HE'S FINE.
GIVE HIM OUR REGARDS.
I'M AFRAID A SMALL CHURCHYARD LIKE THIS, WELL, WE'RE NEVER GOING TO MEET AN ACTUAL MEMBER OF THE HONOUR GUARD.
STILL, IT'S GOOD TO KNOW THAT THEY'RE THERE.
BOD HAD NO IDEA WHAT THE MAN WAS TALKING ABOUT, BUT HE FILED IT AWAY FOR LATER.
I'LL TELL HIM.
GOOD NIGHT.

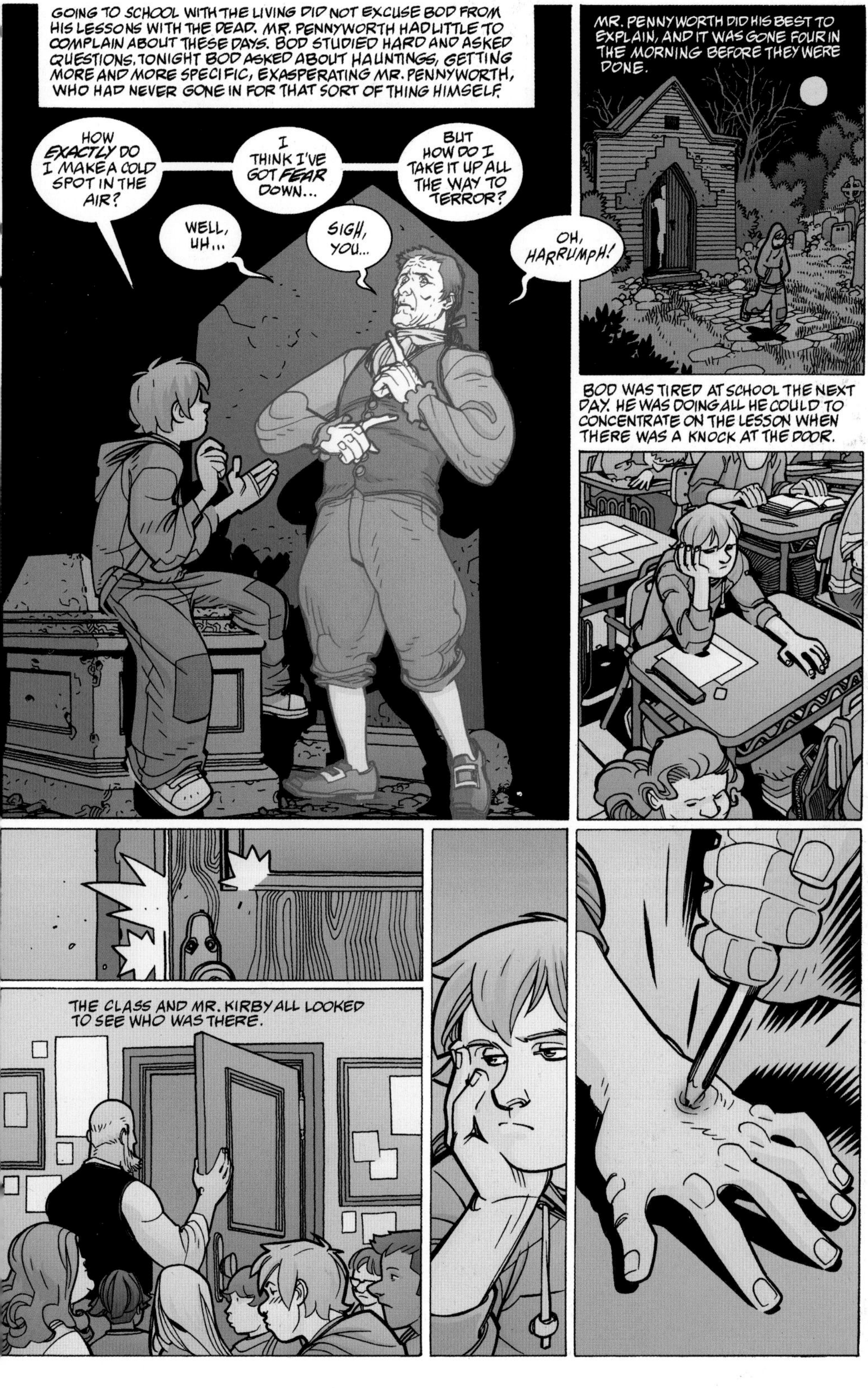
GOING TO SCHOOL WITH THE LIVING DID NOT EXCUSE BOD FROM HIS LESSONS WITH THE DEAD. MR. PENNYWORTH HAD LITTLE TO COMPLAIN ABOUT THESE DAYS. BOD STUDIED HARD AND ASKED QUESTIONS. TONIGHT BOD ASKED ABOUT HAUNTINGS, GETTING MORE AND MORE SPECIFIC, EXASPERATING MR. PENNYWORTH, WHO HAD NEVER GONE IN FOR THAT SORT OF THING HIMSELF.
HOW EXACTLY DO I MAKE A COLD SPOT IN THE AIR?
WELL, UH...
I THINK I'VE GOT FEAR DOWN...
SIGH, YOU...
BUT HOW DO I TAKE IT UP ALL THE WAY TO TERROR?
OH, HARRUMPH!
MR. PENNYWORTH DID HIS BEST TO EXPLAIN, AND IT WAS GONE FOUR IN THE MORNING BEFORE THEY WERE DONE.
BOD WAS TIRED AT SCHOOL THE NEXT DAY. HE WAS DOING ALL HE COULD TO CONCENTRATE ON THE LESSON WHEN THERE WAS A KNOCK AT THE DOOR.
THE CLASS AND MR. KIRBY ALL LOOKED TO SEE WHO WAS THERE.

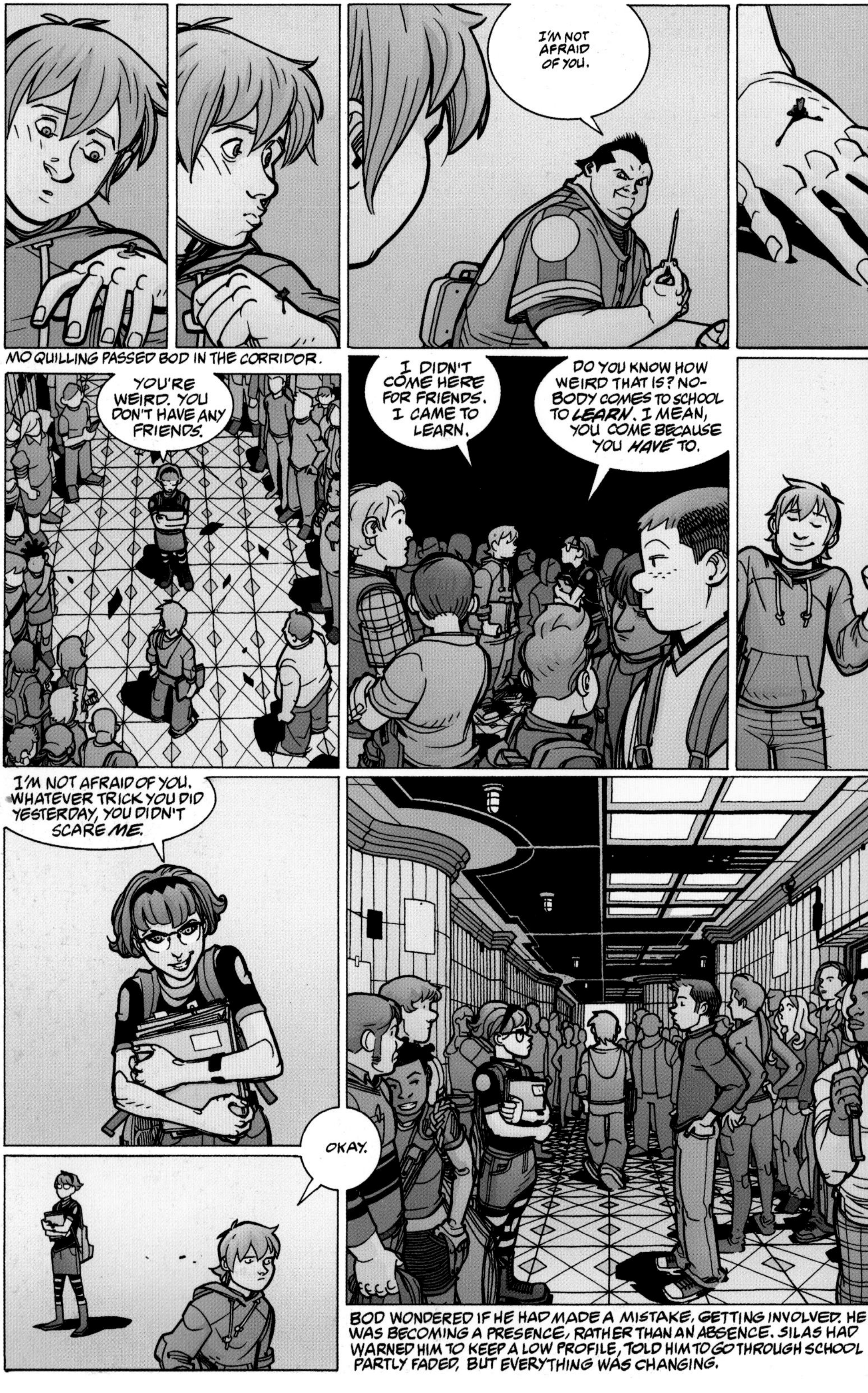
I'M NOT AFRAID OF YOU.
MO QUILLING PASSED BOD IN THE CORRIDOR.
YOU'RE WEIRD. YOU DON'T HAVE ANY FRIENDS.
I DIDN'T COME HERE FOR FRIENDS. I CAME TO LEARN.
DO YOU KNOW HOW WEIRD THAT IS? NO-BODY COMES TO SCHOOL TO LEARN. I MEAN, YOU COME BECAUSE YOU HAVE TO.
I'M NOT AFRAID OF YOU. WHATEVER TRICK YOU DID YESTERDAY, YOU DIDN'T SCARE ME.
OKAY.
BOD WONDERED IF HE HAD MADE A MISTAKE, GETTING INVOLVED. HE WAS BECOMING A PRESENCE, RATHER THAN AN ABSENCE. SILAS HAD WARNED HIM TO KEEP A LOW PROFILE, TOLD HIM TO GO THROUGH SCHOOL PARTLY FADED, BUT EVERYTHING WAS CHANGING.

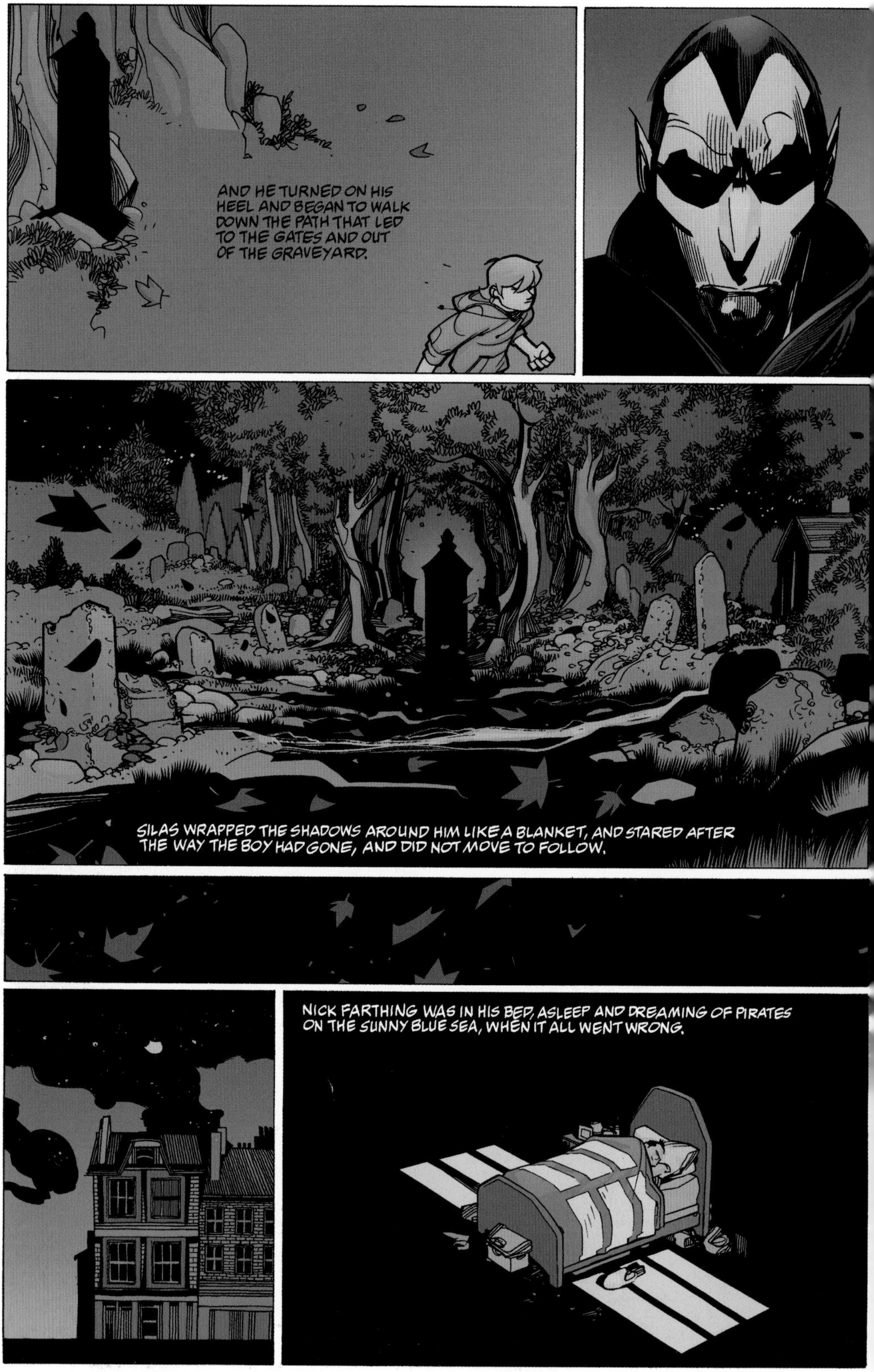
AND HE TURNED ON HIS HEEL AND BEGAN TO WALK DOWN THE PATH THAT LED TO THE GATES AND OUT OF THE GRAVEYARD.
SILAS WRAPPED THE SHADOWS AROUND HIM LIKE A BLANKET, AND STARED AFTER THE WAY THE BOY HAD GONE, AND DID NOT MOVE TO FOLLOW.
NICK FARTHING WAS IN HIS BED, ASLEEP AND DREAMING OF PIRATES ON THE SUNNY BLUE SEA, WHEN IT ALL WENT WRONG.

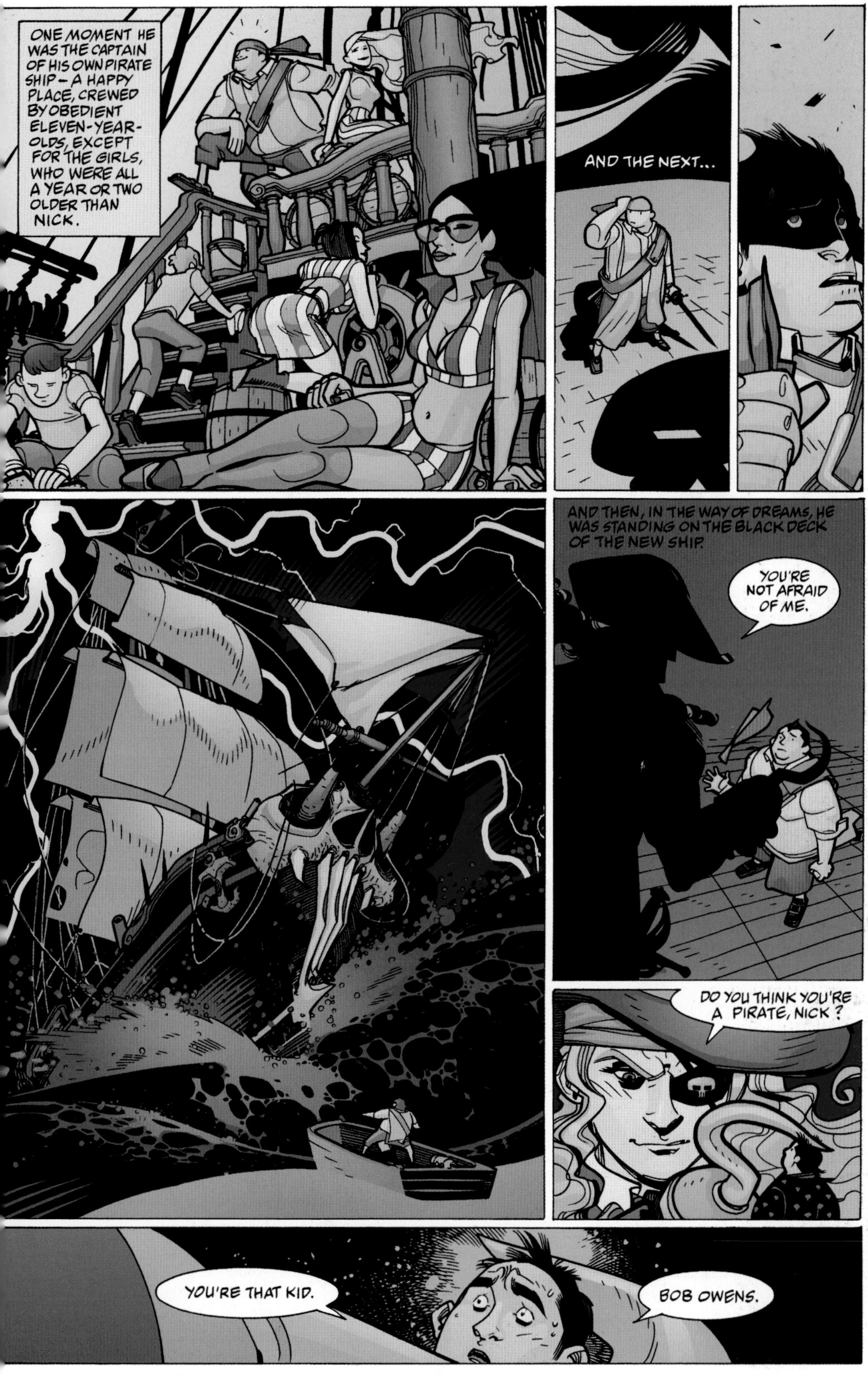
ONE MOMENT HE WAS THE CAPTAIN OF HIS OWN PIRATE SHIP – A HAPPY PLACE, CREWED BY OBEDIENT ELEVEN-YEAR-OLDS, EXCEPT FOR THE GIRLS, WHO WERE ALL A YEAR OR TWO OLDER THAN NICK.
AND THE NEXT...
AND THEN, IN THE WAY OF DREAMS, HE WAS STANDING ON THE BLACK DECK OF THE NEW SHIP.
YOU'RE NOT AFRAID OF ME.
DO YOU THINK YOU'RE A PIRATE, NICK?
YOU'RE THAT KID.
BOB OWENS.

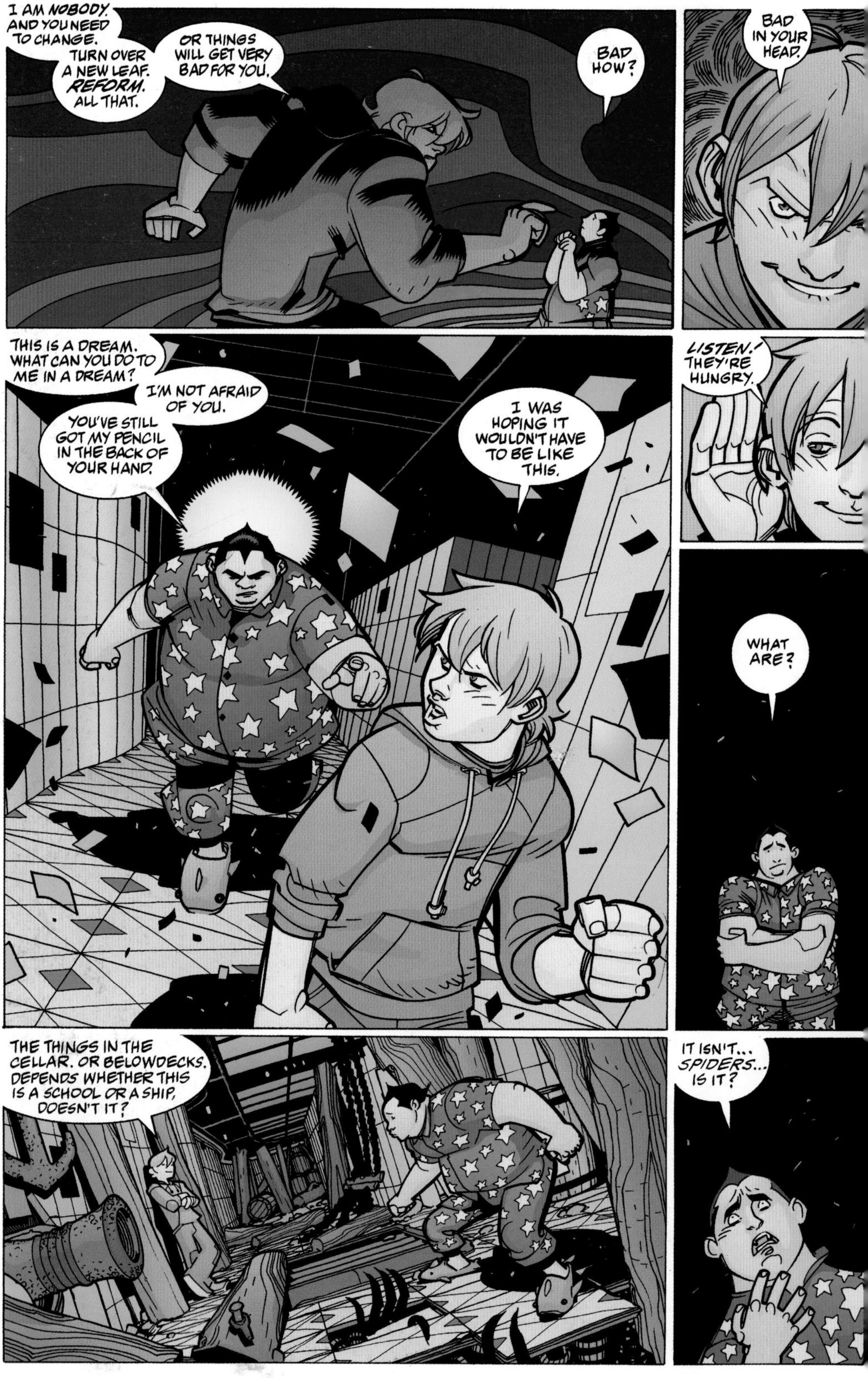
I AM NOBODY. AND YOU NEED TO CHANGE. TURN OVER A NEW LEAF. REFORM. ALL THAT.
OR THINGS WILL GET VERY BAD FOR YOU.
BAD HOW?
BAD IN YOUR HEAD.
THIS IS A DREAM. WHAT CAN YOU DO TO ME IN A DREAM?
I'M NOT AFRAID OF YOU.
YOU'VE STILL GOT MY PENCIL IN THE BACK OF YOUR HAND.
I WAS HOPING IT WOULDN'T HAVE TO BE LIKE THIS.
LISTEN! THEY'RE HUNGRY.
WHAT ARE?
THE THINGS IN THE CELLAR. OR BELOWDECKS. DEPENDS WHETHER THIS IS A SCHOOL OR A SHIP, DOESN'T IT?
IT ISN'T... SPIDERS... IS IT?

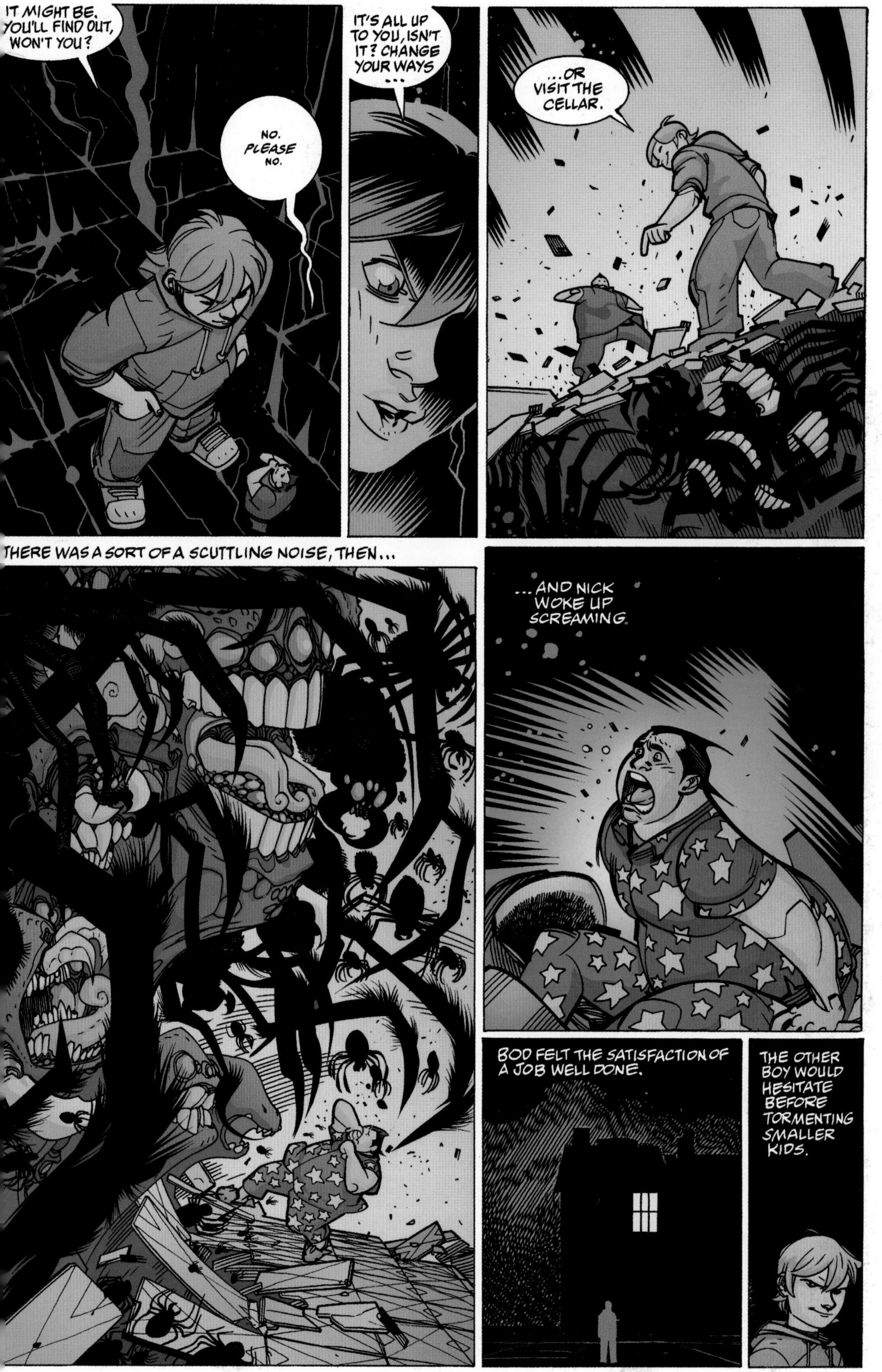
IT MIGHT BE. YOU'LL FIND OUT, WON'T YOU?
NO. PLEASE NO.
IT'S ALL UP TO YOU, ISN'T IT? CHANGE YOUR WAYS ...
...OR VISIT THE CELLAR.
THERE WAS A SORT OF A SCUTTLING NOISE, THEN...
...AND NICK WOKE UP SCREAMING.
BOD FELT THE SATISFACTION OF A JOB WELL DONE.
THE OTHER BOY WOULD HESITATE BEFORE TORMENTING SMALLER KIDS.

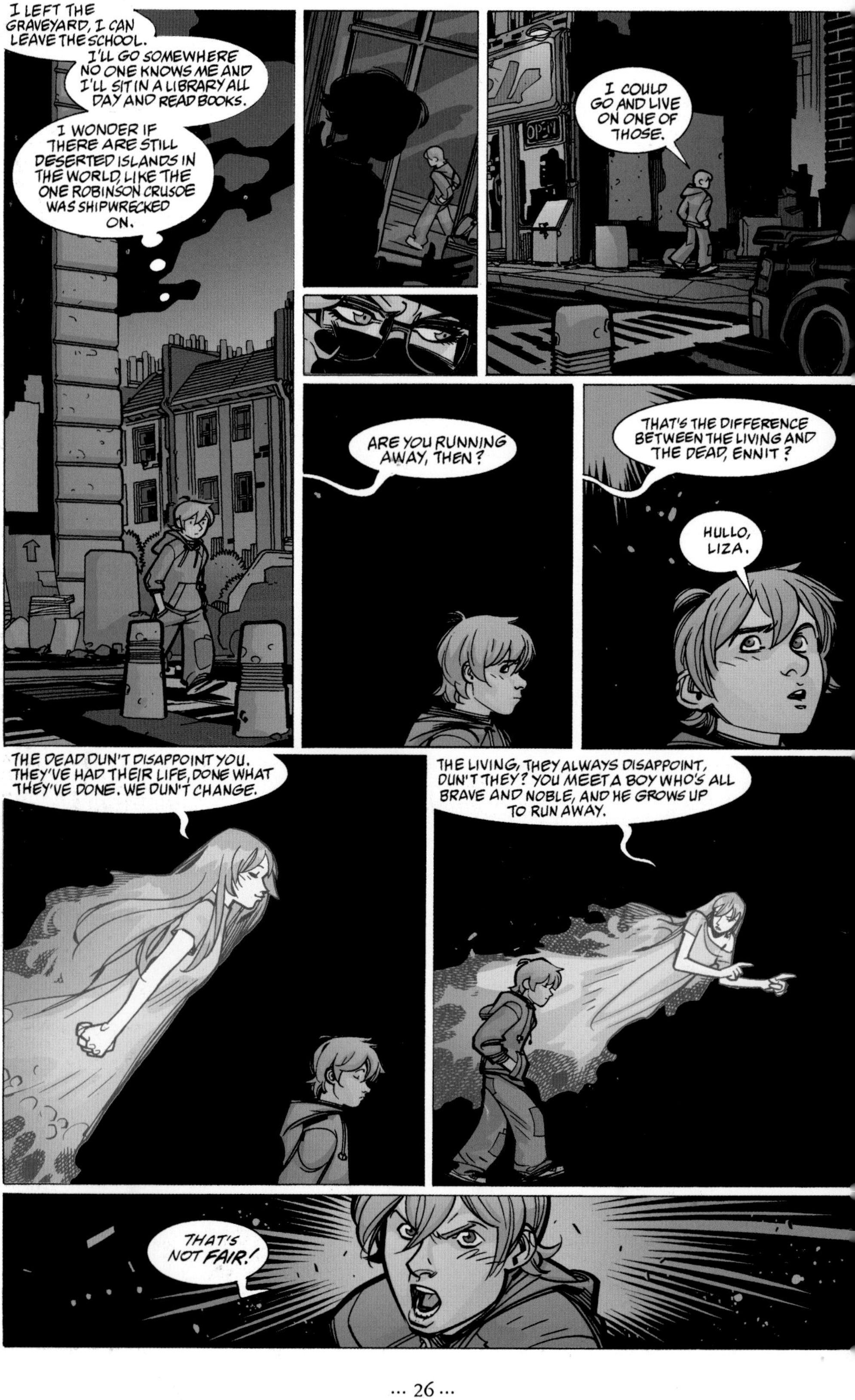
I LEFT THE GRAVEYARD, I CAN LEAVE THE SCHOOL.
I'LL GO SOMEWHERE NO ONE KNOWS ME AND I'LL SIT IN A LIBRARY ALL DAY AND READ BOOKS.
I WONDER IF THERE ARE STILL DESERTED ISLANDS IN THE WORLD, LIKE THE ONE ROBINSON CRUSOE WAS SHIPWRECKED ON.
OPEN
I COULD GO AND LIVE ON ONE OF THOSE.
ARE YOU RUNNING AWAY, THEN?
THAT'S THE DIFFERENCE BETWEEN THE LIVING AND THE DEAD, ENNIT?
HULLO, LIZA.
THE DEAD DUN'T DISAPPOINT YOU. THEY'VE HAD THEIR LIFE, DONE WHAT THEY'VE DONE. WE DUN'T CHANGE.
THE LIVING, THEY ALWAYS DISAPPOINT, DUN'T THEY? YOU MEET A BOY WHO'S ALL BRAVE AND NOBLE, AND HE GROWS UP TO RUN AWAY.
THAT'S NOT FAIR!

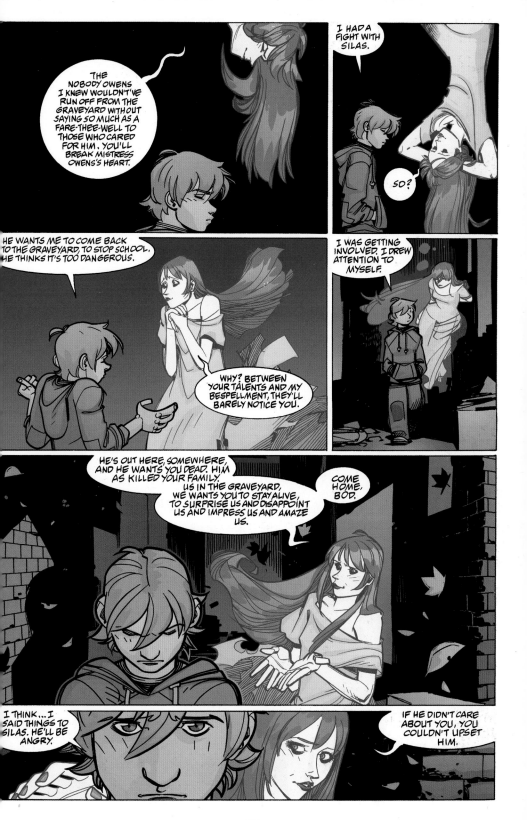

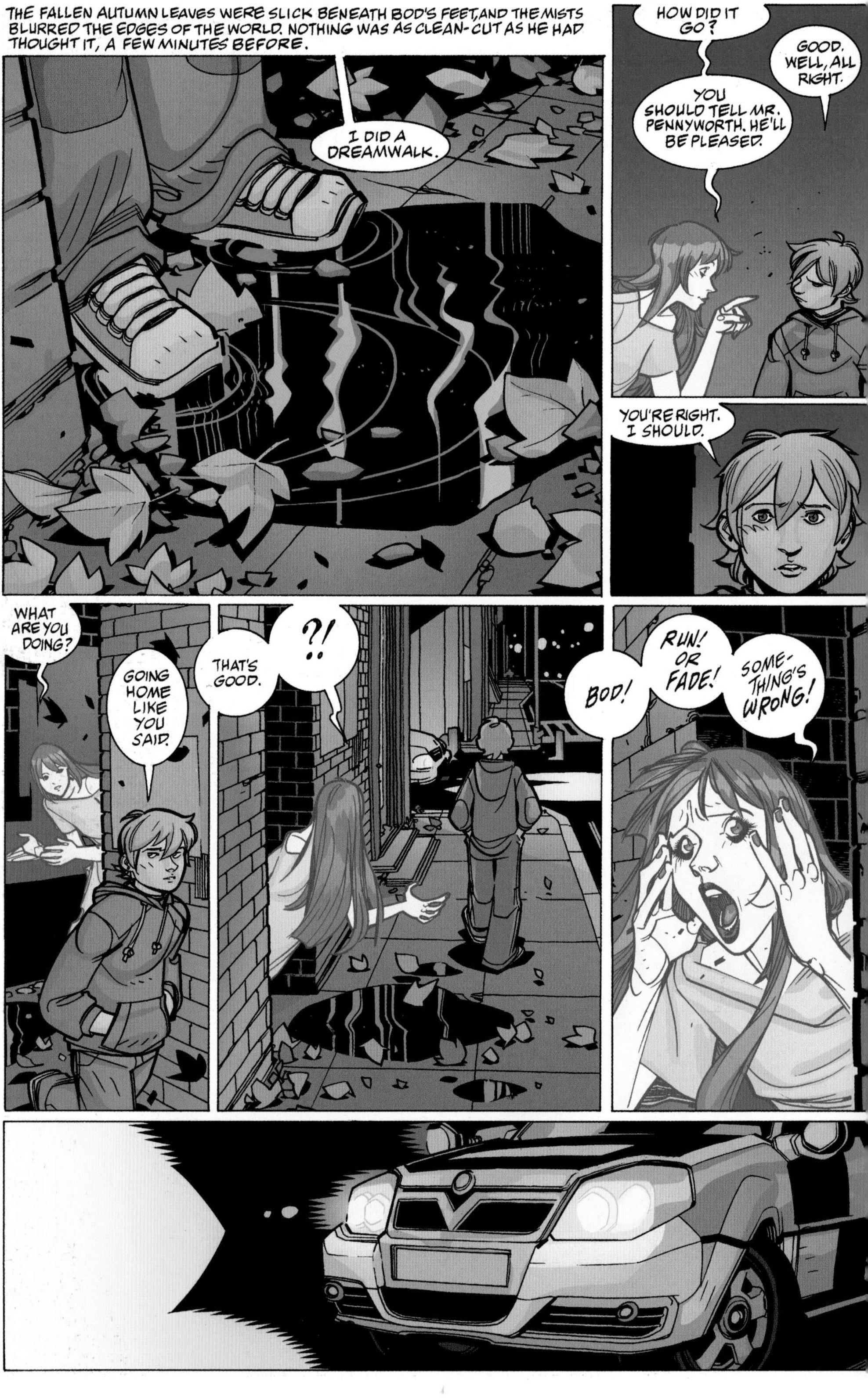
THE FALLEN AUTUMN LEAVES WERE SLICK BENEATH BOD'S FEET, AND THE MISTS BLURRED THE EDGES OF THE WORLD. NOTHING WAS AS CLEAN-CUT AS HE HAD THOUGHT IT, A FEW MINUTES BEFORE.
HOW DID IT GO?
I DID A DREAMWALK.
YOU SHOULD TELL MR. PENNYWORTH. HE'LL BE PLEASED.
GOOD. WELL, ALL RIGHT.
YOU'RE RIGHT. I SHOULD.
WHAT ARE YOU DOING?
GOING HOME LIKE YOU SAID.
THAT'S GOOD.
?!
BOD!
RUN! OR FADE!
SOME-THING'S WRONG!

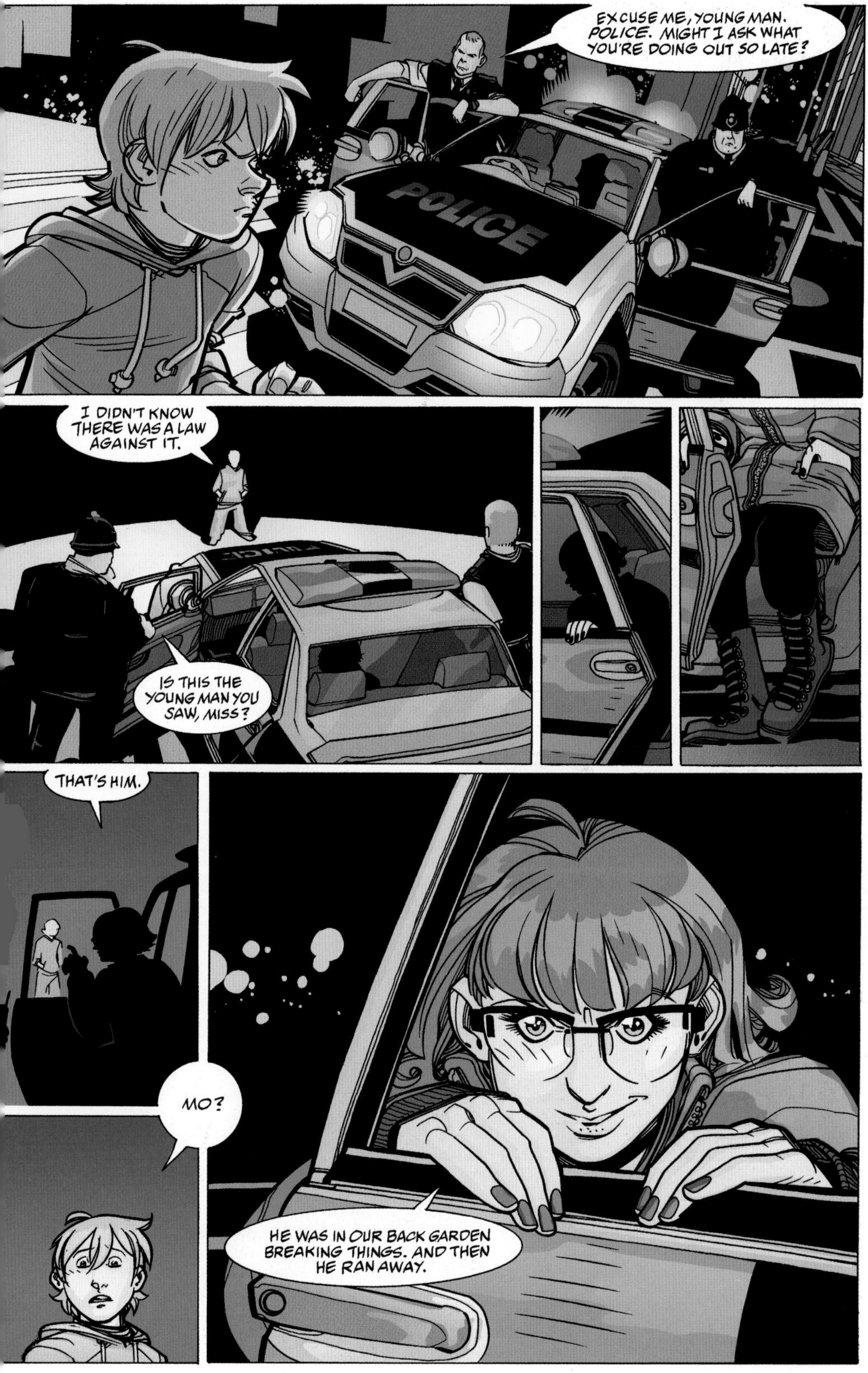
EXCUSE ME, YOUNG MAN. POLICE. MIGHT I ASK WHAT YOU'RE DOING OUT SO LATE?
POLICE
I DIDN'T KNOW THERE WAS A LAW AGAINST IT.
IS THIS THE YOUNG MAN YOU SAW, MISS?
THAT'S HIM.
MO?
HE WAS IN OUR BACK GARDEN BREAKING THINGS. AND THEN HE RAN AWAY.

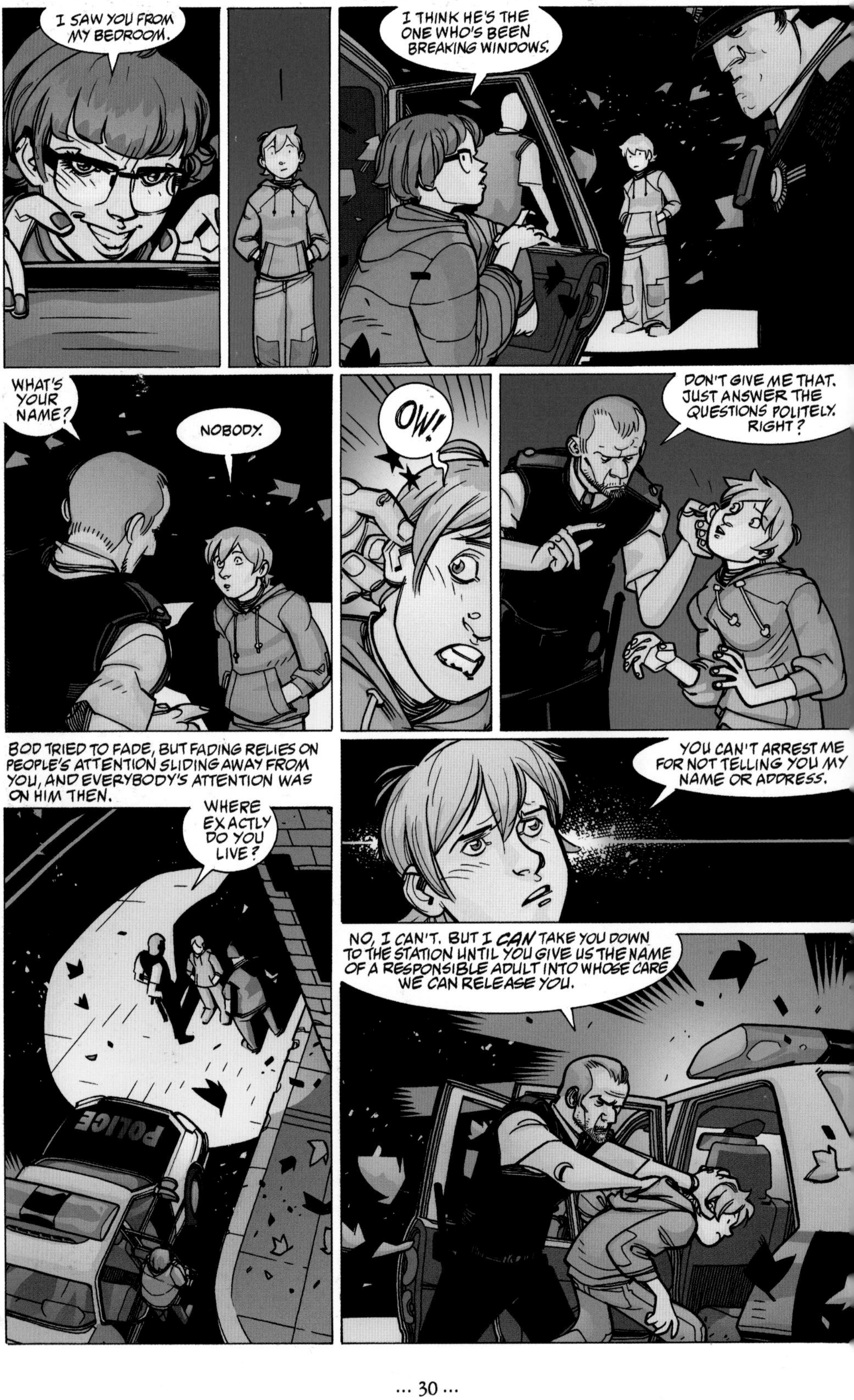
I SAW YOU FROM MY BEDROOM.
I THINK HE'S THE ONE WHO'S BEEN BREAKING WINDOWS.
WHAT'S YOUR NAME?
NOBODY.
OW!
DON'T GIVE ME THAT. JUST ANSWER THE QUESTIONS POLITELY. RIGHT?
BOD TRIED TO FADE, BUT FADING RELIES ON PEOPLE'S ATTENTION SLIDING AWAY FROM YOU, AND EVERYBODY'S ATTENTION WAS ON HIM THEN.
WHERE EXACTLY DO YOU LIVE?
YOU CAN'T ARREST ME FOR NOT TELLING YOU MY NAME OR ADDRESS.
NO, I CAN'T. BUT I CAN TAKE YOU DOWN TO THE STATION UNTIL YOU GIVE US THE NAME OF A RESPONSIBLE ADULT INTO WHOSE CARE WE CAN RELEASE YOU.
POLICE

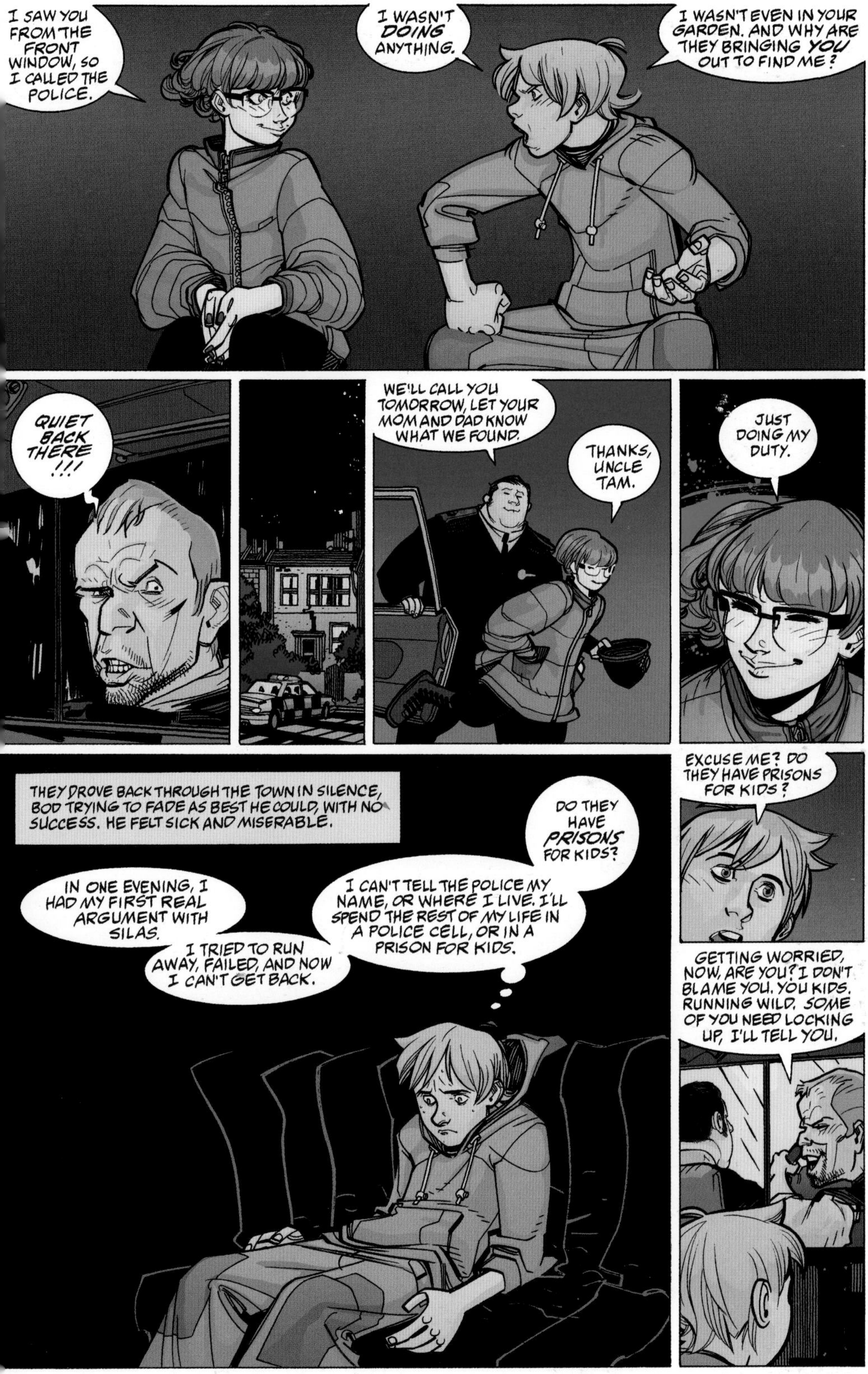
I SAW YOU FROM THE FRONT WINDOW, SO I CALLED THE POLICE.
I WASN'T *DOING* ANYTHING.
I WASN'T EVEN IN YOUR GARDEN. AND WHY ARE THEY BRINGING *YOU* OUT TO FIND ME?
QUIET BACK THERE!!!
WE'LL CALL YOU TOMORROW, LET YOUR MOM AND DAD KNOW WHAT WE FOUND.
THANKS, UNCLE TAM.
JUST DOING MY DUTY.
THEY DROVE BACK THROUGH THE TOWN IN SILENCE, BOD TRYING TO FADE AS BEST HE COULD, WITH NO SUCCESS. HE FELT SICK AND MISERABLE.
IN ONE EVENING, I HAD MY FIRST REAL ARGUMENT WITH SILAS.
I TRIED TO RUN AWAY, FAILED, AND NOW I CAN'T GET BACK.
I CAN'T TELL THE POLICE MY NAME, OR WHERE I LIVE. I'LL SPEND THE REST OF MY LIFE IN A POLICE CELL, OR IN A PRISON FOR KIDS.
DO THEY HAVE *PRISONS* FOR KIDS?
EXCUSE ME? DO THEY HAVE PRISONS FOR KIDS?
GETTING WORRIED, NOW, ARE YOU? I DON'T BLAME YOU. YOU KIDS. RUNNING WILD. SOME OF YOU NEED LOCKING UP, I'LL TELL YOU.

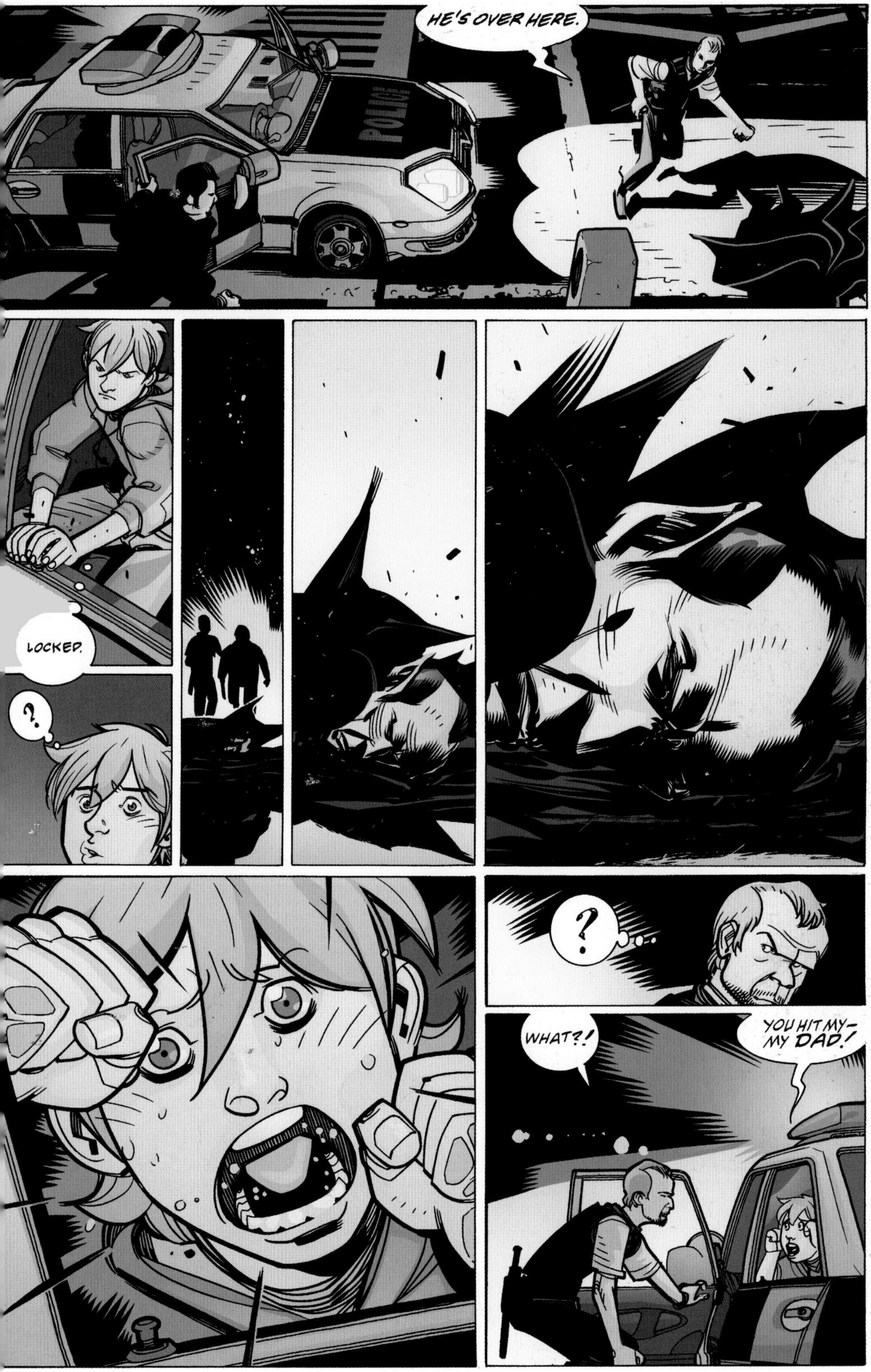
HE'S OVER HERE.
LOCKED.
?
?
WHAT?!
YOU HIT MY— MY DAD!

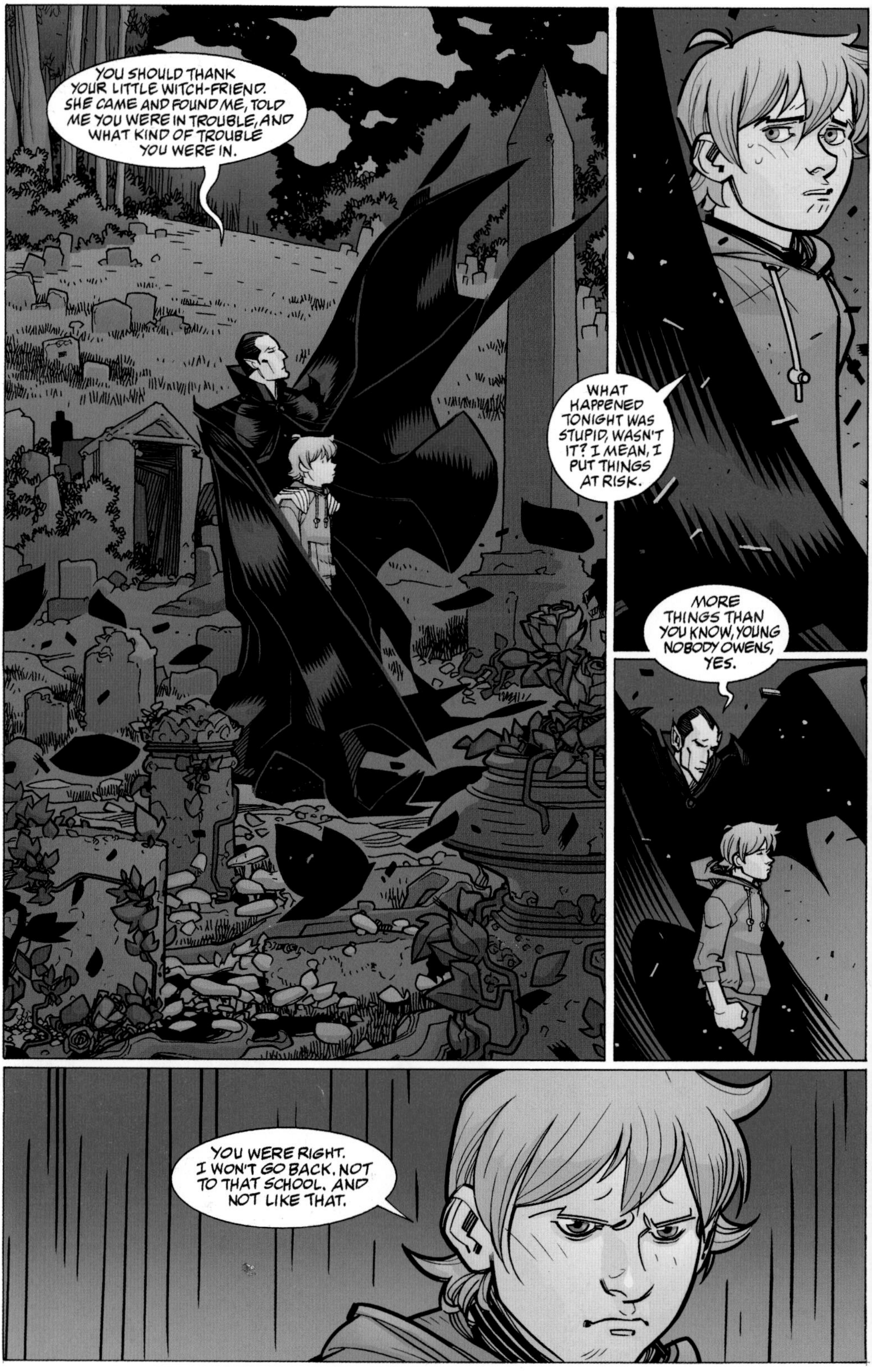
YOU SHOULD THANK YOUR LITTLE WITCH-FRIEND. SHE CAME AND FOUND ME, TOLD ME YOU WERE IN TROUBLE, AND WHAT KIND OF TROUBLE YOU WERE IN.
WHAT HAPPENED TONIGHT WAS STUPID, WASN'T IT? I MEAN, I PUT THINGS AT RISK.
MORE THINGS THAN YOU KNOW, YOUNG NOBODY OWENS, YES.
YOU WERE RIGHT. I WON'T GO BACK. NOT TO THAT SCHOOL. AND NOT LIKE THAT.

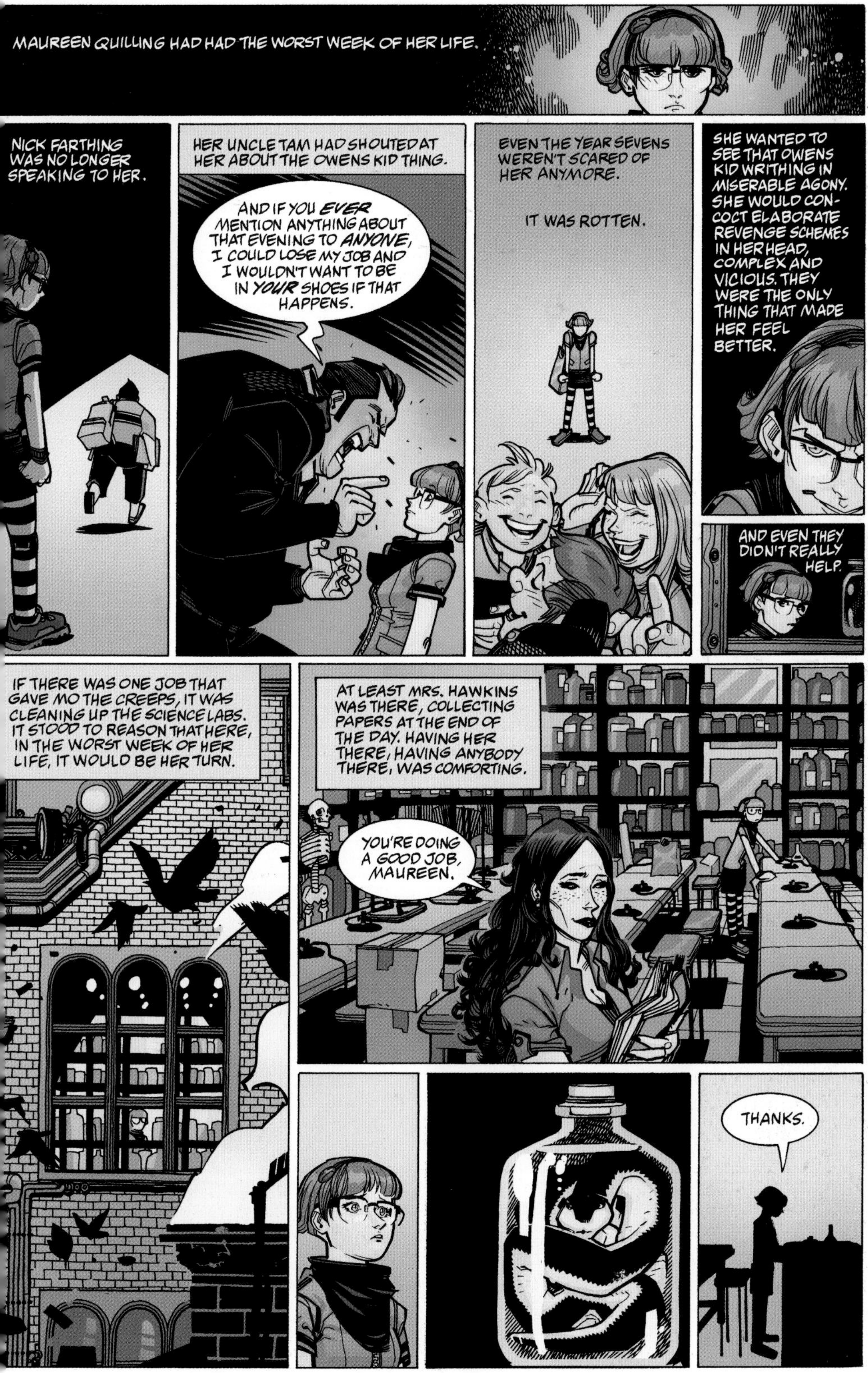
MAUREEN QUILLING HAD HAD THE WORST WEEK OF HER LIFE. . .
NICK FARTHING WAS NO LONGER SPEAKING TO HER.
HER UNCLE TAM HAD SHOUTED AT HER ABOUT THE OWENS KID THING.
AND IF YOU EVER MENTION ANYTHING ABOUT THAT EVENING TO ANYONE, I COULD LOSE MY JOB AND I WOULDN'T WANT TO BE IN YOUR SHOES IF THAT HAPPENS.
EVEN THE YEAR SEVENS WEREN'T SCARED OF HER ANYMORE.
IT WAS ROTTEN.
SHE WANTED TO SEE THAT OWENS KID WRITHING IN MISERABLE AGONY. SHE WOULD CONCOCT ELABORATE REVENGE SCHEMES IN HER HEAD, COMPLEX AND VICIOUS. THEY WERE THE ONLY THING THAT MADE HER FEEL BETTER.
AND EVEN THEY DIDN'T REALLY HELP.
IF THERE WAS ONE JOB THAT GAVE MO THE CREEPS, IT WAS CLEANING UP THE SCIENCE LABS. IT STOOD TO REASON THAT HERE, IN THE WORST WEEK OF HER LIFE, IT WOULD BE HER TURN.
AT LEAST MRS. HAWKINS WAS THERE, COLLECTING PAPERS AT THE END OF THE DAY. HAVING HER THERE, HAVING ANYBODY THERE, WAS COMFORTING.
YOU'RE DOING A GOOD JOB, MAUREEN.
THANKS.

... 39 ...

... 40 ...

... 41 ...

HE'S STILL OUT THERE, THE MAN WHO KILLED MY FIRST FAMILY. I STILL NEED TO LEARN ABOUT PEOPLE. ARE YOU GOING TO STOP ME FROM LEAVING THE GRAVEYARD?

NO. THAT WAS A MISTAKE, AND ONE THAT WE HAVE BOTH LEARNED FROM.

THEN WHAT?

THERE ARE OTHER WAYS TO SATISFY YOUR INTEREST IN STORIES, AND BOOKS, AND IN THE WORLD, AND MANY SITUATIONS IN WHICH THERE MIGHT BE OTHER LIVING PEOPLE AROUND YOU, LIKE LIBRARIES, THE THEATER, OR THE CINEMA.

WHAT'S THAT? IS IT LIKE FOOTBALL?

FOOTBALL. HMM. THAT'S USUALLY A LITTLE EARLY IN THE DAY FOR ME. BUT MISS LUPESCU COULD TAKE YOU TO SEE A FOOTBALL MATCH THE NEXT TIME SHE'S HERE.

WE HAVE BOTH LEFT TOO MANY TRACKS AND TRACES IN THE LAST FEW WEEKS.

I'D LIKE THAT.

THOMAS R. STOUT
1817 - 1851
DEEPLY REGRETTED
BY ALL WHO
KNEW HIM.

THEY ARE STILL LOOKING FOR YOU, YOU KNOW.

YOU SAID THAT BEFORE. HOW DO YOU KNOW? AND WHO **ARE** THEY? AND WHAT DO THEY WANT?

BUT SILAS ONLY SHOOK HIS HEAD AND WOULD BE DRAWN NO FURTHER, AND WITH THAT, FOR THE TIME BEING, BOD HAD TO BE SATISFIED.

LAFUENTE

7
Every Man Jack

Illustrated by Scott Hampton

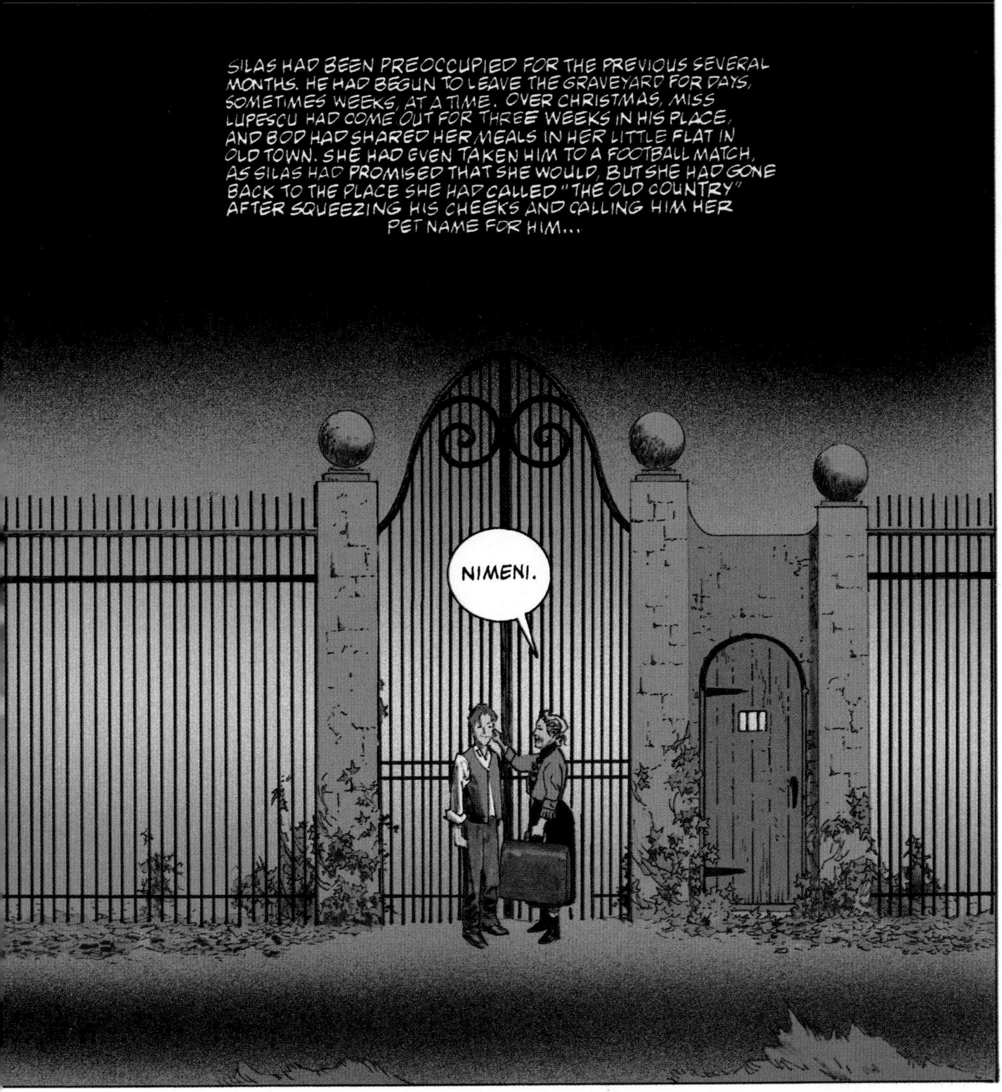
SILAS HAD BEEN PREOCCUPIED FOR THE PREVIOUS SEVERAL MONTHS. HE HAD BEGUN TO LEAVE THE GRAVEYARD FOR DAYS, SOMETIMES WEEKS, AT A TIME. OVER CHRISTMAS, MISS LUPESCU HAD COME OUT FOR THREE WEEKS IN HIS PLACE, AND BOD HAD SHARED HER MEALS IN HER LITTLE FLAT IN OLD TOWN. SHE HAD EVEN TAKEN HIM TO A FOOTBALL MATCH, AS SILAS HAD PROMISED THAT SHE WOULD, BUT SHE HAD GONE BACK TO THE PLACE SHE HAD CALLED "THE OLD COUNTRY" AFTER SQUEEZING HIS CHEEKS AND CALLING HIM HER PET NAME FOR HIM...
NIMENI.

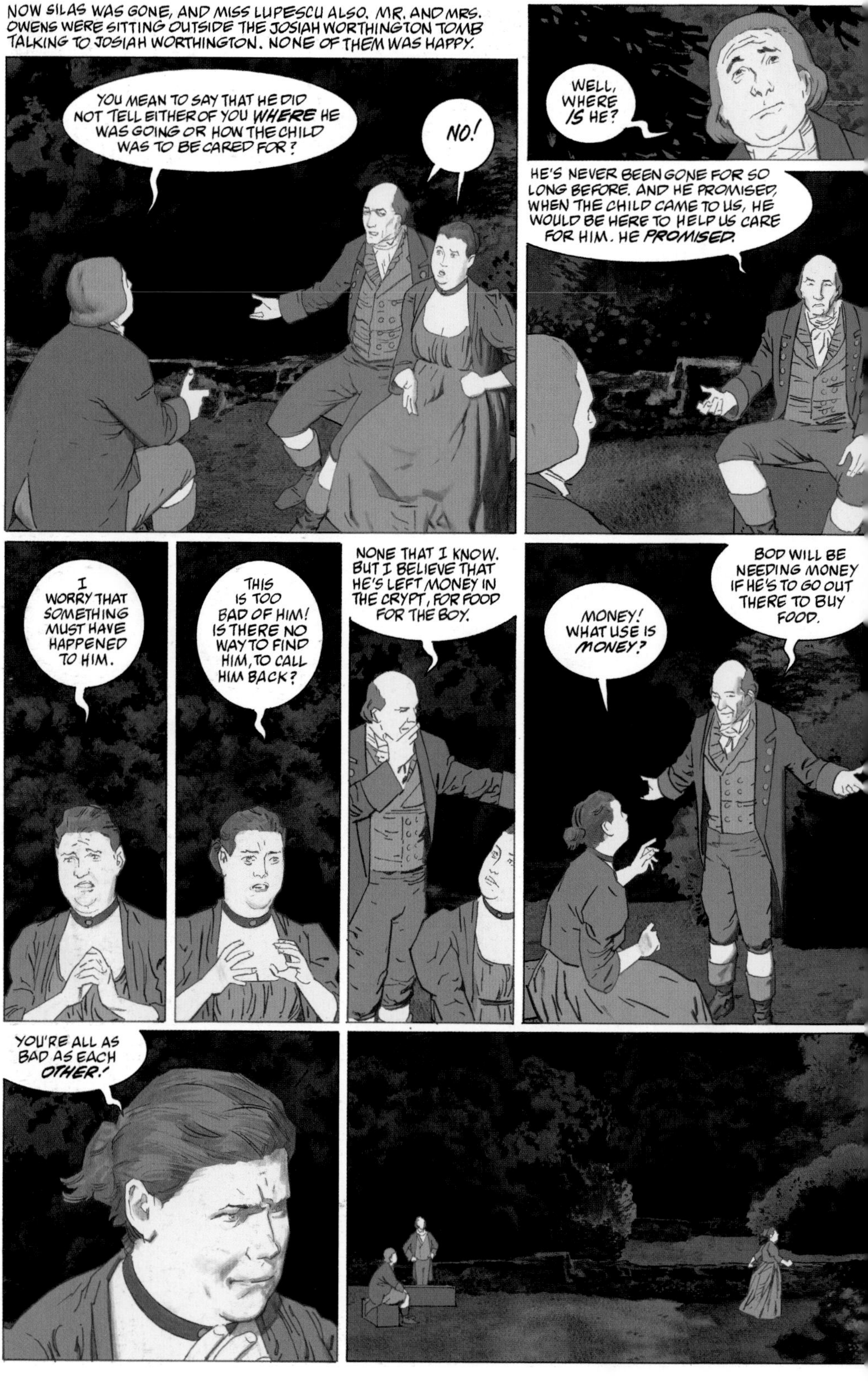
NOW SILAS WAS GONE, AND MISS LUPESCU ALSO. MR. AND MRS. OWENS WERE SITTING OUTSIDE THE JOSIAH WORTHINGTON TOMB TALKING TO JOSIAH WORTHINGTON. NONE OF THEM WAS HAPPY.
YOU MEAN TO SAY THAT HE DID NOT TELL EITHER OF YOU WHERE HE WAS GOING OR HOW THE CHILD WAS TO BE CARED FOR?
NO!
WELL, WHERE IS HE?
HE'S NEVER BEEN GONE FOR SO LONG BEFORE. AND HE PROMISED, WHEN THE CHILD CAME TO US, HE WOULD BE HERE TO HELP US CARE FOR HIM. HE PROMISED.
I WORRY THAT SOMETHING MUST HAVE HAPPENED TO HIM.
THIS IS TOO BAD OF HIM! IS THERE NO WAY TO FIND HIM, TO CALL HIM BACK?
NONE THAT I KNOW. BUT I BELIEVE THAT HE'S LEFT MONEY IN THE CRYPT, FOR FOOD FOR THE BOY.
MONEY! WHAT USE IS MONEY?
BOD WILL BE NEEDING MONEY IF HE'S TO GO OUT THERE TO BUY FOOD.
YOU'RE ALL AS BAD AS EACH OTHER!

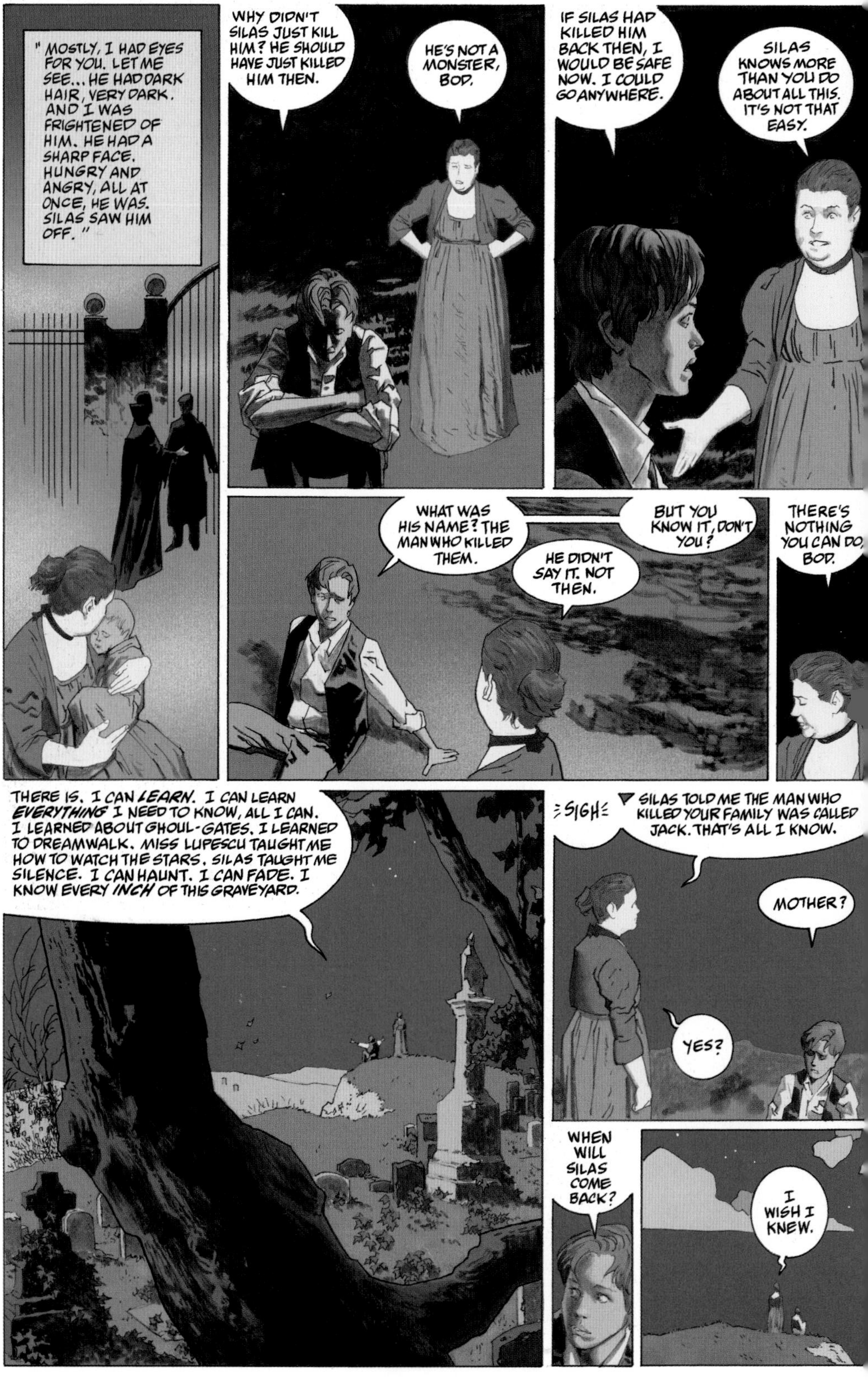
"MOSTLY, I HAD EYES FOR YOU. LET ME SEE... HE HAD DARK HAIR, VERY DARK. AND I WAS FRIGHTENED OF HIM. HE HAD A SHARP FACE. HUNGRY AND ANGRY, ALL AT ONCE, HE WAS. SILAS SAW HIM OFF."
WHY DIDN'T SILAS JUST KILL HIM? HE SHOULD HAVE JUST KILLED HIM THEN.
HE'S NOT A MONSTER, BOD.
IF SILAS HAD KILLED HIM BACK THEN, I WOULD BE SAFE NOW. I COULD GO ANYWHERE.
SILAS KNOWS MORE THAN YOU DO ABOUT ALL THIS. IT'S NOT THAT EASY.
WHAT WAS HIS NAME? THE MAN WHO KILLED THEM.
HE DIDN'T SAY IT. NOT THEN.
BUT YOU KNOW IT, DON'T YOU?
THERE'S NOTHING YOU CAN DO, BOD.
THERE IS. I CAN *LEARN*. I CAN LEARN *EVERYTHING* I NEED TO KNOW, ALL I CAN. I LEARNED ABOUT GHOUL-GATES. I LEARNED TO DREAMWALK. MISS LUPESCU TAUGHT ME HOW TO WATCH THE STARS. SILAS TAUGHT ME SILENCE. I CAN HAUNT. I CAN FADE. I KNOW EVERY *INCH* OF THIS GRAVEYARD.
SIGH
SILAS TOLD ME THE MAN WHO KILLED YOUR FAMILY WAS CALLED JACK. THAT'S ALL I KNOW.
MOTHER?
YES?
WHEN WILL SILAS COME BACK?
I WISH I KNEW.

... 47 ...

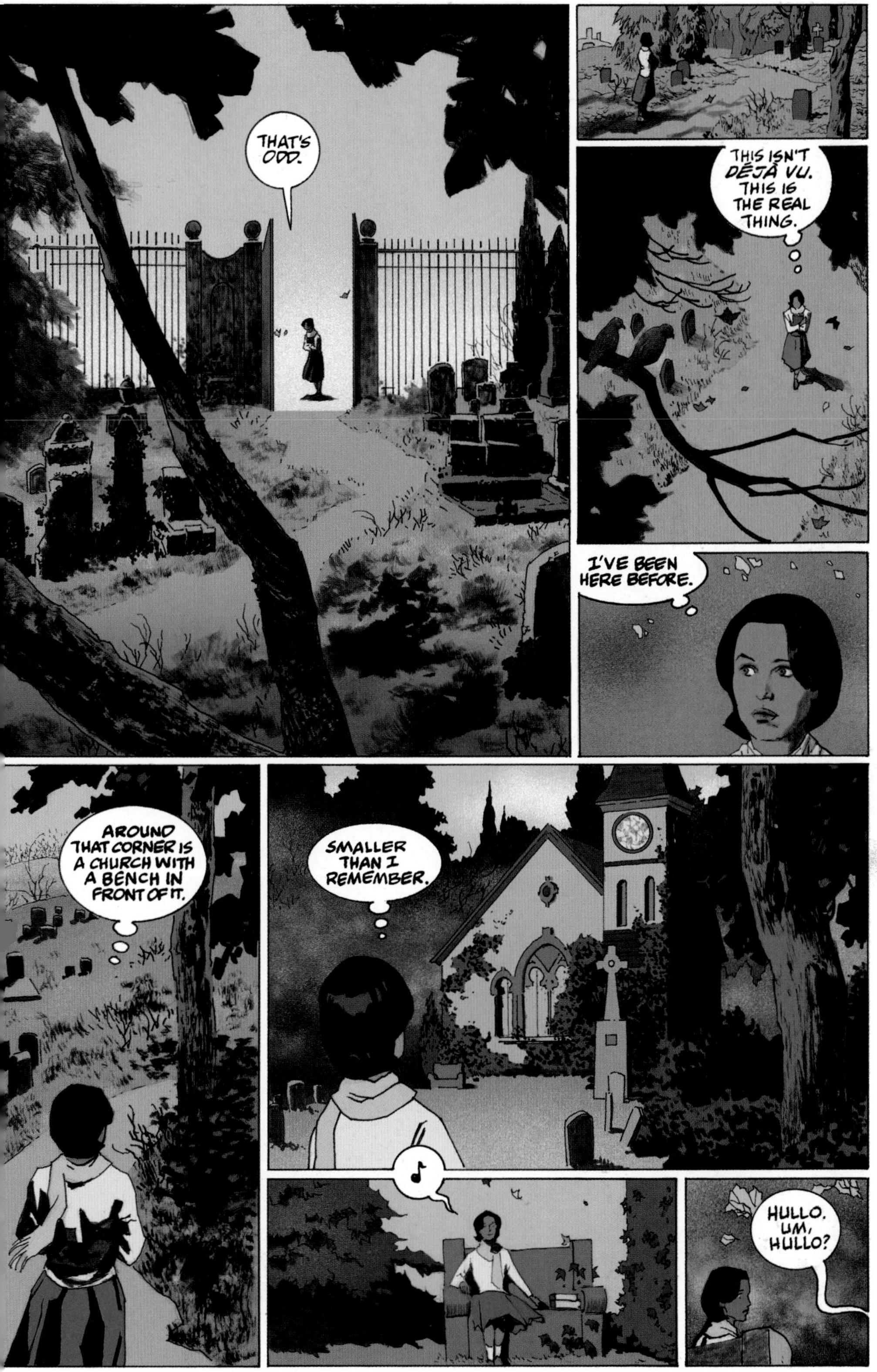
THAT'S ODD.
THIS ISN'T DÉJÀ VU. THIS IS THE REAL THING.
I'VE BEEN HERE BEFORE.
AROUND THAT CORNER IS A CHURCH WITH A BENCH IN FRONT OF IT.
SMALLER THAN I REMEMBER.
HULLO. UM, HULLO?

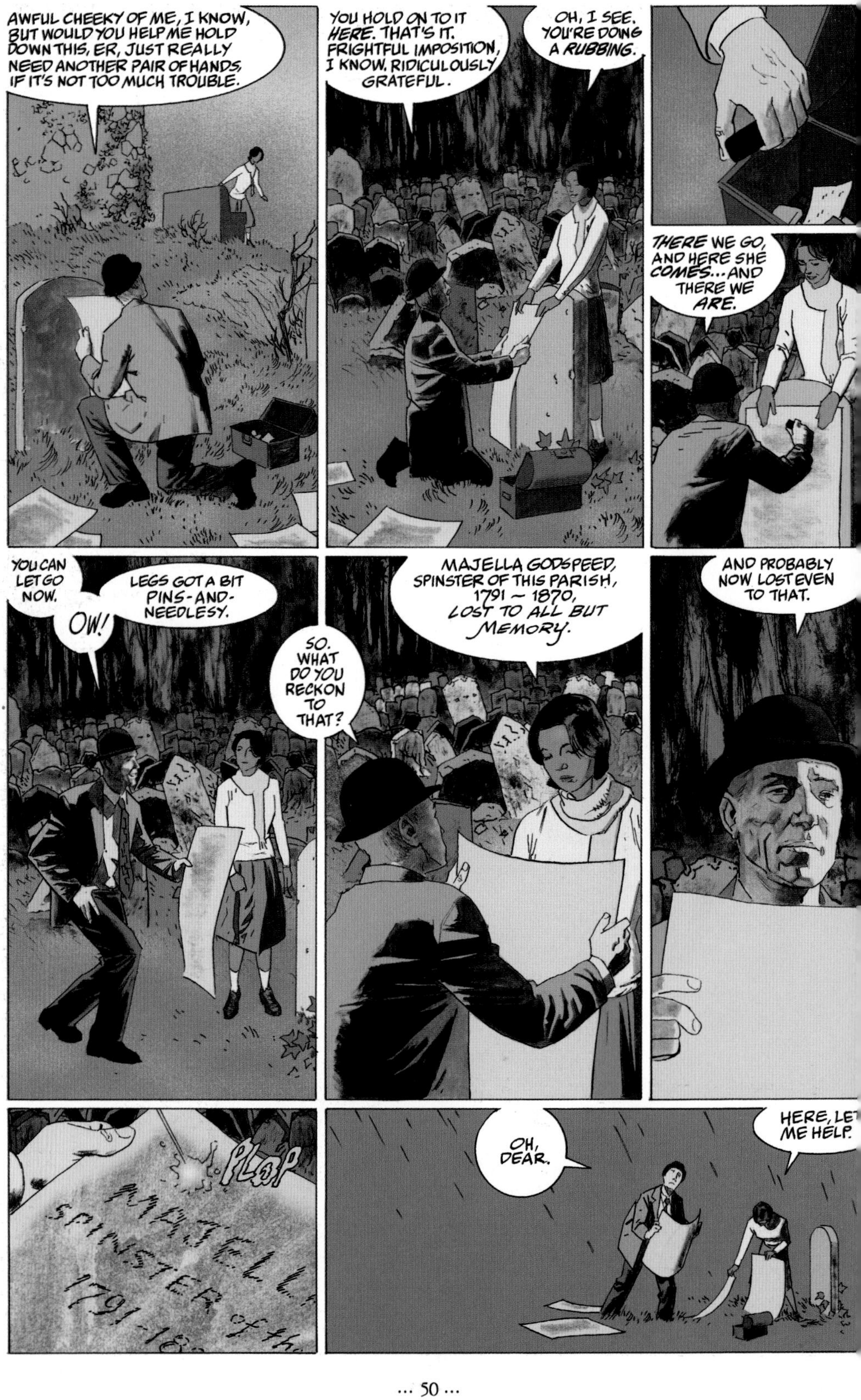
AWFUL CHEEKY OF ME, I KNOW, BUT WOULD YOU HELP ME HOLD DOWN THIS, ER, JUST REALLY NEED ANOTHER PAIR OF HANDS, IF IT'S NOT TOO MUCH TROUBLE.
YOU HOLD ON TO IT *HERE*. THAT'S IT. FRIGHTFUL IMPOSITION, I KNOW. RIDICULOUSLY GRATEFUL.
OH, I SEE. YOU'RE DOING A *RUBBING*.
THERE WE GO, AND HERE SHE *COMES*... AND THERE WE *ARE*.
YOU CAN LET GO NOW.
OW!
LEGS GOT A BIT PINS-AND-NEEDLESY.
SO. WHAT DO YOU RECKON TO THAT?
MAJELLA GODSPEED, SPINSTER OF THIS PARISH, 1791 ~ 1870, LOST TO ALL BUT MEMORY.
AND PROBABLY NOW LOST EVEN TO THAT.
PLOP
OH, DEAR.
HERE, LET ME HELP.

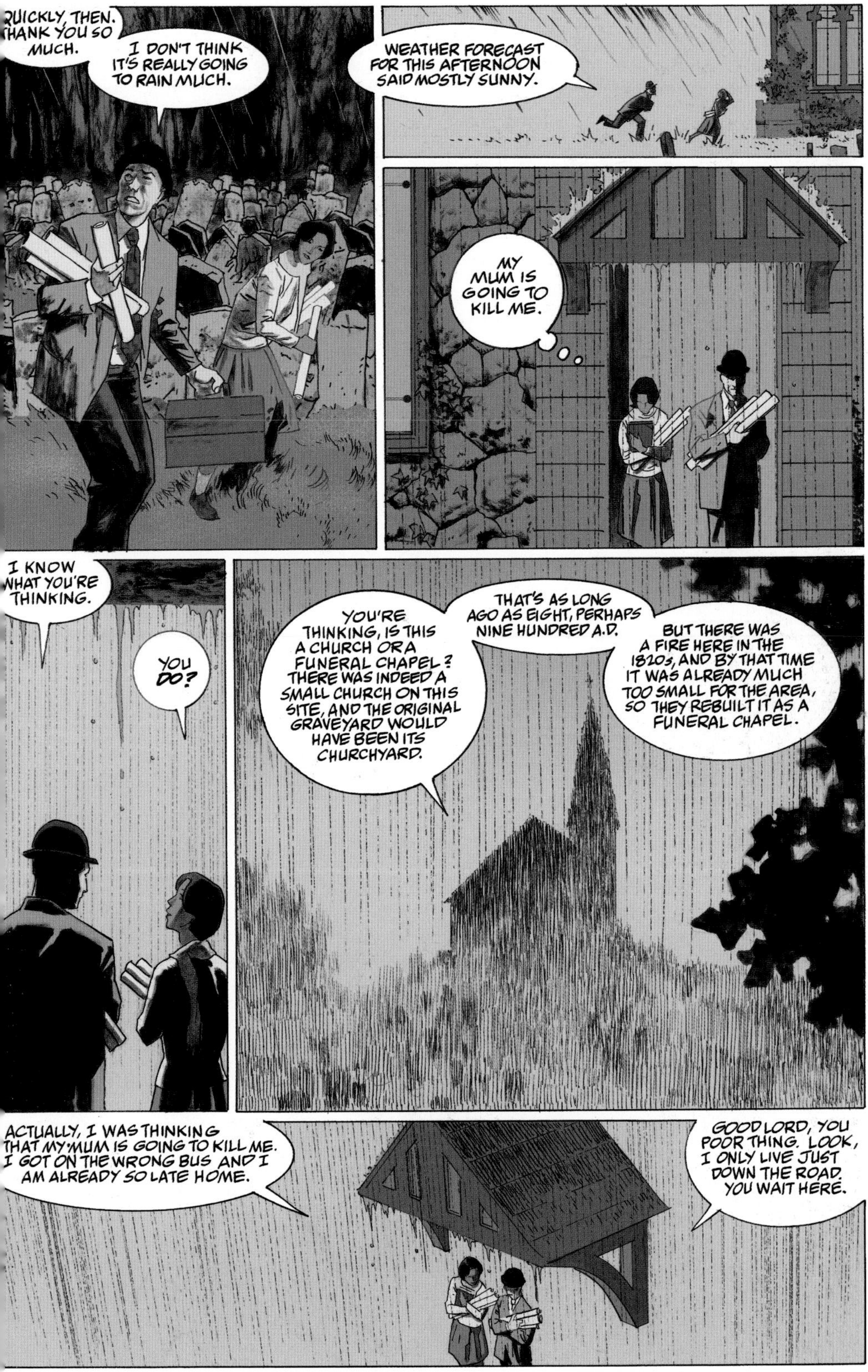
QUICKLY, THEN. THANK YOU SO MUCH.
I DON'T THINK IT'S REALLY GOING TO RAIN MUCH.
WEATHER FORECAST FOR THIS AFTERNOON SAID MOSTLY SUNNY.
MY MUM IS GOING TO KILL ME.
I KNOW WHAT YOU'RE THINKING.
YOU DO?
YOU'RE THINKING, IS THIS A CHURCH OR A FUNERAL CHAPEL? THERE WAS INDEED A SMALL CHURCH ON THIS SITE, AND THE ORIGINAL GRAVEYARD WOULD HAVE BEEN ITS CHURCHYARD.
THAT'S AS LONG AGO AS EIGHT, PERHAPS NINE HUNDRED A.D.
BUT THERE WAS A FIRE HERE IN THE 1820s, AND BY THAT TIME IT WAS ALREADY MUCH TOO SMALL FOR THE AREA, SO THEY REBUILT IT AS A FUNERAL CHAPEL.
ACTUALLY, I WAS THINKING THAT MY MUM IS GOING TO KILL ME. I GOT ON THE WRONG BUS AND I AM ALREADY SO LATE HOME.
GOOD LORD, YOU POOR THING. LOOK, I ONLY LIVE JUST DOWN THE ROAD. YOU WAIT HERE.

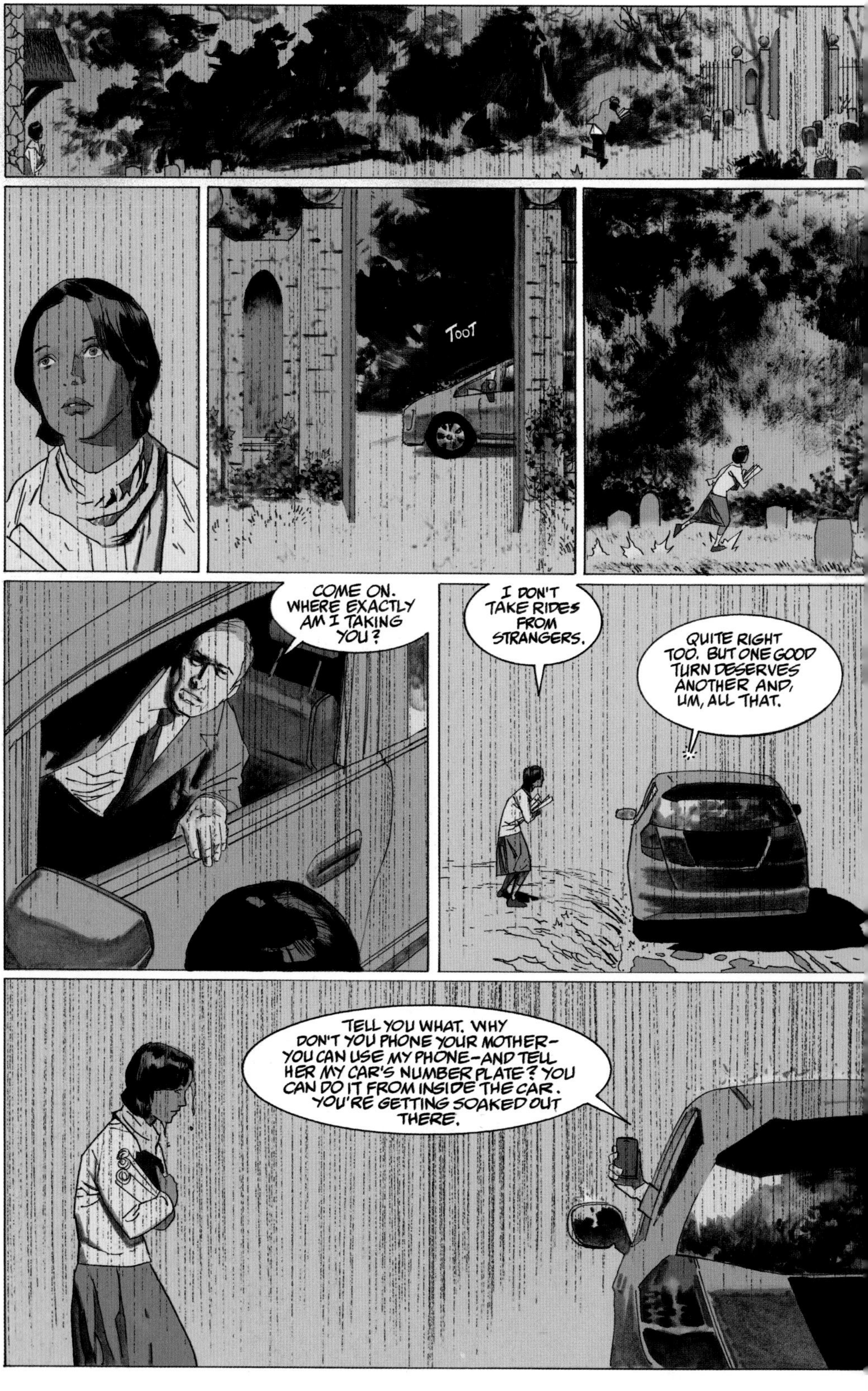
TOOT
COME ON. WHERE EXACTLY AM I TAKING YOU?
I DON'T TAKE RIDES FROM STRANGERS.
QUITE RIGHT TOO. BUT ONE GOOD TURN DESERVES ANOTHER AND, UM, ALL THAT.
TELL YOU WHAT. WHY DON'T YOU PHONE YOUR MOTHER-YOU CAN USE MY PHONE-AND TELL HER MY CAR'S NUMBER PLATE? YOU CAN DO IT FROM INSIDE THE CAR. YOU'RE GETTING SOAKED OUT THERE.

... 55 ...

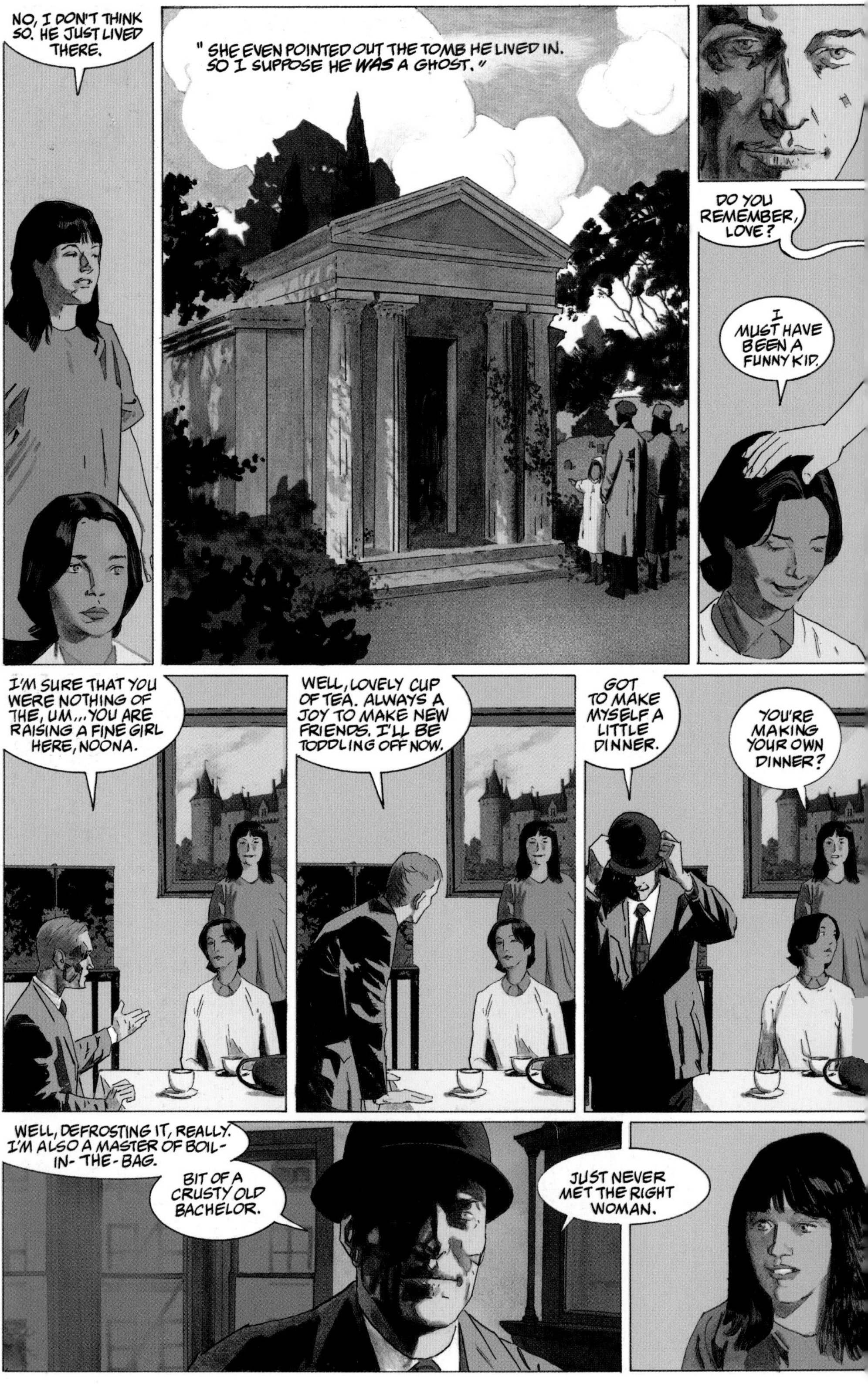
NO, I DON'T THINK SO. HE JUST LIVED THERE.
" SHE EVEN POINTED OUT THE TOMB HE LIVED IN. SO I SUPPOSE HE WAS A GHOST. "
DO YOU REMEMBER, LOVE?
I MUST HAVE BEEN A FUNNY KID.
I'M SURE THAT YOU WERE NOTHING OF THE, UM... YOU ARE RAISING A FINE GIRL HERE, NOONA.
WELL, LOVELY CUP OF TEA. ALWAYS A JOY TO MAKE NEW FRIENDS. I'LL BE TODDLING OFF NOW.
GOT TO MAKE MYSELF A LITTLE DINNER.
YOU'RE MAKING YOUR OWN DINNER?
WELL, DEFROSTING IT, REALLY. I'M ALSO A MASTER OF BOIL-IN-THE-BAG.
BIT OF A CRUSTY OLD BACHELOR.
JUST NEVER MET THE RIGHT WOMAN.

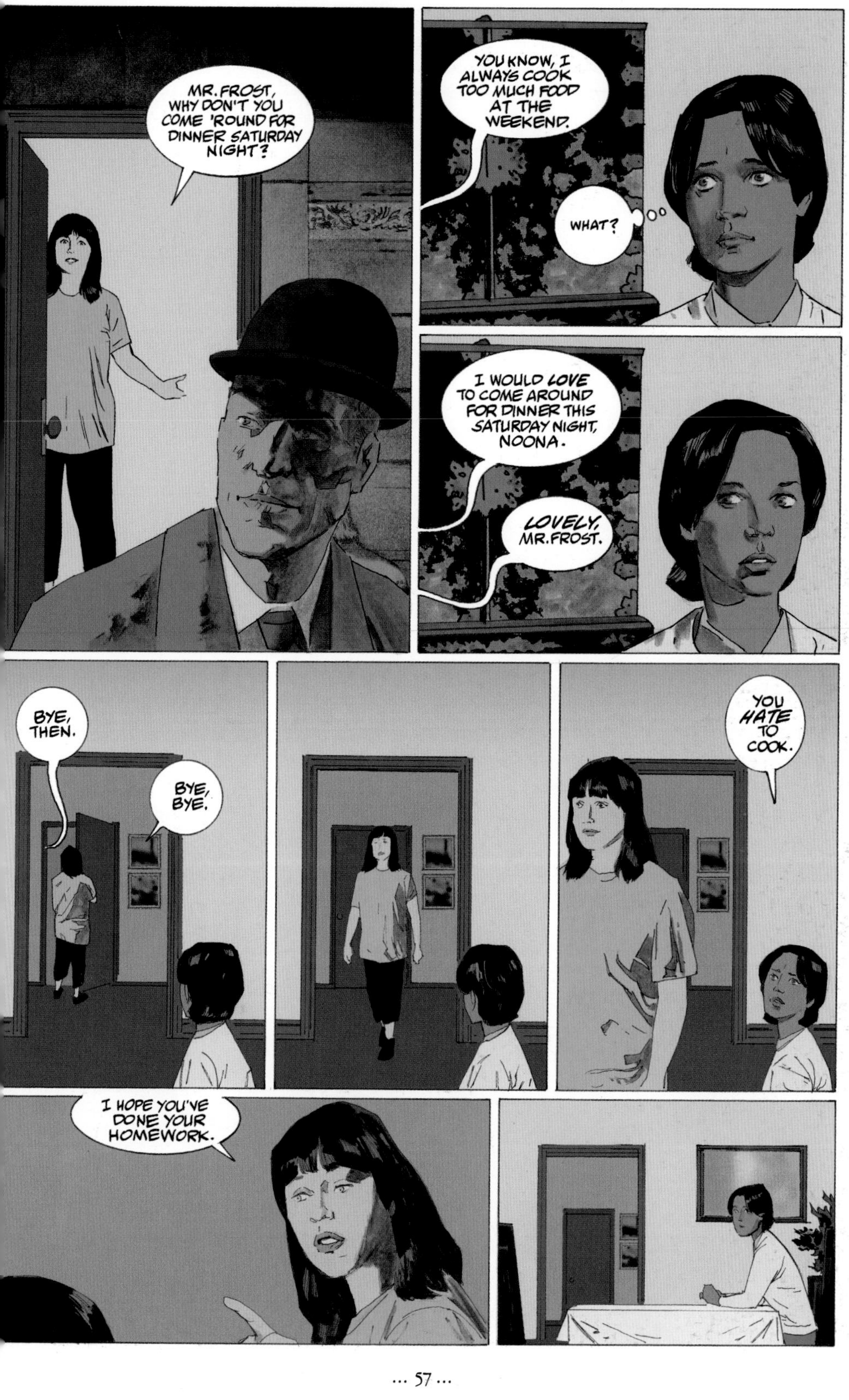
MR. FROST, WHY DON'T YOU COME 'ROUND FOR DINNER SATURDAY NIGHT?
YOU KNOW, I ALWAYS COOK TOO MUCH FOOD AT THE WEEKEND.
WHAT?
I WOULD LOVE TO COME AROUND FOR DINNER THIS SATURDAY NIGHT, NOONA.
LOVELY, MR. FROST.
BYE, THEN.
BYE, BYE.
YOU HATE TO COOK.
I HOPE YOU'VE DONE YOUR HOMEWORK.

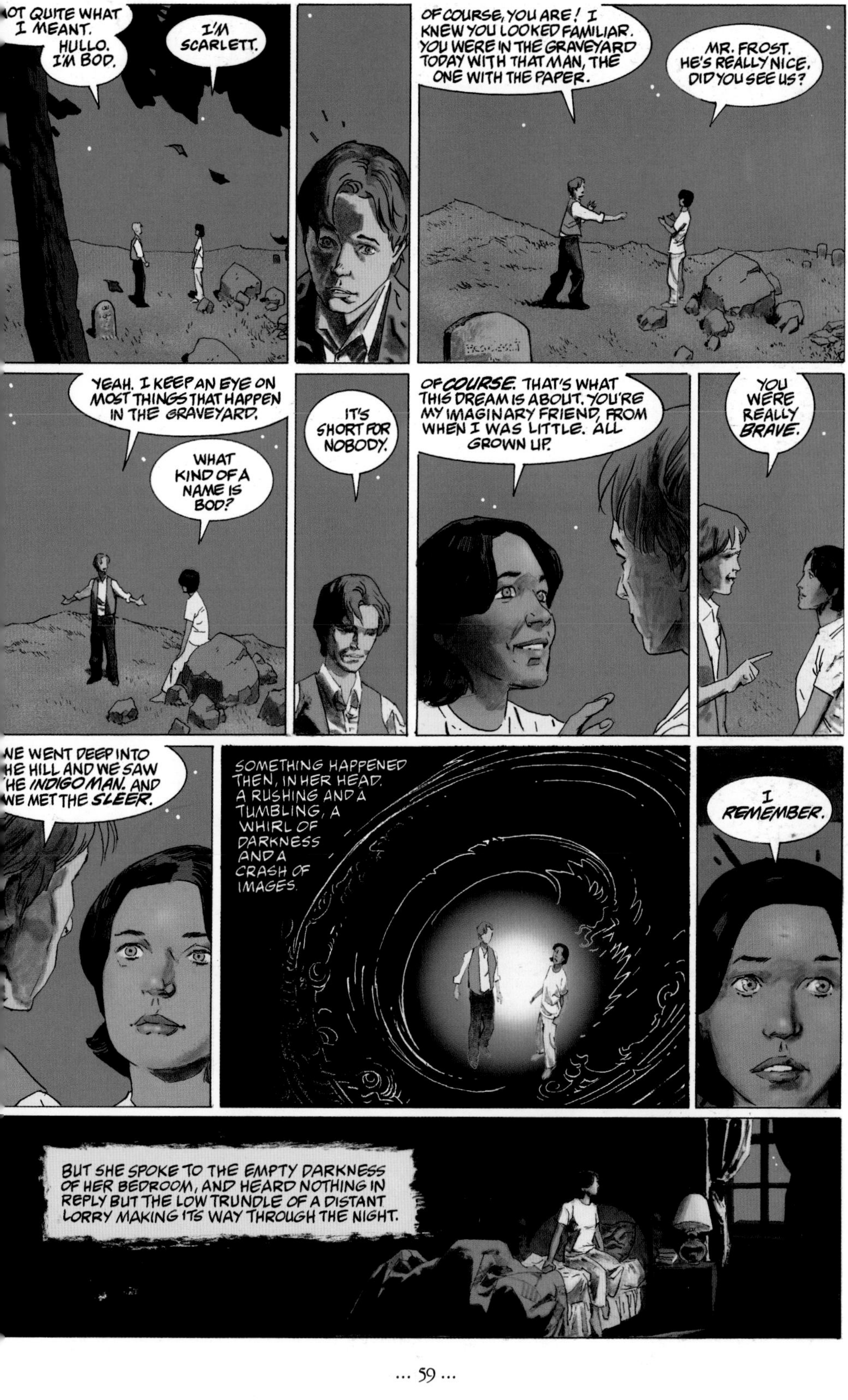
OT QUITE WHAT I MEANT. HULLO. I'M BOD.
I'M SCARLETT.
OF COURSE, YOU ARE! I KNEW YOU LOOKED FAMILIAR. YOU WERE IN THE GRAVEYARD TODAY WITH THAT MAN, THE ONE WITH THE PAPER.
MR. FROST. HE'S REALLY NICE. DID YOU SEE US?
YEAH. I KEEP AN EYE ON MOST THINGS THAT HAPPEN IN THE GRAVEYARD.
WHAT KIND OF A NAME IS BOD?
IT'S SHORT FOR NOBODY.
OF COURSE. THAT'S WHAT THIS DREAM IS ABOUT. YOU'RE MY IMAGINARY FRIEND, FROM WHEN I WAS LITTLE. ALL GROWN UP.
YOU WERE REALLY BRAVE.
WE WENT DEEP INTO HE HILL AND WE SAW HE INDIGO MAN. AND WE MET THE SLEER.
SOMETHING HAPPENED THEN, IN HER HEAD. A RUSHING AND A TUMBLING, A WHIRL OF DARKNESS AND A CRASH OF IMAGES.
I REMEMBER.
BUT SHE SPOKE TO THE EMPTY DARKNESS OF HER BEDROOM, AND HEARD NOTHING IN REPLY BUT THE LOW TRUNDLE OF A DISTANT LORRY MAKING ITS WAY THROUGH THE NIGHT.

BOD HAD STORES OF FOOD, THE KIND THAT LASTED, CACHED IN THE CRYPT. HE HAD ENOUGH TO KEEP HIM GOING FOR A COUPLE OF MONTHS. SILAS HAD MADE SURE OF THAT.

THE GRAVEYARD, THOUGH, WAS HIS WORLD AND HIS DOMAIN, AND HE LOVED IT AS ONLY A FOURTEEN-YEAR-OLD BOY CAN LOVE ANYTHING.

HE MISSED THE WORLD BEYOND THE GRAVEYARD GATES, BUT HE KNEW IT WAS NOT SAFE OUT THERE.

NOT YET.

AND YET...

IN THE GRAVEYARD, NO ONE EVER CHANGED. THE LITTLE CHILDREN BOD HAD PLAYED WITH WHEN HE WAS SMALL, WERE STILL LITTLE CHILDREN.

FORTINBRAS BARTLEBY, WHO HAD ONCE BEEN HIS BEST FRIEND, WAS NOW FOUR OR FIVE YEARS YOUNGER THAN BOD WAS, AND THEY HAD LESS TO TALK ABOUT EACH TIME THEY SAW EACH OTHER.

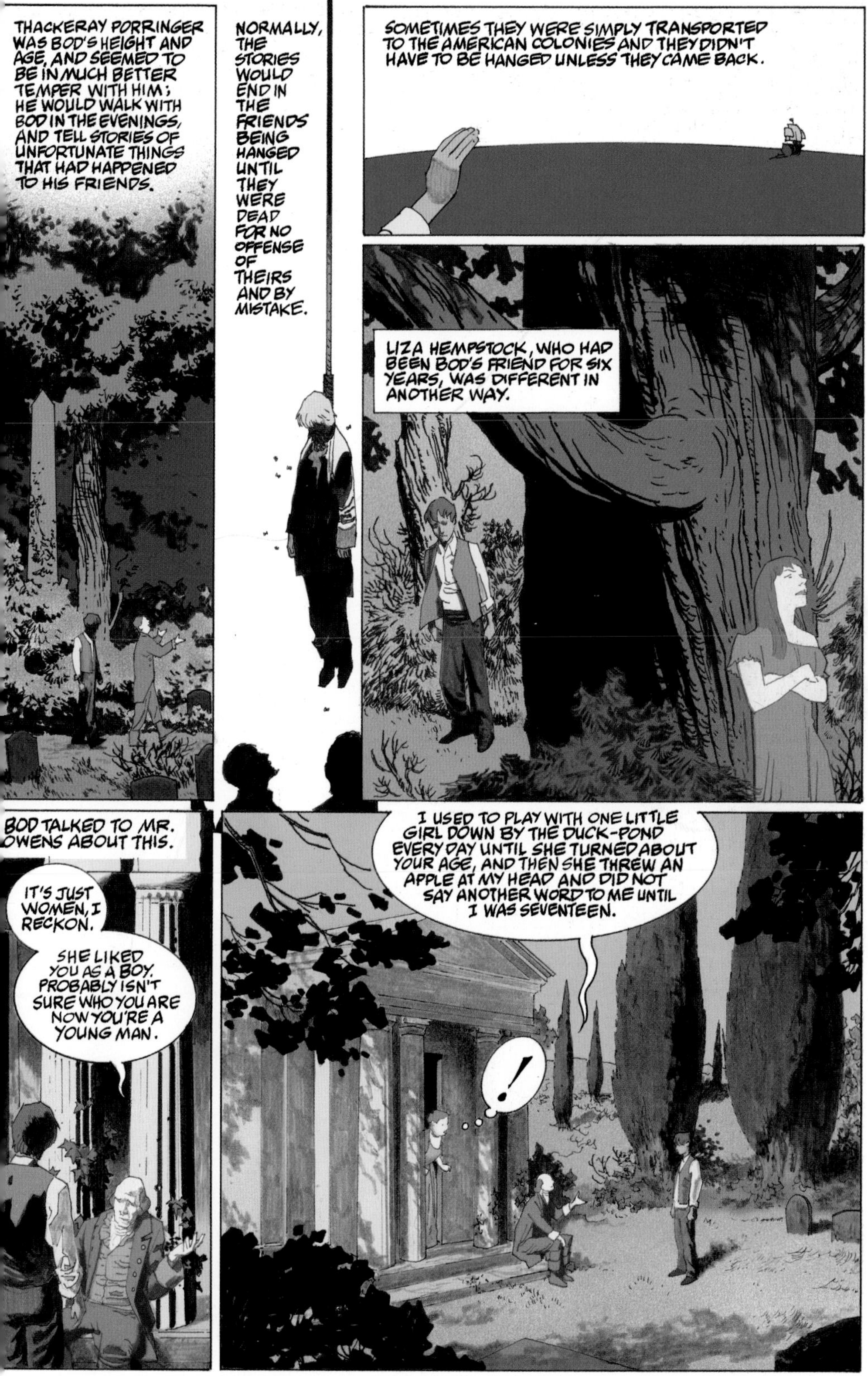
THACKERAY PORRINGER WAS BOD'S HEIGHT AND AGE, AND SEEMED TO BE IN MUCH BETTER TEMPER WITH HIM; HE WOULD WALK WITH BOD IN THE EVENINGS, AND TELL STORIES OF UNFORTUNATE THINGS THAT HAD HAPPENED TO HIS FRIENDS.
NORMALLY, THE STORIES WOULD END IN THE FRIENDS BEING HANGED UNTIL THEY WERE DEAD FOR NO OFFENSE OF THEIRS AND BY MISTAKE.
SOMETIMES THEY WERE SIMPLY TRANSPORTED TO THE AMERICAN COLONIES AND THEY DIDN'T HAVE TO BE HANGED UNLESS THEY CAME BACK.
LIZA HEMPSTOCK, WHO HAD BEEN BOD'S FRIEND FOR SIX YEARS, WAS DIFFERENT IN ANOTHER WAY.
BOD TALKED TO MR. OWENS ABOUT THIS.
IT'S JUST WOMEN, I RECKON.
SHE LIKED YOU AS A BOY. PROBABLY ISN'T SURE WHO YOU ARE NOW YOU'RE A YOUNG MAN.
I USED TO PLAY WITH ONE LITTLE GIRL DOWN BY THE DUCK-POND EVERY DAY UNTIL SHE TURNED ABOUT YOUR AGE, AND THEN SHE THREW AN APPLE AT MY HEAD AND DID NOT SAY ANOTHER WORD TO ME UNTIL I WAS SEVENTEEN.
!

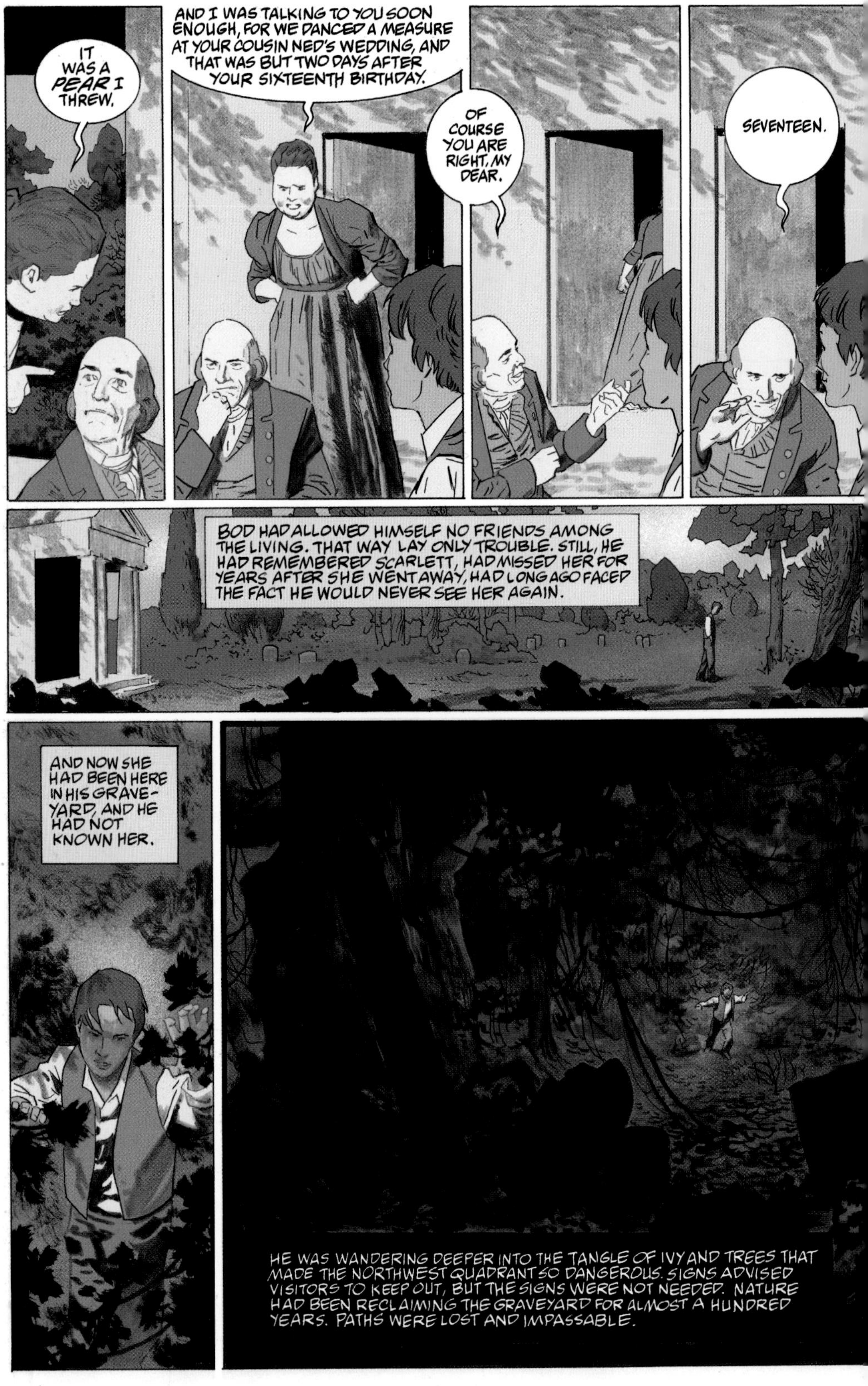

IT WAS A PEAR I THREW.
AND I WAS TALKING TO YOU SOON ENOUGH, FOR WE DANCED A MEASURE AT YOUR COUSIN NED'S WEDDING, AND THAT WAS BUT TWO DAYS AFTER YOUR SIXTEENTH BIRTHDAY.
OF COURSE YOU ARE RIGHT, MY DEAR.
SEVENTEEN.
BOD HAD ALLOWED HIMSELF NO FRIENDS AMONG THE LIVING. THAT WAY LAY ONLY TROUBLE. STILL, HE HAD REMEMBERED SCARLETT, HAD MISSED HER FOR YEARS AFTER SHE WENT AWAY, HAD LONG AGO FACED THE FACT HE WOULD NEVER SEE HER AGAIN.
AND NOW SHE HAD BEEN HERE IN HIS GRAVEYARD, AND HE HAD NOT KNOWN HER.
HE WAS WANDERING DEEPER INTO THE TANGLE OF IVY AND TREES THAT MADE THE NORTHWEST QUADRANT SO DANGEROUS. SIGNS ADVISED VISITORS TO KEEP OUT, BUT THE SIGNS WERE NOT NEEDED. NATURE HAD BEEN RECLAIMING THE GRAVEYARD FOR ALMOST A HUNDRED YEARS. PATHS WERE LOST AND IMPASSABLE.

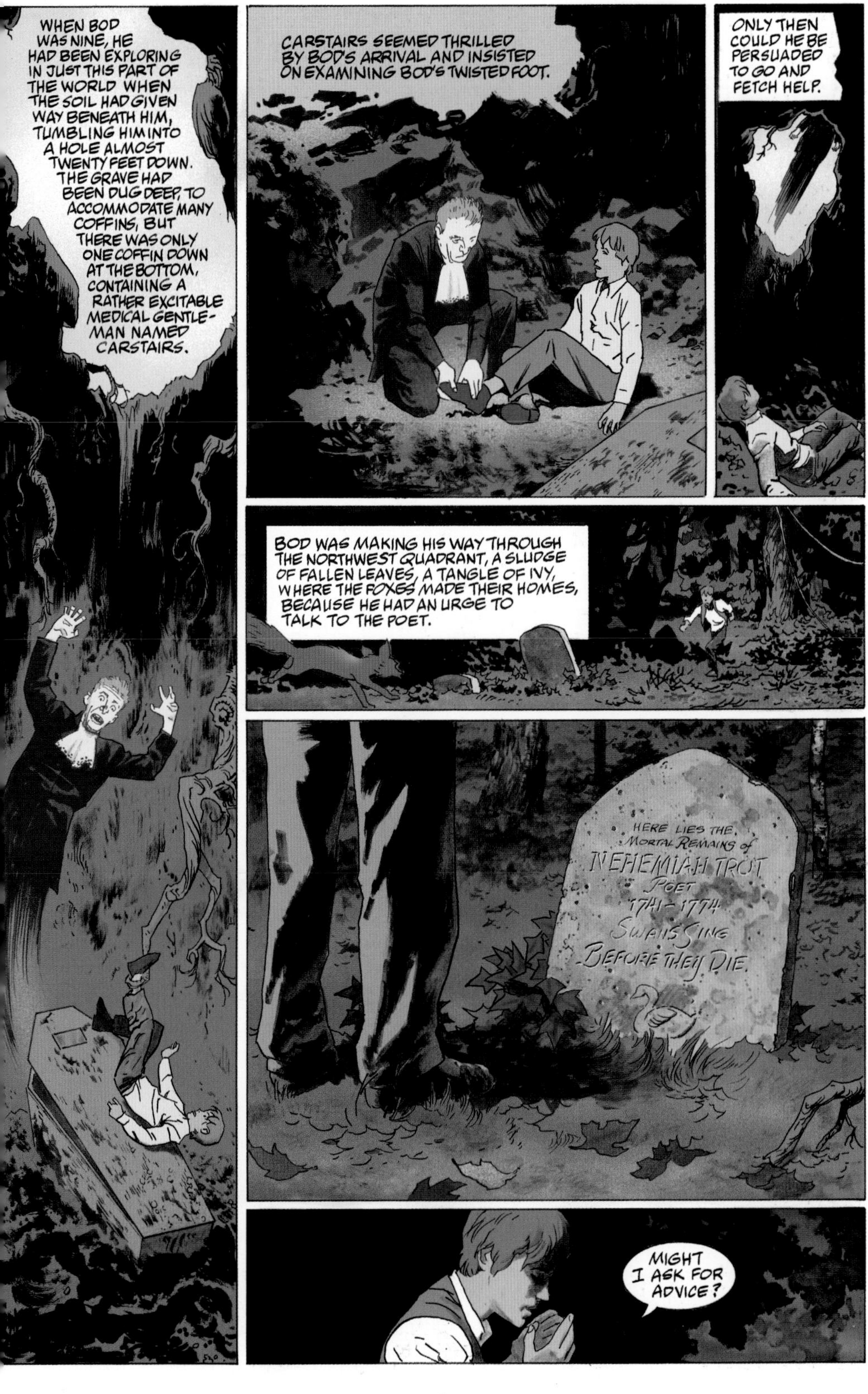
WHEN BOD WAS NINE, HE HAD BEEN EXPLORING IN JUST THIS PART OF THE WORLD WHEN THE SOIL HAD GIVEN WAY BENEATH HIM, TUMBLING HIM INTO A HOLE ALMOST TWENTY FEET DOWN. THE GRAVE HAD BEEN DUG DEEP, TO ACCOMMODATE MANY COFFINS, BUT THERE WAS ONLY ONE COFFIN DOWN AT THE BOTTOM, CONTAINING A RATHER EXCITABLE MEDICAL GENTLEMAN NAMED CARSTAIRS.
CARSTAIRS SEEMED THRILLED BY BOD'S ARRIVAL AND INSISTED ON EXAMINING BOD'S TWISTED FOOT.
ONLY THEN COULD HE BE PERSUADED TO GO AND FETCH HELP.
BOD WAS MAKING HIS WAY THROUGH THE NORTHWEST QUADRANT, A SLUDGE OF FALLEN LEAVES, A TANGLE OF IVY, WHERE THE FOXES MADE THEIR HOMES, BECAUSE HE HAD AN URGE TO TALK TO THE POET.
HERE LIES THE MORTAL REMAINS OF NEHEMIAH TROT POET 1741 - 1774 SWANS SING BEFORE THEY DIE
MIGHT I ASK FOR ADVICE?

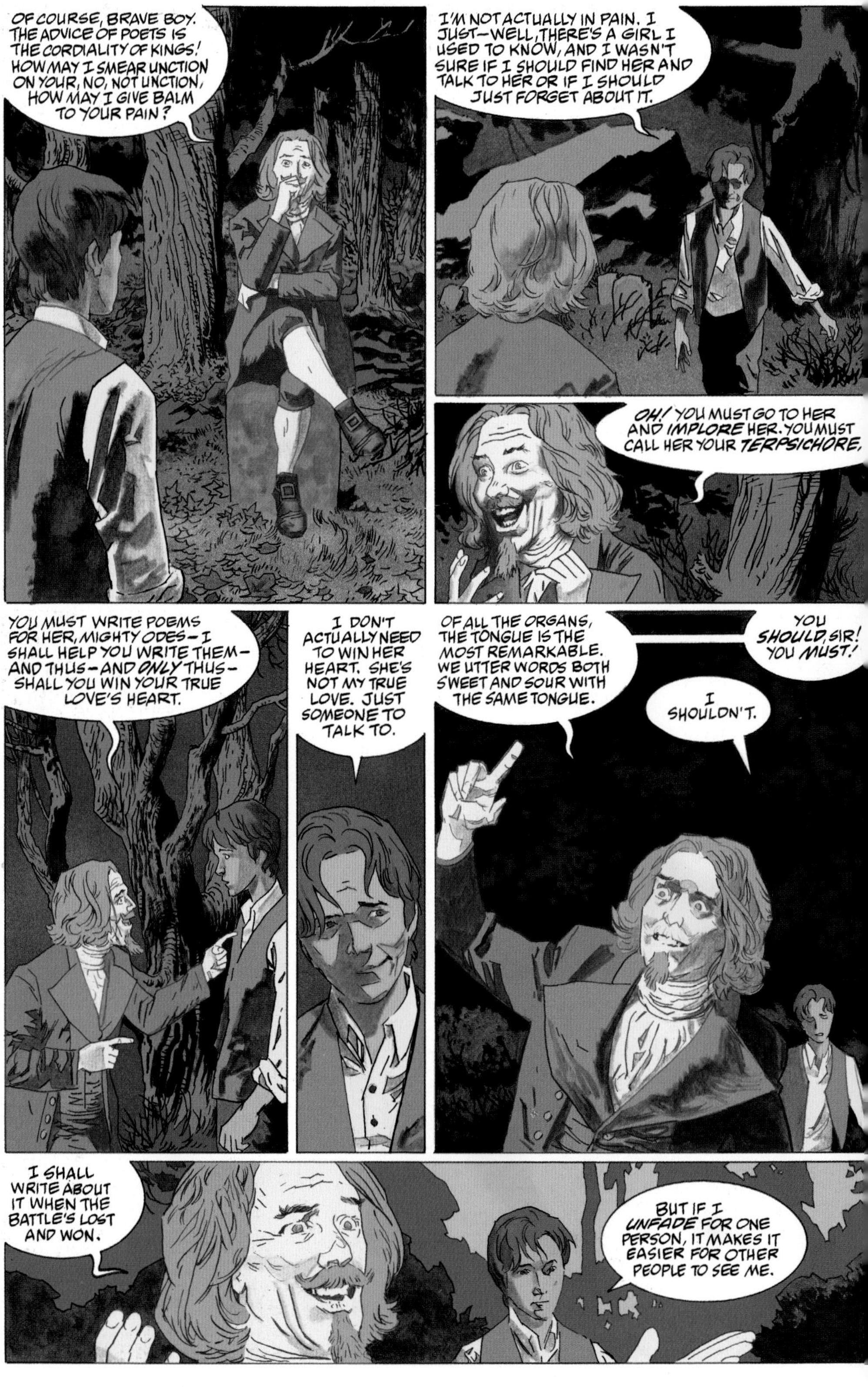
OF COURSE, BRAVE BOY. THE ADVICE OF POETS IS THE CORDIALITY OF KINGS! HOW MAY I SMEAR UNCTION ON YOUR, NO, NOT UNCTION, HOW MAY I GIVE BALM TO YOUR PAIN?
I'M NOT ACTUALLY IN PAIN. I JUST—WELL, THERE'S A GIRL I USED TO KNOW, AND I WASN'T SURE IF I SHOULD FIND HER AND TALK TO HER OR IF I SHOULD JUST FORGET ABOUT IT.
OH! YOU MUST GO TO HER AND IMPLORE HER. YOU MUST CALL HER YOUR TERPSICHORE.
YOU MUST WRITE POEMS FOR HER, MIGHTY ODES—I SHALL HELP YOU WRITE THEM—AND THUS—AND ONLY THUS—SHALL YOU WIN YOUR TRUE LOVE'S HEART.
I DON'T ACTUALLY NEED TO WIN HER HEART. SHE'S NOT MY TRUE LOVE. JUST SOMEONE TO TALK TO.
OF ALL THE ORGANS, THE TONGUE IS THE MOST REMARKABLE. WE UTTER WORDS BOTH SWEET AND SOUR WITH THE SAME TONGUE.
YOU SHOULD, SIR! YOU MUST!
I SHOULDN'T.
I SHALL WRITE ABOUT IT WHEN THE BATTLE'S LOST AND WON.
BUT IF I UNFADE FOR ONE PERSON, IT MAKES IT EASIER FOR OTHER PEOPLE TO SEE ME.

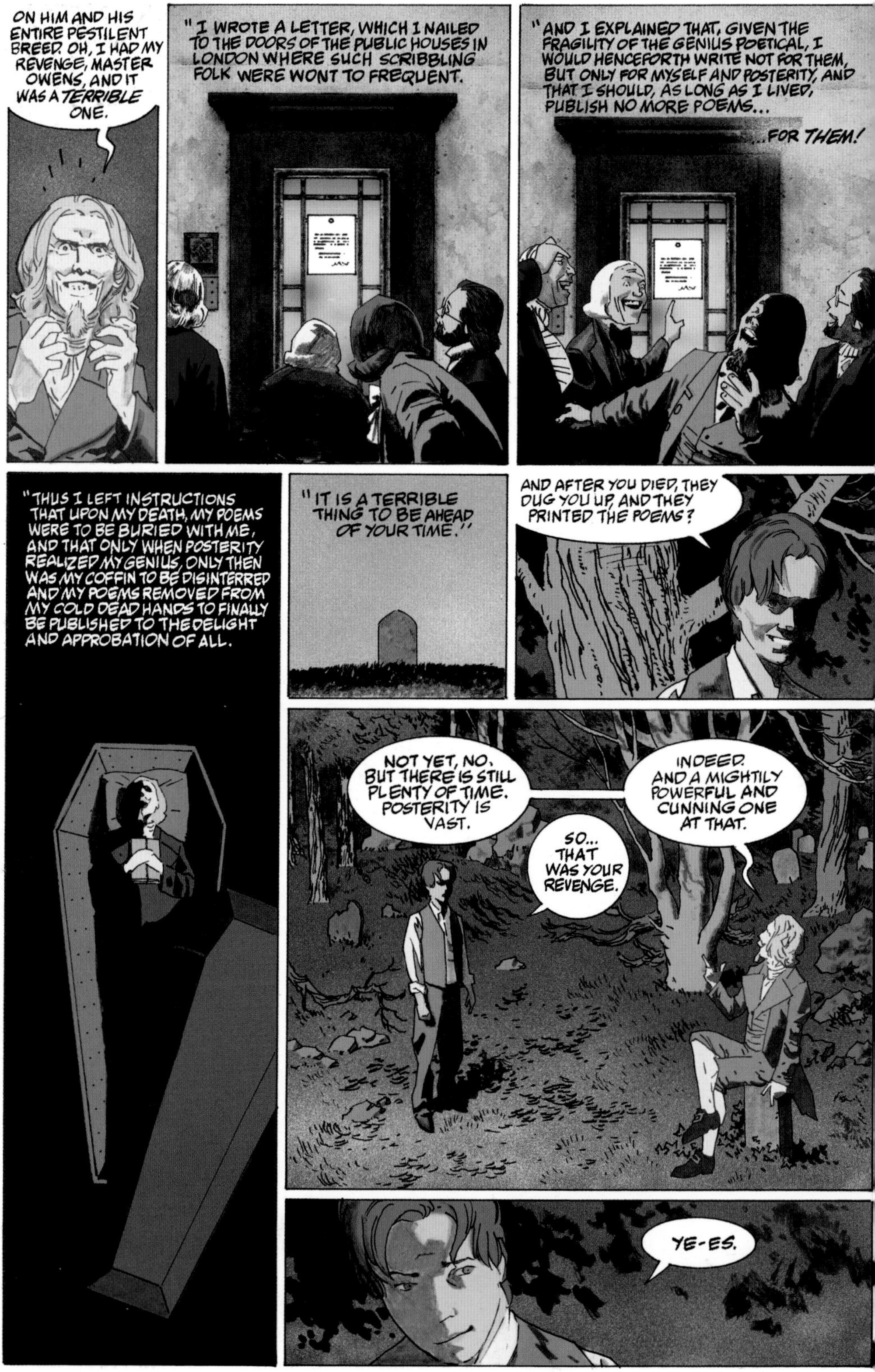

ON HIM AND HIS ENTIRE PESTILENT BREED. OH, I HAD MY REVENGE, MASTER OWENS, AND IT WAS A TERRIBLE ONE.
"I WROTE A LETTER, WHICH I NAILED TO THE DOORS OF THE PUBLIC HOUSES IN LONDON WHERE SUCH SCRIBBLING FOLK WERE WONT TO FREQUENT.
"AND I EXPLAINED THAT, GIVEN THE FRAGILITY OF THE GENIUS POETICAL, I WOULD HENCEFORTH WRITE NOT FOR THEM, BUT ONLY FOR MYSELF AND POSTERITY, AND THAT I SHOULD, AS LONG AS I LIVED, PUBLISH NO MORE POEMS...
...FOR THEM!
"THUS I LEFT INSTRUCTIONS THAT UPON MY DEATH, MY POEMS WERE TO BE BURIED WITH ME, AND THAT ONLY WHEN POSTERITY REALIZED MY GENIUS, ONLY THEN WAS MY COFFIN TO BE DISINTERRED AND MY POEMS REMOVED FROM MY COLD DEAD HANDS TO FINALLY BE PUBLISHED TO THE DELIGHT AND APPROBATION OF ALL.
"IT IS A TERRIBLE THING TO BE AHEAD OF YOUR TIME."
AND AFTER YOU DIED, THEY DUG YOU UP, AND THEY PRINTED THE POEMS?
NOT YET, NO. BUT THERE IS STILL PLENTY OF TIME. POSTERITY IS VAST.
SO... THAT WAS YOUR REVENGE.
INDEED. AND A MIGHTILY POWERFUL AND CUNNING ONE AT THAT.
YE-ES.

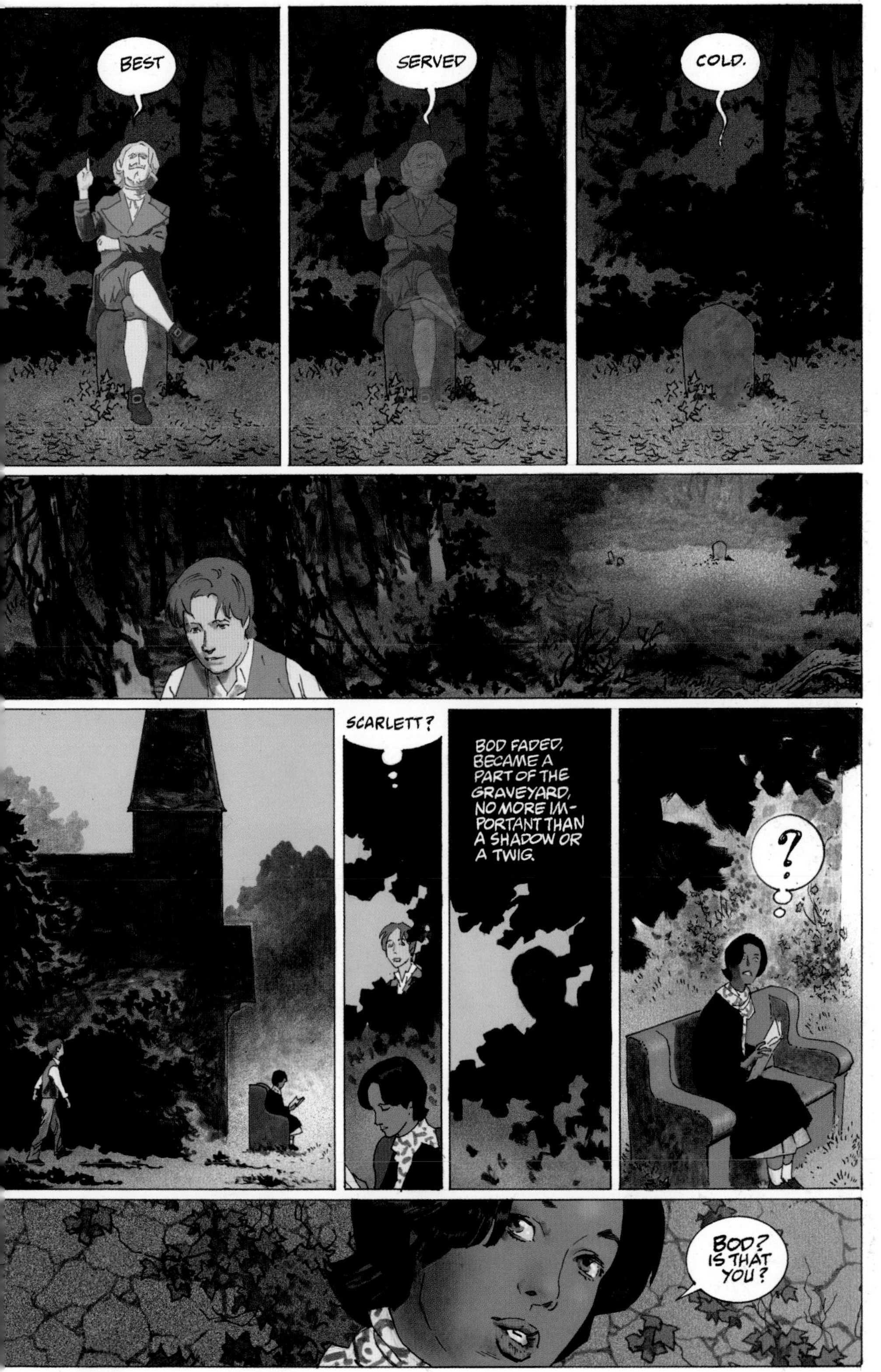
BEST
SERVED
COLD.
SCARLETT?
BOD FADED, BECAME A PART OF THE GRAVEYARD, NO MORE IMPORTANT THAN A SHADOW OR A TWIG.
?
BOD? IS THAT YOU?

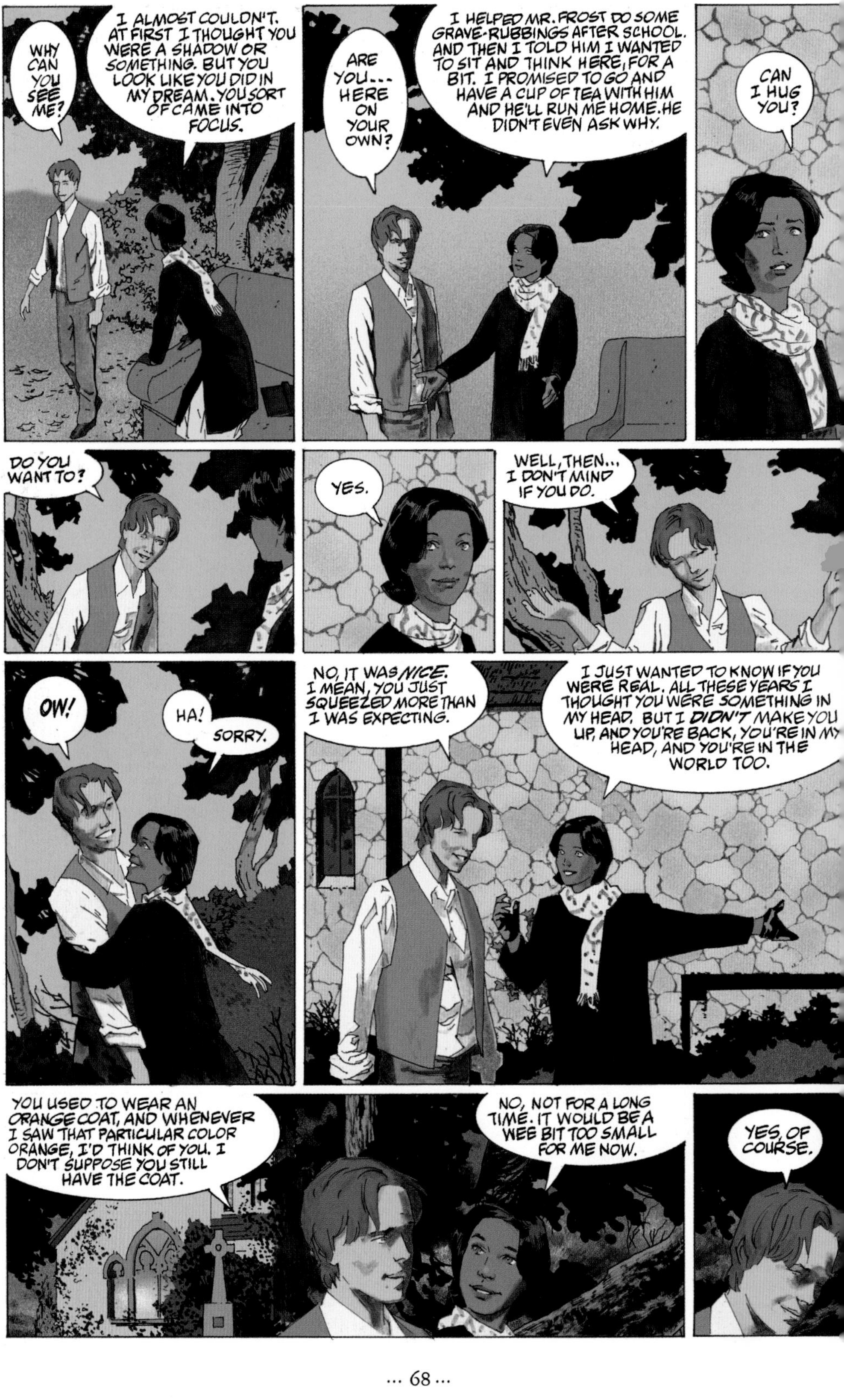
WHY CAN YOU SEE ME?
I ALMOST COULDN'T. AT FIRST I THOUGHT YOU WERE A SHADOW OR SOMETHING. BUT YOU LOOK LIKE YOU DID IN MY DREAM. YOU SORT OF CAME INTO FOCUS.
ARE YOU... HERE ON YOUR OWN?
I HELPED MR. FROST DO SOME GRAVE-RUBBINGS AFTER SCHOOL. AND THEN I TOLD HIM I WANTED TO SIT AND THINK HERE, FOR A BIT. I PROMISED TO GO AND HAVE A CUP OF TEA WITH HIM AND HE'LL RUN ME HOME. HE DIDN'T EVEN ASK WHY.
CAN I HUG YOU?
DO YOU WANT TO?
YES.
WELL, THEN... I DON'T MIND IF YOU DO.
OW!
HA!
SORRY.
NO, IT WAS NICE. I MEAN, YOU JUST SQUEEZED MORE THAN I WAS EXPECTING.
I JUST WANTED TO KNOW IF YOU WERE REAL. ALL THESE YEARS I THOUGHT YOU WERE SOMETHING IN MY HEAD. BUT I DIDN'T MAKE YOU UP, AND YOU'RE BACK, YOU'RE IN MY HEAD, AND YOU'RE IN THE WORLD TOO.
YOU USED TO WEAR AN ORANGE COAT, AND WHENEVER I SAW THAT PARTICULAR COLOR ORANGE, I'D THINK OF YOU. I DON'T SUPPOSE YOU STILL HAVE THE COAT.
NO, NOT FOR A LONG TIME. IT WOULD BE A WEE BIT TOO SMALL FOR ME NOW.
YES, OF COURSE.

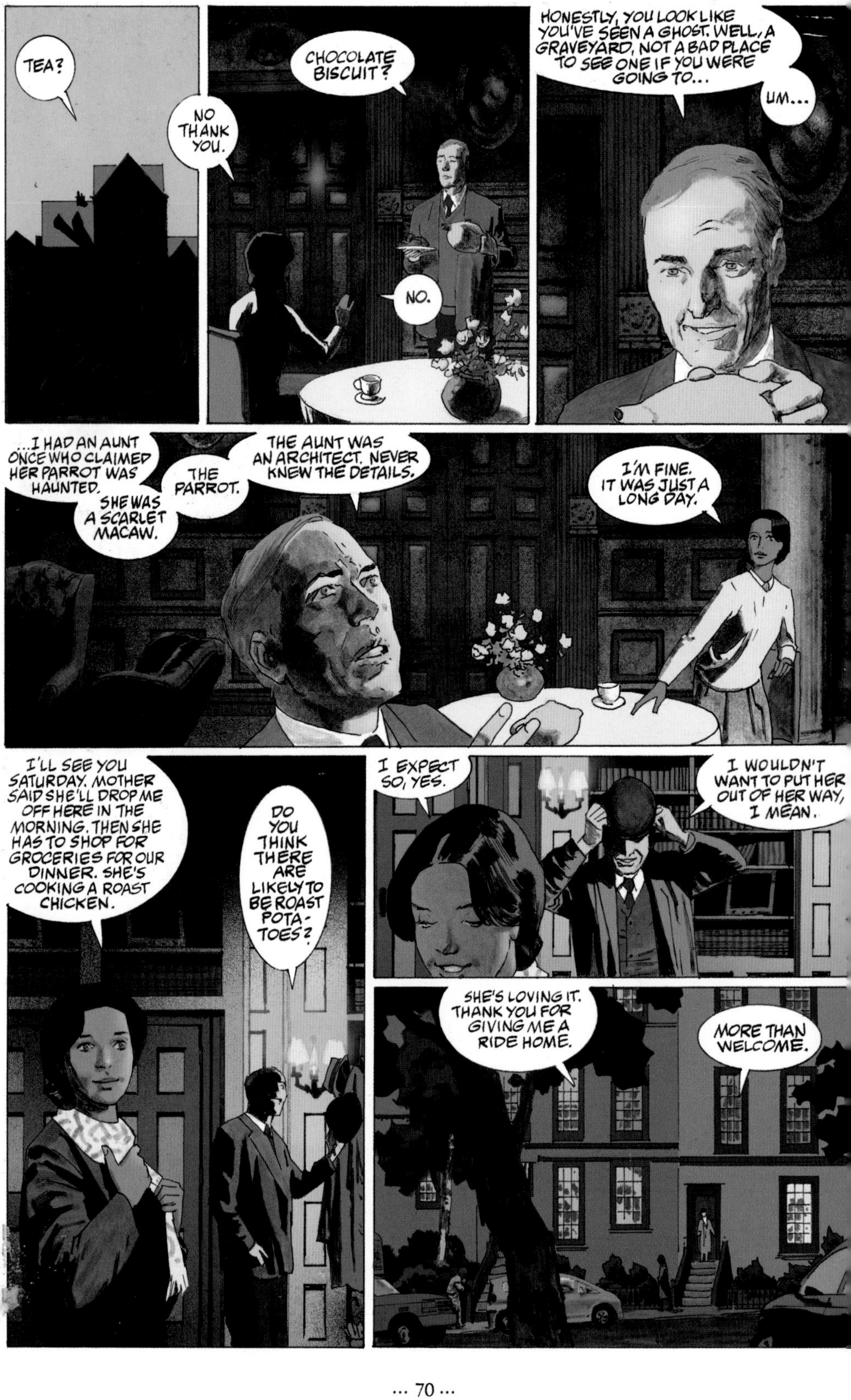
TEA?
NO THANK YOU.
CHOCOLATE BISCUIT?
NO.
HONESTLY, YOU LOOK LIKE YOU'VE SEEN A GHOST. WELL, A GRAVEYARD, NOT A BAD PLACE TO SEE ONE IF YOU WERE GOING TO...
UM...
...I HAD AN AUNT ONCE WHO CLAIMED HER PARROT WAS HAUNTED.
THE PARROT.
SHE WAS A SCARLET MACAW.
THE AUNT WAS AN ARCHITECT. NEVER KNEW THE DETAILS.
I'M FINE. IT WAS JUST A LONG DAY.
I'LL SEE YOU SATURDAY. MOTHER SAID SHE'LL DROP ME OFF HERE IN THE MORNING. THEN SHE HAS TO SHOP FOR GROCERIES FOR OUR DINNER. SHE'S COOKING A ROAST CHICKEN.
DO YOU THINK THERE ARE LIKELY TO BE ROAST POTATOES?
I EXPECT SO, YES.
I WOULDN'T WANT TO PUT HER OUT OF HER WAY, I MEAN.
SHE'S LOVING IT. THANK YOU FOR GIVING ME A RIDE HOME.
MORE THAN WELCOME.

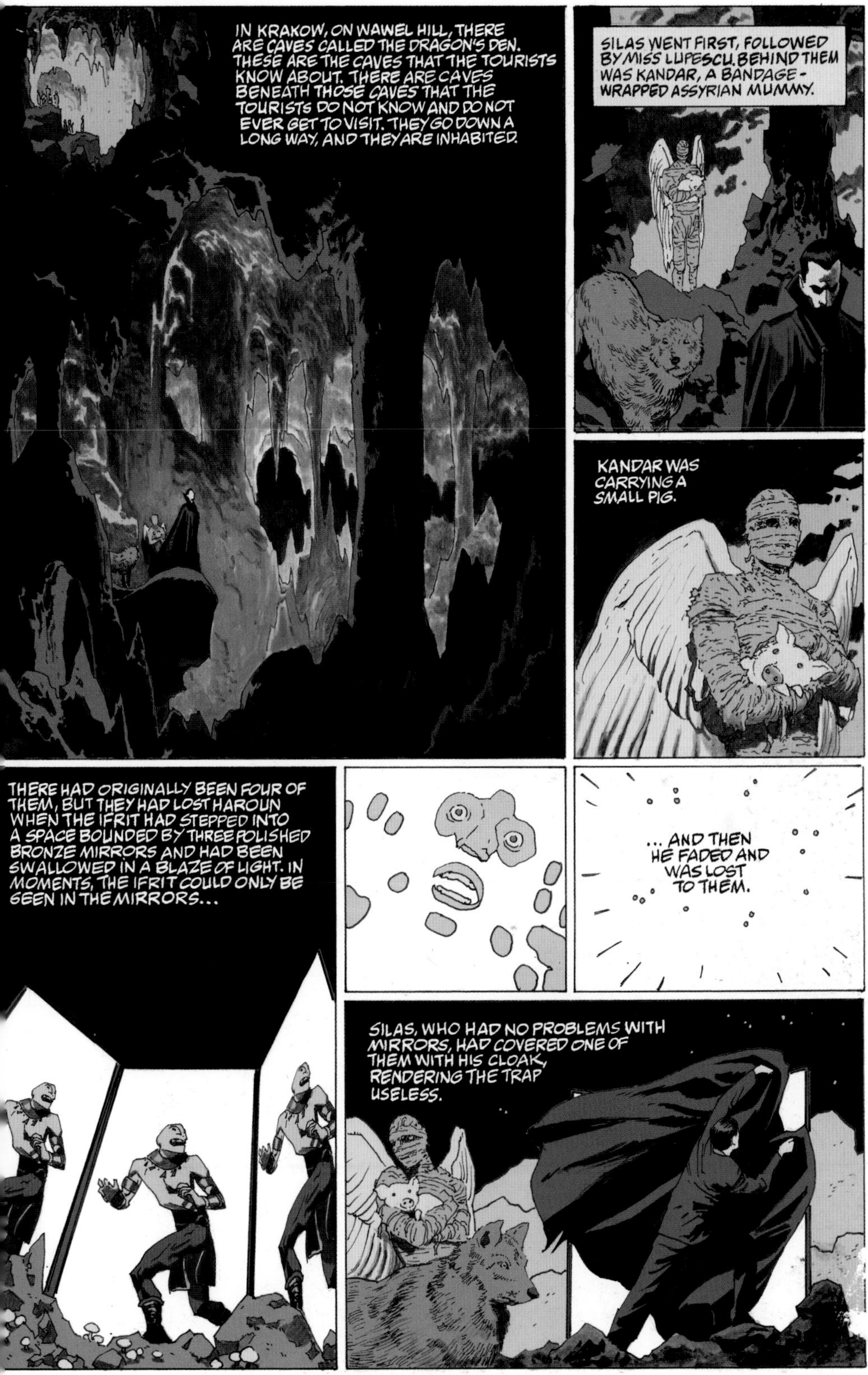
IN KRAKOW, ON WAWEL HILL, THERE ARE CAVES CALLED THE DRAGON'S DEN. THESE ARE THE CAVES THAT THE TOURISTS KNOW ABOUT. THERE ARE CAVES BENEATH THOSE CAVES THAT THE TOURISTS DO NOT KNOW AND DO NOT EVER GET TO VISIT. THEY GO DOWN A LONG WAY, AND THEY ARE INHABITED.
SILAS WENT FIRST, FOLLOWED BY MISS LUPESCU. BEHIND THEM WAS KANDAR, A BANDAGE-WRAPPED ASSYRIAN MUMMY.
KANDAR WAS CARRYING A SMALL PIG.
THERE HAD ORIGINALLY BEEN FOUR OF THEM, BUT THEY HAD LOST HAROUN WHEN THE IFRIT HAD STEPPED INTO A SPACE BOUNDED BY THREE POLISHED BRONZE MIRRORS AND HAD BEEN SWALLOWED IN A BLAZE OF LIGHT. IN MOMENTS, THE IFRIT COULD ONLY BE SEEN IN THE MIRRORS...
... AND THEN HE FADED AND WAS LOST TO THEM.
SILAS, WHO HAD NO PROBLEMS WITH MIRRORS, HAD COVERED ONE OF THEM WITH HIS CLOAK, RENDERING THE TRAP USELESS.

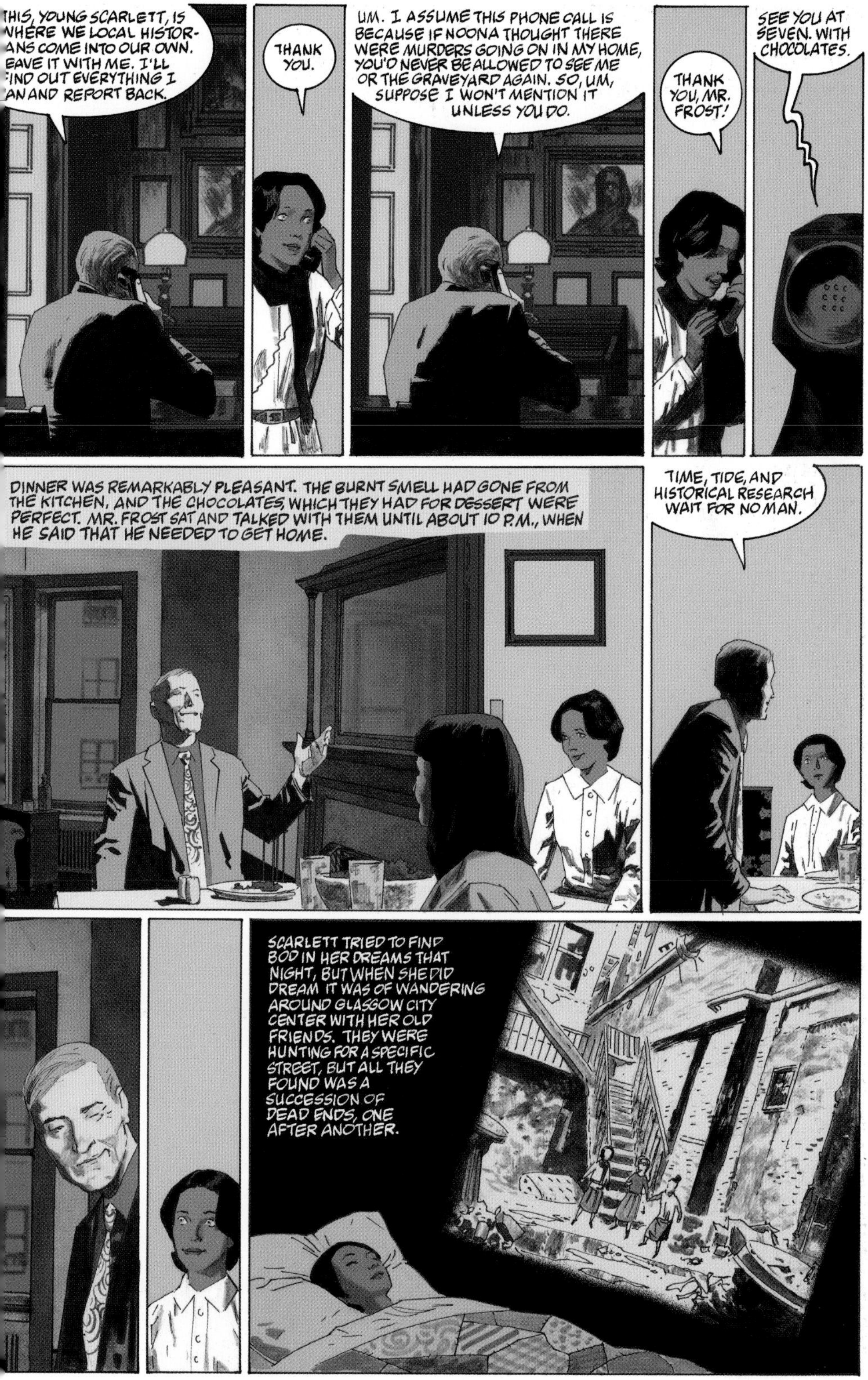
THIS, YOUNG SCARLETT, IS WHERE WE LOCAL HISTORIANS COME INTO OUR OWN. LEAVE IT WITH ME. I'LL FIND OUT EVERYTHING I CAN AND REPORT BACK.
THANK YOU.
UM. I ASSUME THIS PHONE CALL IS BECAUSE IF NOONA THOUGHT THERE WERE MURDERS GOING ON IN MY HOME, YOU'D NEVER BE ALLOWED TO SEE ME OR THE GRAVEYARD AGAIN. SO, UM, SUPPOSE I WON'T MENTION IT UNLESS YOU DO.
THANK YOU, MR. FROST!
SEE YOU AT SEVEN. WITH CHOCOLATES.
DINNER WAS REMARKABLY PLEASANT. THE BURNT SMELL HAD GONE FROM THE KITCHEN, AND THE CHOCOLATES, WHICH THEY HAD FOR DESSERT WERE PERFECT. MR. FROST SAT AND TALKED WITH THEM UNTIL ABOUT 10 P.M., WHEN HE SAID THAT HE NEEDED TO GET HOME.
TIME, TIDE, AND HISTORICAL RESEARCH WAIT FOR NO MAN.
SCARLETT TRIED TO FIND BOD IN HER DREAMS THAT NIGHT, BUT WHEN SHE DID DREAM IT WAS OF WANDERING AROUND GLASGOW CITY CENTER WITH HER OLD FRIENDS. THEY WERE HUNTING FOR A SPECIFIC STREET, BUT ALL THEY FOUND WAS A SUCCESSION OF DEAD ENDS, ONE AFTER ANOTHER.

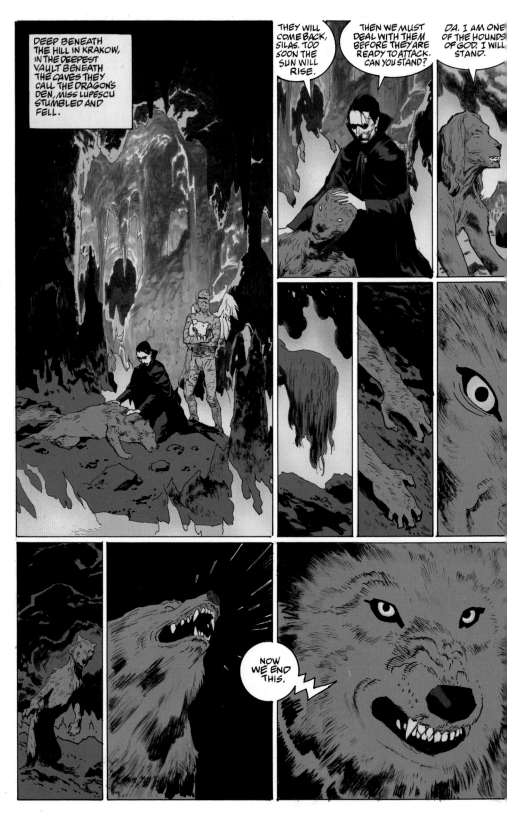

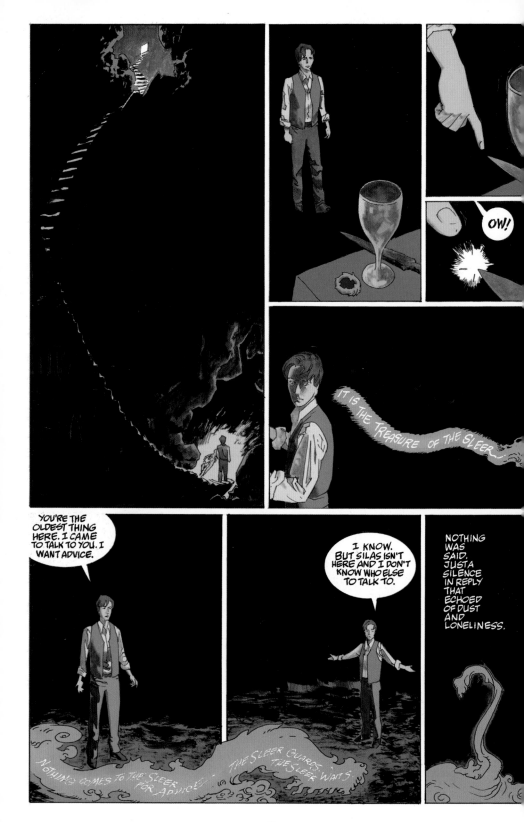

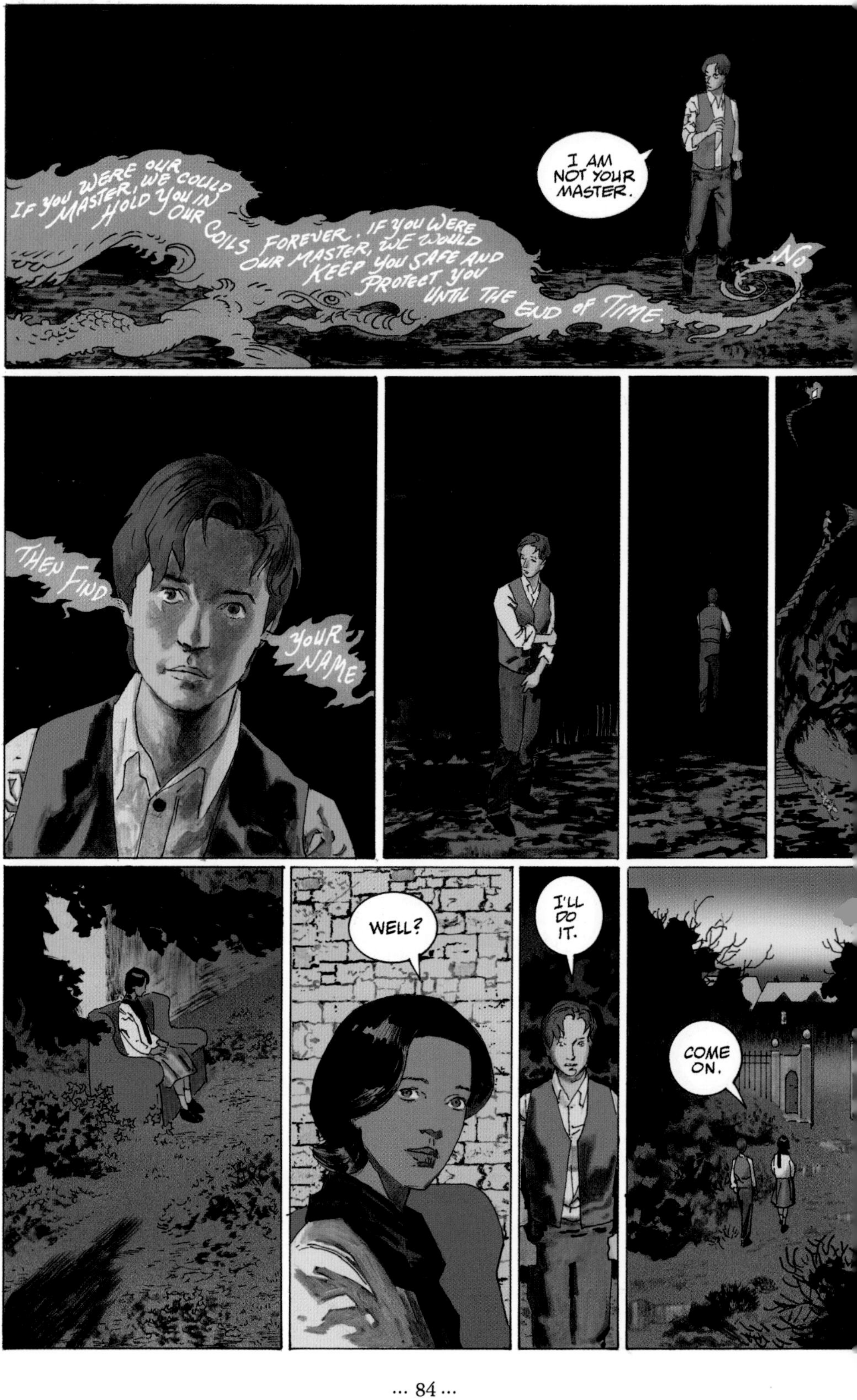
IF YOU WERE OUR MASTER, WE COULD HOLD YOU IN OUR COILS FOREVER. IF YOU WERE OUR MASTER, WE WOULD KEEP YOU SAFE AND PROTECT YOU UNTIL THE END OF TIME.
I AM NOT YOUR MASTER.
NO
THEN FIND
YOUR NAME
WELL?
I'LL DO IT.
COME ON.

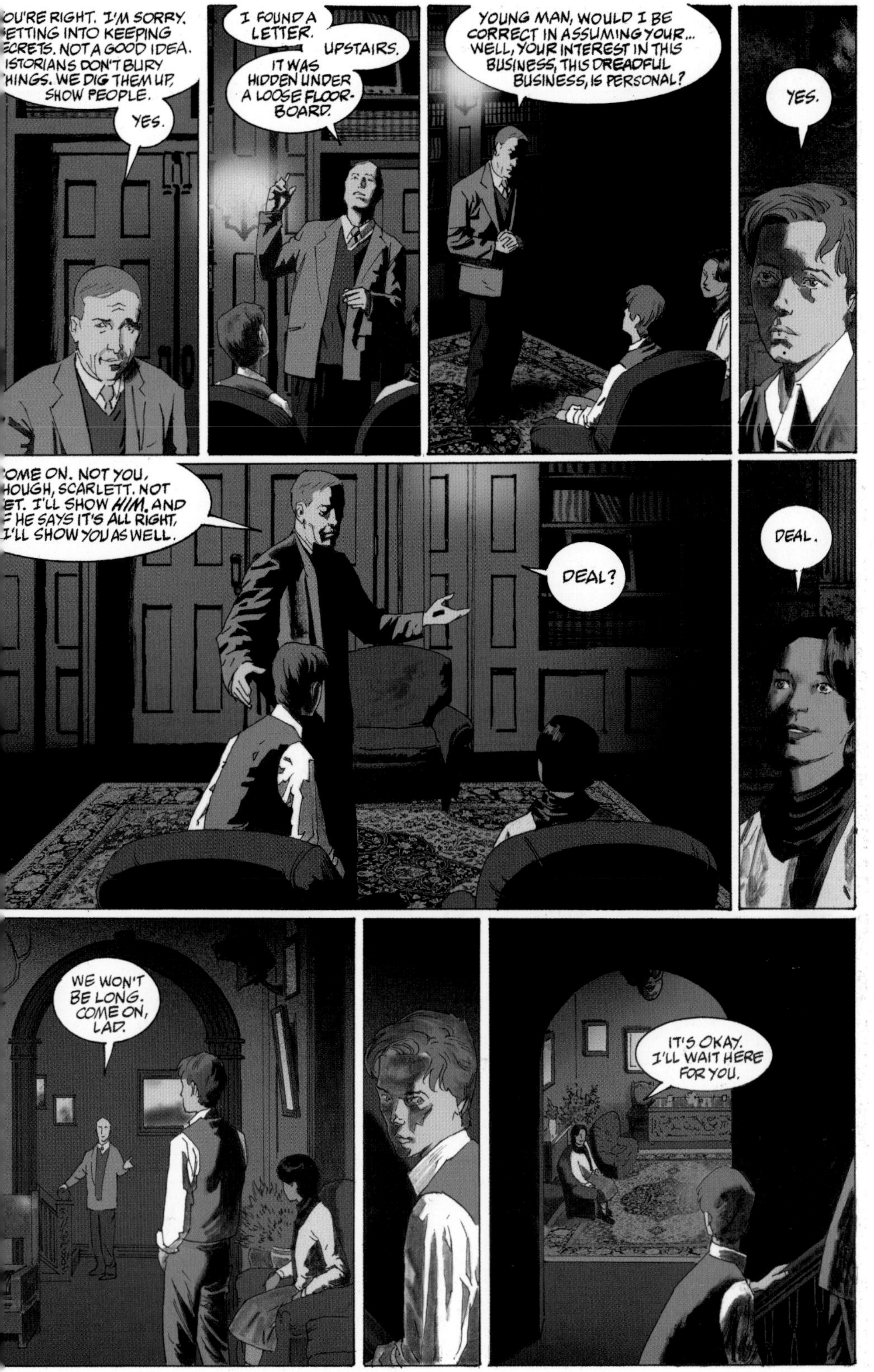
OU'RE RIGHT. I'M SORRY. ETTING INTO KEEPING ECRETS. NOT A GOOD IDEA. ISTORIANS DON'T BURY HINGS. WE DIG THEM UP, SHOW PEOPLE.
YES.
I FOUND A LETTER.
UPSTAIRS.
IT WAS HIDDEN UNDER A LOOSE FLOOR-BOARD.
YOUNG MAN, WOULD I BE CORRECT IN ASSUMING YOUR... WELL, YOUR INTEREST IN THIS BUSINESS, THIS DREADFUL BUSINESS, IS PERSONAL?
YES.
OME ON. NOT YOU, HOUGH, SCARLETT. NOT ET. I'LL SHOW HIM. AND F HE SAYS IT'S ALL RIGHT, I'LL SHOW YOU AS WELL.
DEAL?
DEAL.
WE WON'T BE LONG. COME ON, LAD.
IT'S OKAY. I'LL WAIT HERE FOR YOU.

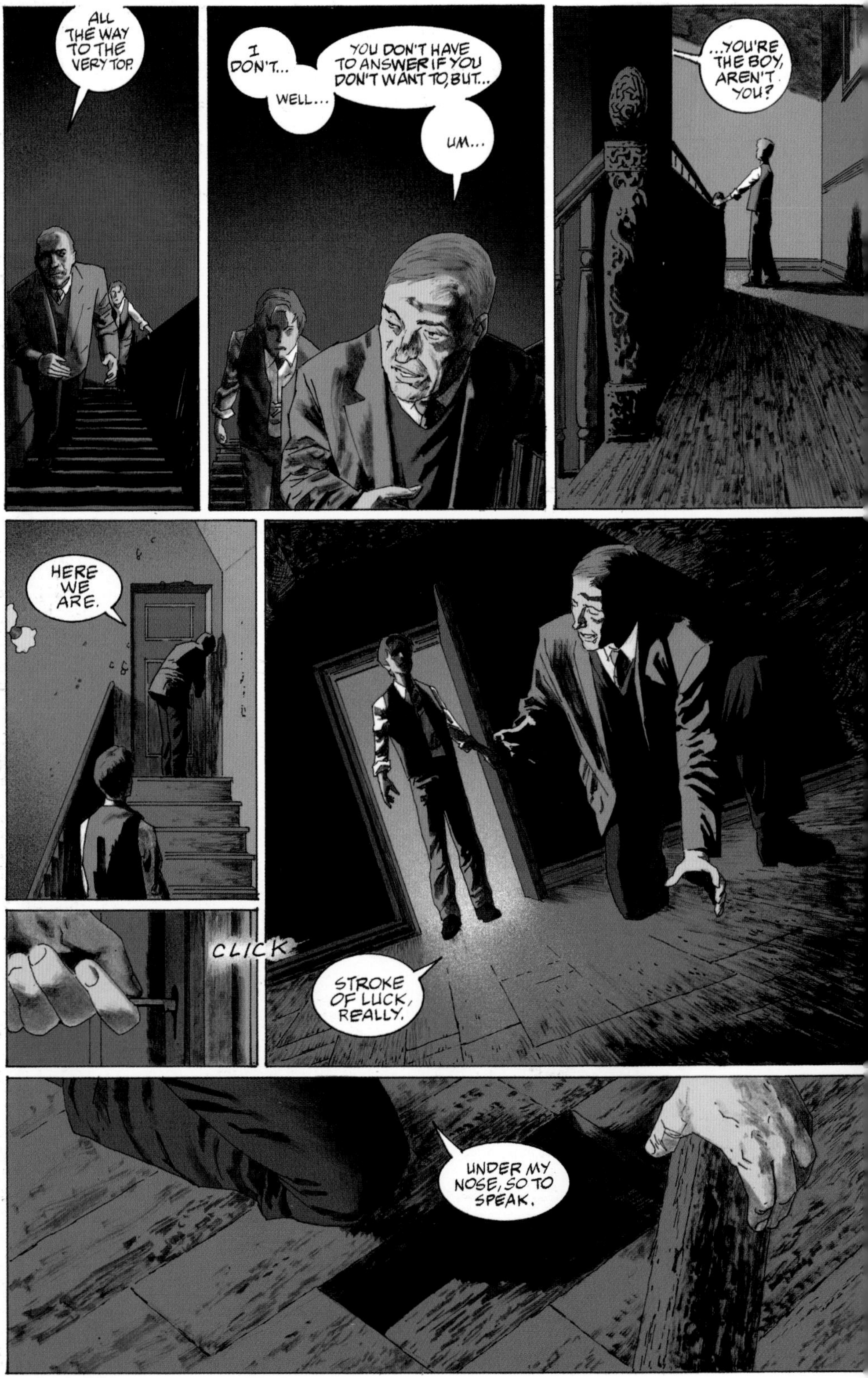
ALL THE WAY TO THE VERY TOP.
I DON'T...
WELL...
YOU DON'T HAVE TO ANSWER IF YOU DON'T WANT TO, BUT...
UM...
...YOU'RE THE BOY, AREN'T YOU?
HERE WE ARE.
CLICK
STROKE OF LUCK, REALLY.
UNDER MY NOSE, SO TO SPEAK.

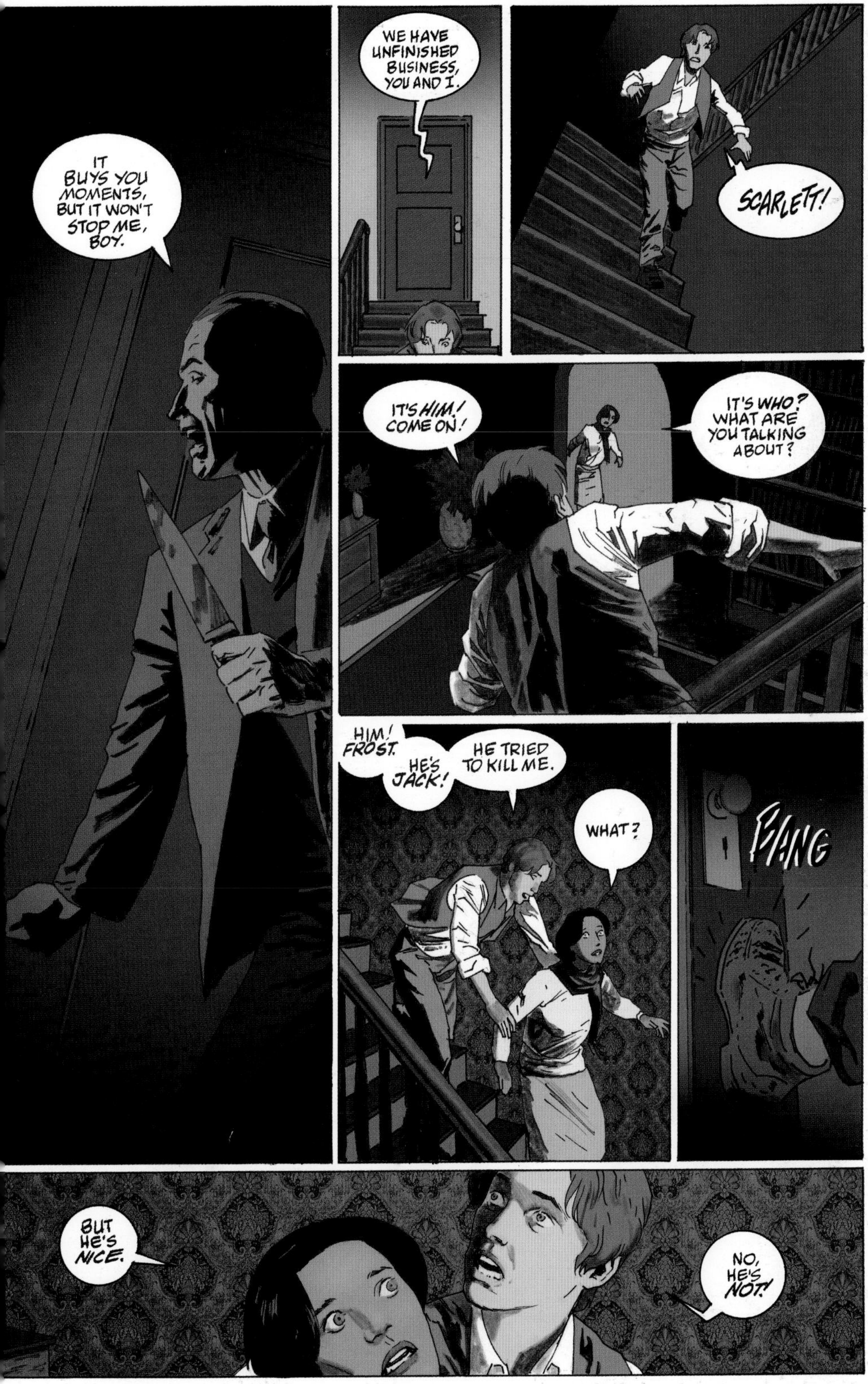
IT BUYS YOU MOMENTS, BUT IT WON'T STOP ME, BOY.
WE HAVE UNFINISHED BUSINESS, YOU AND I.
SCARLETT!
IT'S HIM! COME ON!
IT'S WHO? WHAT ARE YOU TALKING ABOUT?
HIM! FROST.
HE'S JACK!
HE TRIED TO KILL ME.
WHAT?
BANG
BUT HE'S NICE.
NO, HE'S NOT!

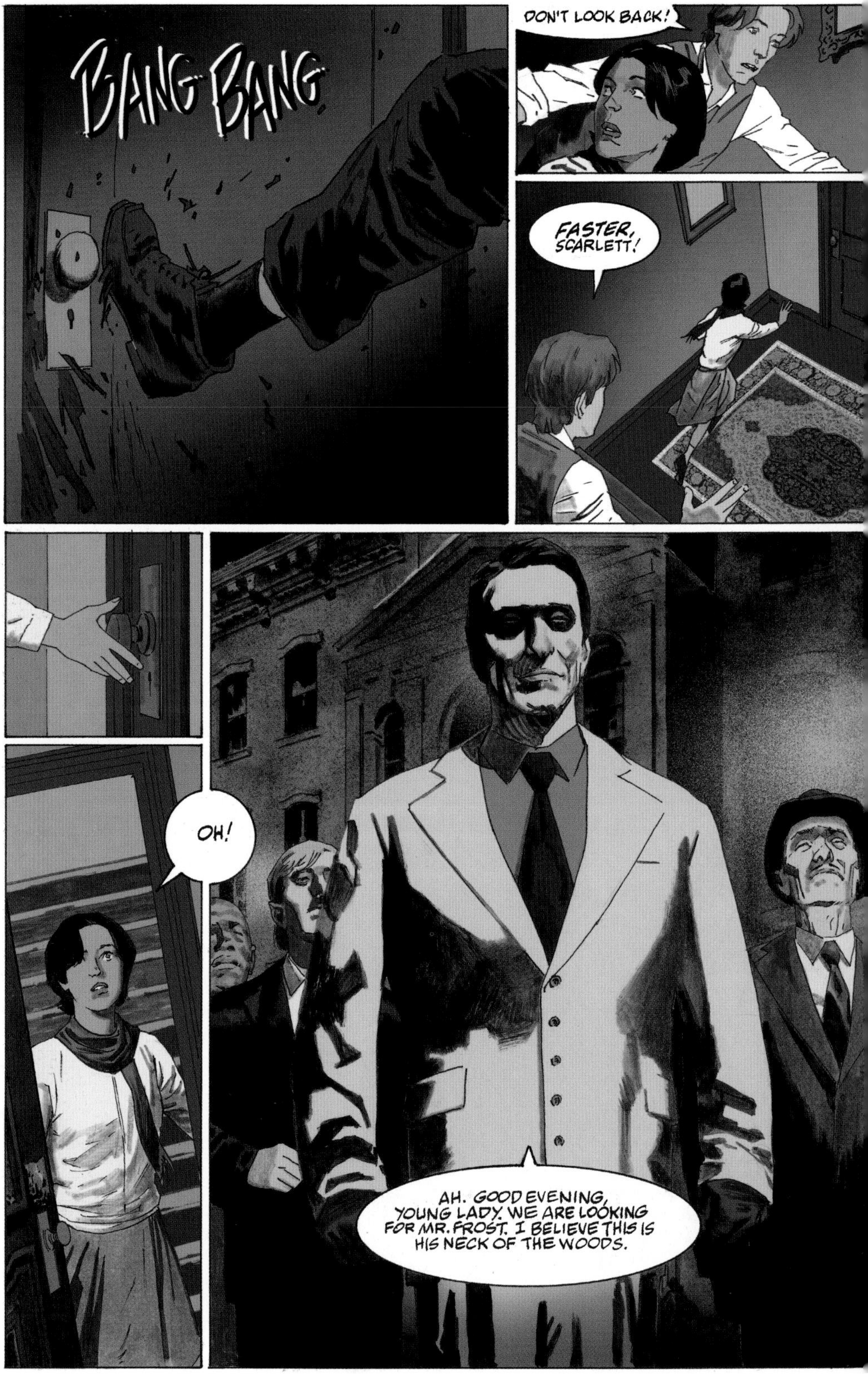
BANG BANG
DON'T LOOK BACK!
FASTER, SCARLETT!
OH!
AH. GOOD EVENING, YOUNG LADY. WE ARE LOOKING FOR MR. FROST. I BELIEVE THIS IS HIS NECK OF THE WOODS.

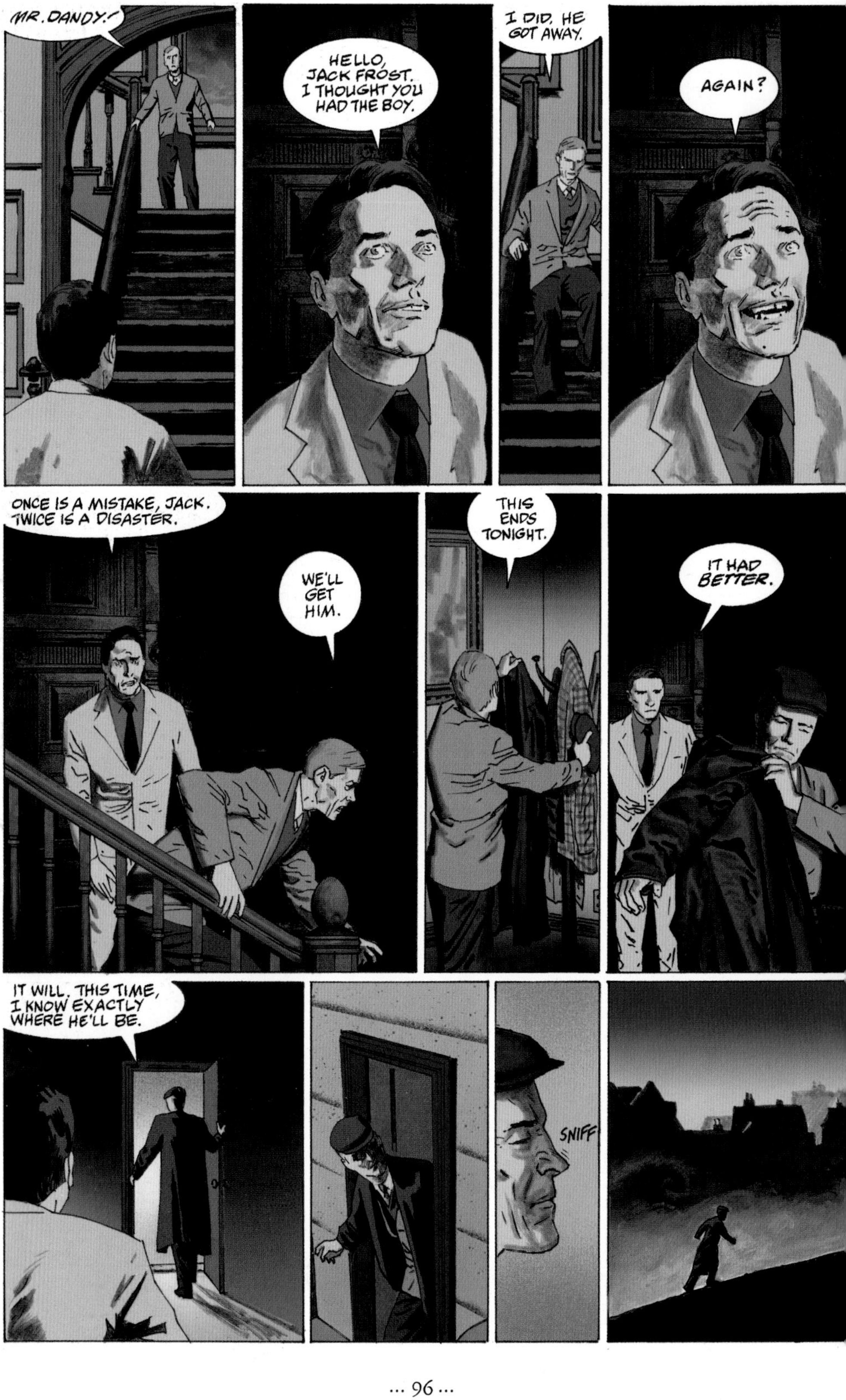
MR. DANDY!
HELLO, JACK FROST. I THOUGHT YOU HAD THE BOY.
I DID, HE GOT AWAY.
AGAIN?
ONCE IS A MISTAKE, JACK. TWICE IS A DISASTER.
WE'LL GET HIM.
THIS ENDS TONIGHT.
IT HAD BETTER.
IT WILL. THIS TIME, I KNOW EXACTLY WHERE HE'LL BE.
SNIFF

... 99 ...

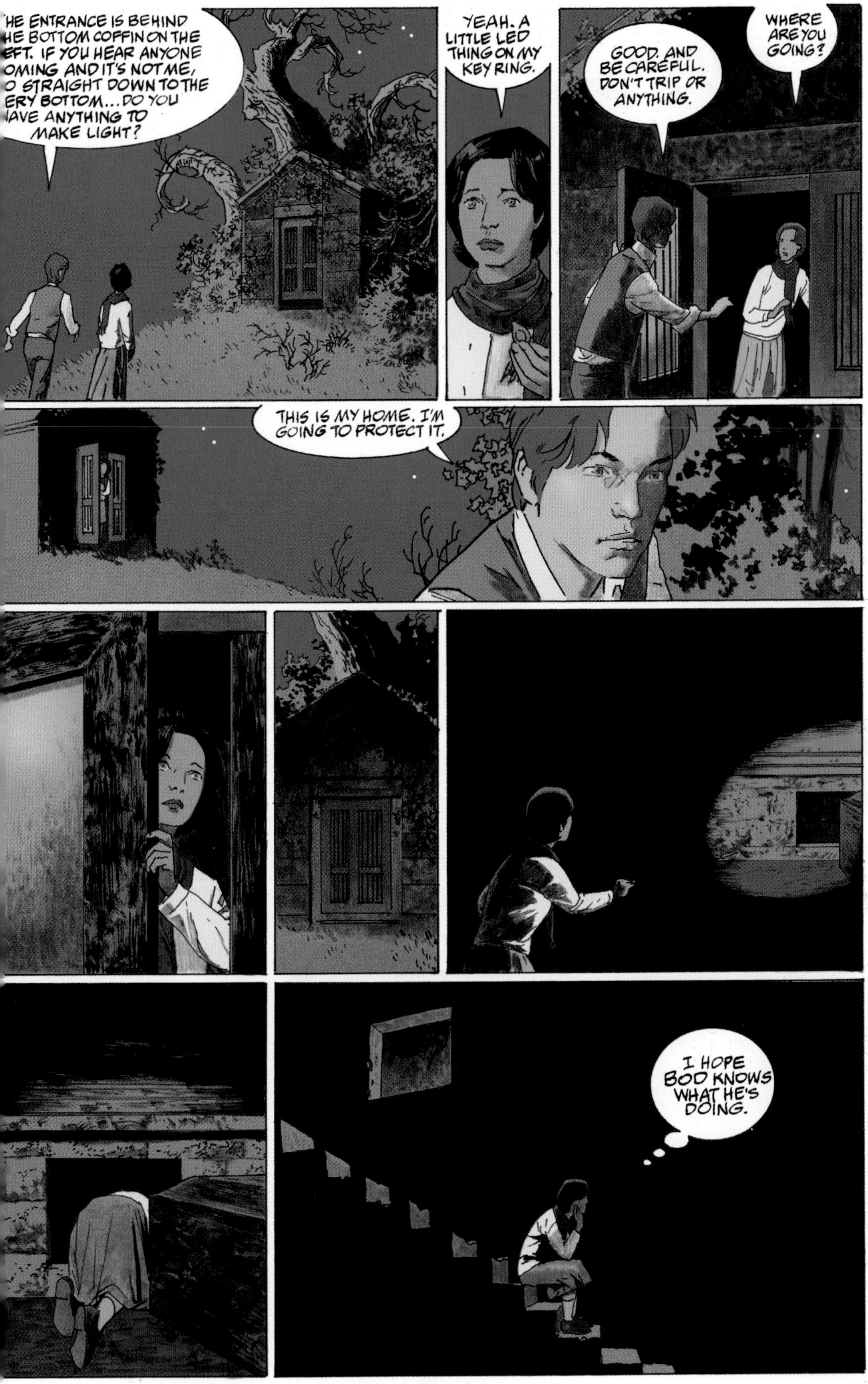
HE ENTRANCE IS BEHIND HE BOTTOM COFFIN ON THE EFT. IF YOU HEAR ANYONE OMING AND IT'S NOT ME, O STRAIGHT DOWN TO THE ERY BOTTOM...DO YOU AVE ANYTHING TO MAKE LIGHT?
YEAH. A LITTLE LED THING ON MY KEY RING.
GOOD. AND BE CAREFUL. DON'T TRIP OR ANYTHING.
WHERE ARE YOU GOING?
THIS IS MY HOME. I'M GOING TO PROTECT IT.
I HOPE BOD KNOWS WHAT HE'S DOING.

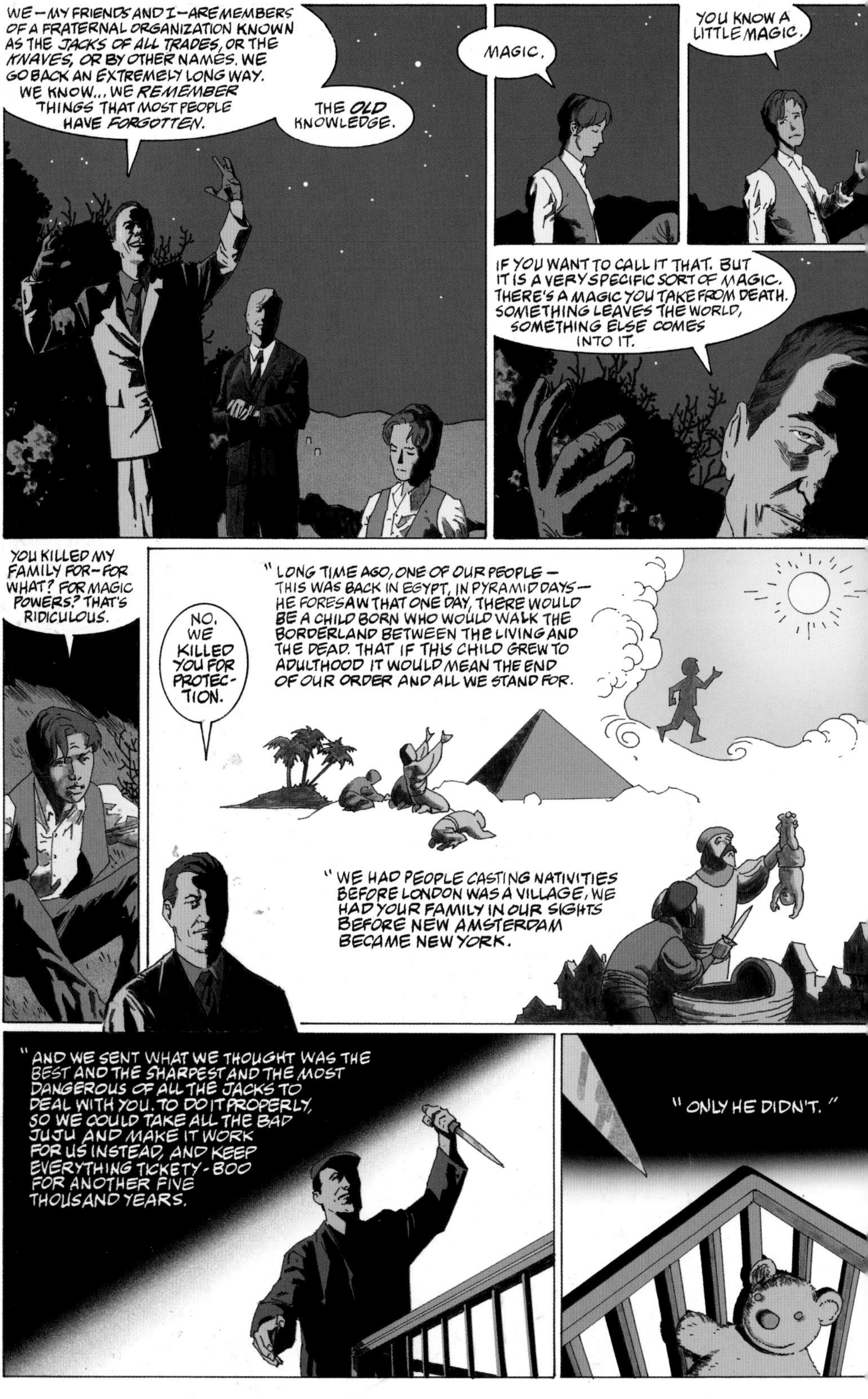
WE—MY FRIENDS AND I—ARE MEMBERS OF A FRATERNAL ORGANIZATION KNOWN AS THE JACKS OF ALL TRADES, OR THE KNAVES, OR BY OTHER NAMES. WE GO BACK AN EXTREMELY LONG WAY. WE KNOW... WE REMEMBER THINGS THAT MOST PEOPLE HAVE FORGOTTEN.
THE OLD KNOWLEDGE.
MAGIC.
YOU KNOW A LITTLE MAGIC.
IF YOU WANT TO CALL IT THAT. BUT IT IS A VERY SPECIFIC SORT OF MAGIC. THERE'S A MAGIC YOU TAKE FROM DEATH. SOMETHING LEAVES THE WORLD, SOMETHING ELSE COMES INTO IT.
YOU KILLED MY FAMILY FOR—FOR WHAT? FOR MAGIC POWERS? THAT'S RIDICULOUS.
NO. WE KILLED YOU FOR PROTECTION.
"LONG TIME AGO, ONE OF OUR PEOPLE—THIS WAS BACK IN EGYPT, IN PYRAMID DAYS—HE FORESAW THAT ONE DAY, THERE WOULD BE A CHILD BORN WHO WOULD WALK THE BORDERLAND BETWEEN THE LIVING AND THE DEAD. THAT IF THIS CHILD GREW TO ADULTHOOD IT WOULD MEAN THE END OF OUR ORDER AND ALL WE STAND FOR.
"WE HAD PEOPLE CASTING NATIVITIES BEFORE LONDON WAS A VILLAGE, WE HAD YOUR FAMILY IN OUR SIGHTS BEFORE NEW AMSTERDAM BECAME NEW YORK.
"AND WE SENT WHAT WE THOUGHT WAS THE BEST AND THE SHARPEST AND THE MOST DANGEROUS OF ALL THE JACKS TO DEAL WITH YOU. TO DO IT PROPERLY, SO WE COULD TAKE ALL THE BAD JUJU AND MAKE IT WORK FOR US INSTEAD, AND KEEP EVERYTHING TICKETY-BOO FOR ANOTHER FIVE THOUSAND YEARS.
"ONLY HE DIDN'T."

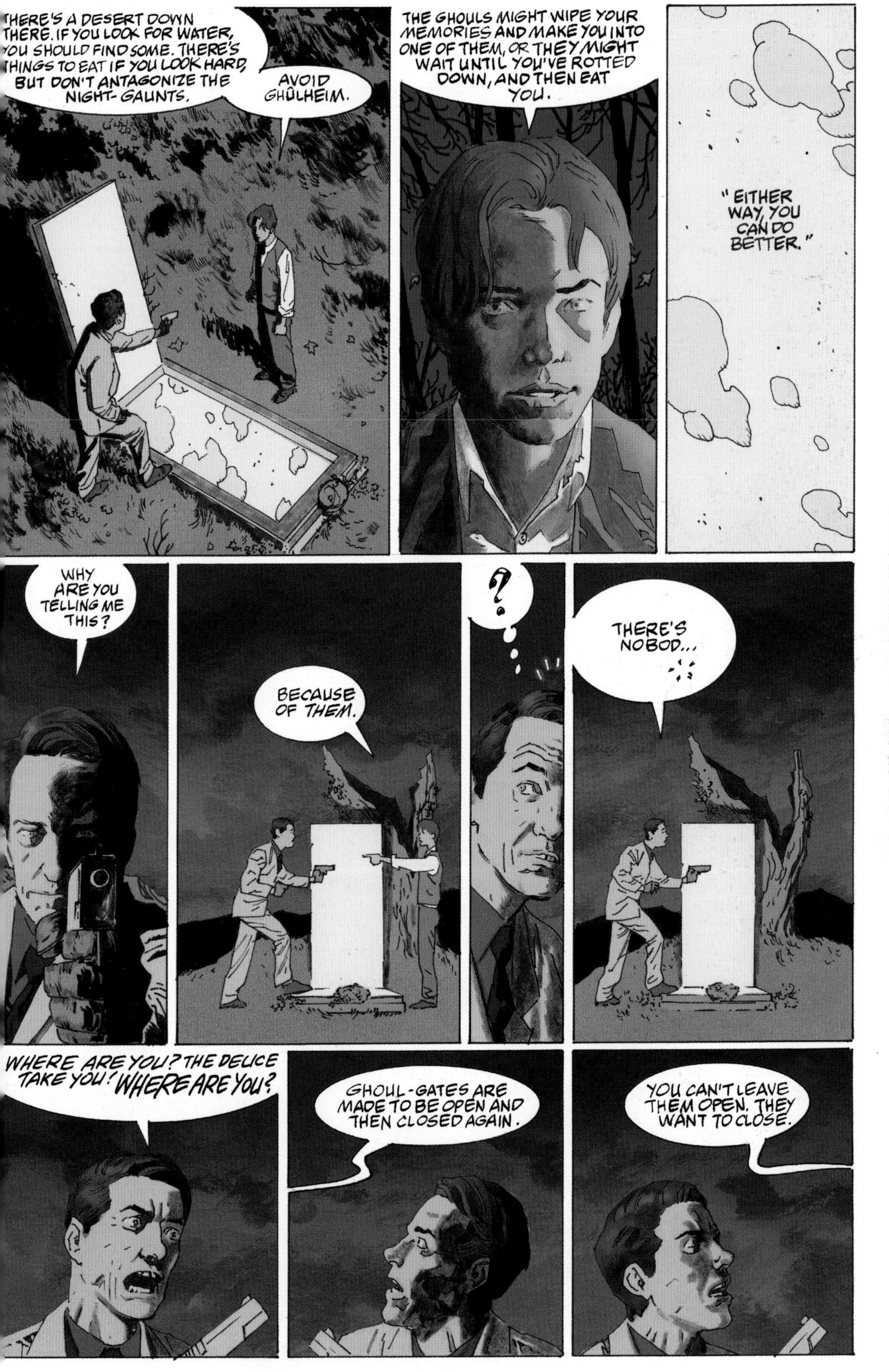
THERE'S A DESERT DOWN THERE. IF YOU LOOK FOR WATER, YOU SHOULD FIND SOME. THERE'S THINGS TO EAT IF YOU LOOK HARD, BUT DON'T ANTAGONIZE THE NIGHT-GAUNTS.
AVOID GHÛLHEIM.
THE GHOULS MIGHT WIPE YOUR MEMORIES AND MAKE YOU INTO ONE OF THEM, OR THEY MIGHT WAIT UNTIL YOU'VE ROTTED DOWN, AND THEN EAT YOU.
"EITHER WAY, YOU CAN DO BETTER."
WHY ARE YOU TELLING ME THIS?
BECAUSE OF THEM.
?
THERE'S NOBOD...
WHERE ARE YOU? THE DEUCE TAKE YOU! WHERE ARE YOU?
GHOUL-GATES ARE MADE TO BE OPEN AND THEN CLOSED AGAIN.
YOU CAN'T LEAVE THEM OPEN. THEY WANT TO CLOSE.

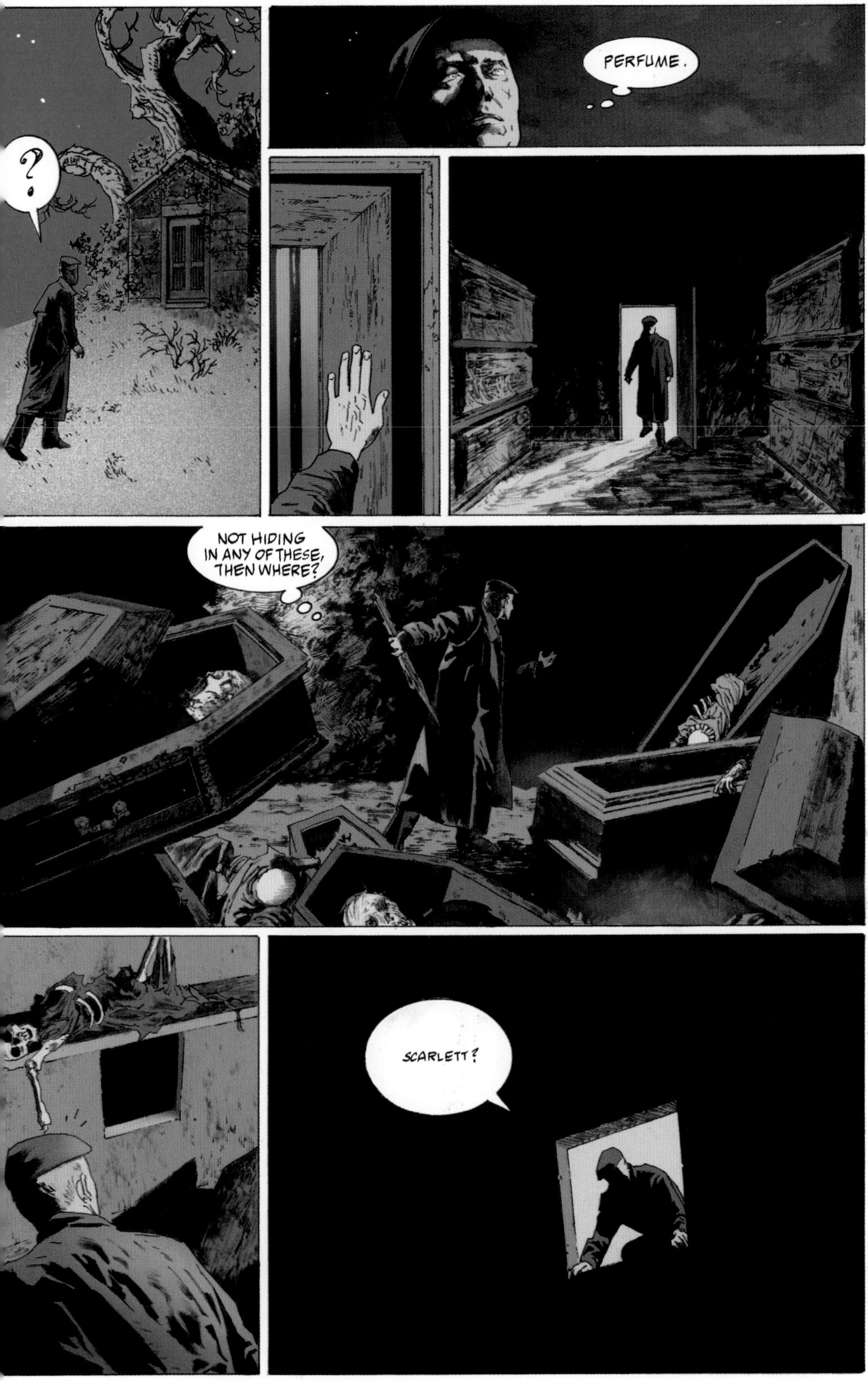
?
PERFUME.
NOT HIDING IN ANY OF THESE, THEN WHERE?
SCARLETT?

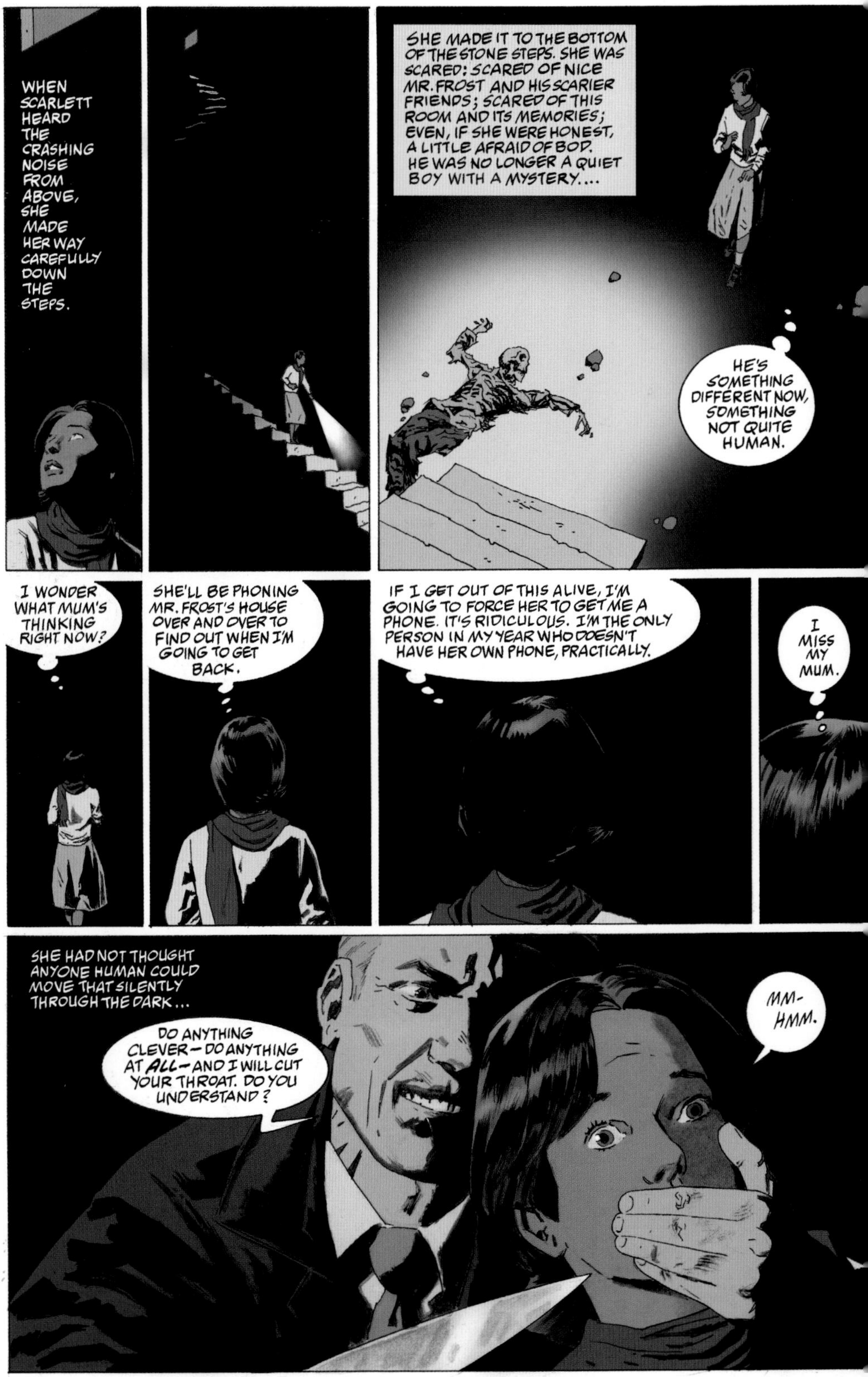
WHEN SCARLETT HEARD THE CRASHING NOISE FROM ABOVE, SHE MADE HER WAY CAREFULLY DOWN THE STEPS.
SHE MADE IT TO THE BOTTOM OF THE STONE STEPS. SHE WAS SCARED: SCARED OF NICE MR. FROST AND HIS SCARIER FRIENDS; SCARED OF THIS ROOM AND ITS MEMORIES; EVEN, IF SHE WERE HONEST, A LITTLE AFRAID OF BOD. HE WAS NO LONGER A QUIET BOY WITH A MYSTERY....
HE'S SOMETHING DIFFERENT NOW, SOMETHING NOT QUITE HUMAN.
I WONDER WHAT MUM'S THINKING RIGHT NOW?
SHE'LL BE PHONING MR. FROST'S HOUSE OVER AND OVER TO FIND OUT WHEN I'M GOING TO GET BACK.
IF I GET OUT OF THIS ALIVE, I'M GOING TO FORCE HER TO GET ME A PHONE. IT'S RIDICULOUS. I'M THE ONLY PERSON IN MY YEAR WHO DOESN'T HAVE HER OWN PHONE, PRACTICALLY.
I MISS MY MUM.
SHE HAD NOT THOUGHT ANYONE HUMAN COULD MOVE THAT SILENTLY THROUGH THE DARK...
DO ANYTHING CLEVER—DO ANYTHING AT ALL—AND I WILL CUT YOUR THROAT. DO YOU UNDERSTAND?
MM-HMM.

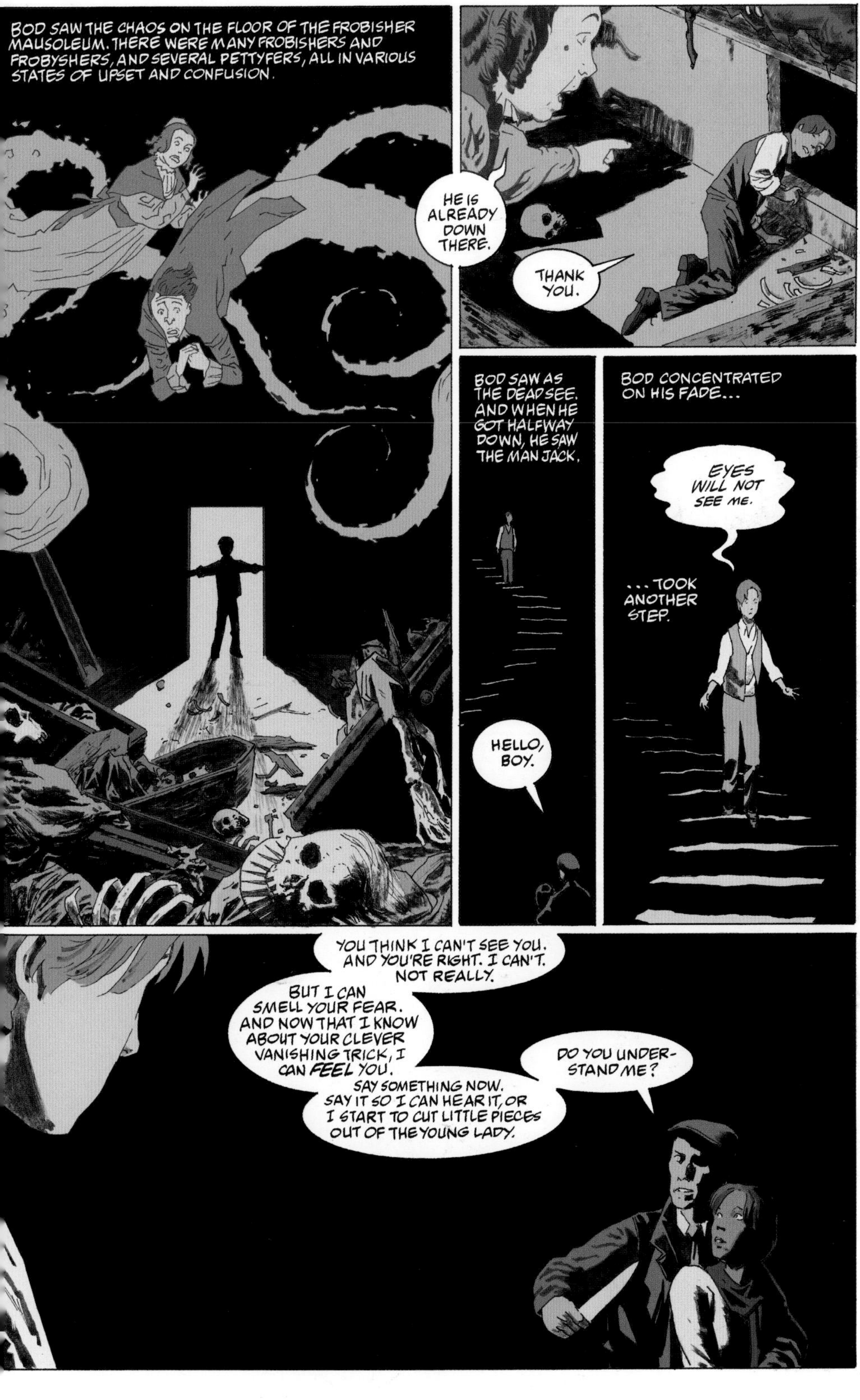

BOD SAW THE CHAOS ON THE FLOOR OF THE FROBISHER MAUSOLEUM. THERE WERE MANY FROBISHERS AND FROBYSHERS, AND SEVERAL PETTYFERS, ALL IN VARIOUS STATES OF UPSET AND CONFUSION.
HE IS ALREADY DOWN THERE.
THANK YOU.
BOD SAW AS THE DEAD SEE. AND WHEN HE GOT HALFWAY DOWN, HE SAW THE MAN JACK.
HELLO, BOY.
BOD CONCENTRATED ON HIS FADE...
EYES WILL NOT SEE ME.
...TOOK ANOTHER STEP.
YOU THINK I CAN'T SEE YOU. AND YOU'RE RIGHT. I CAN'T. NOT REALLY.
BUT I CAN SMELL YOUR FEAR. AND NOW THAT I KNOW ABOUT YOUR CLEVER VANISHING TRICK, I CAN FEEL YOU.
SAY SOMETHING NOW. SAY IT SO I CAN HEAR IT, OR I START TO CUT LITTLE PIECES OUT OF THE YOUNG LADY.
DO YOU UNDERSTAND ME?

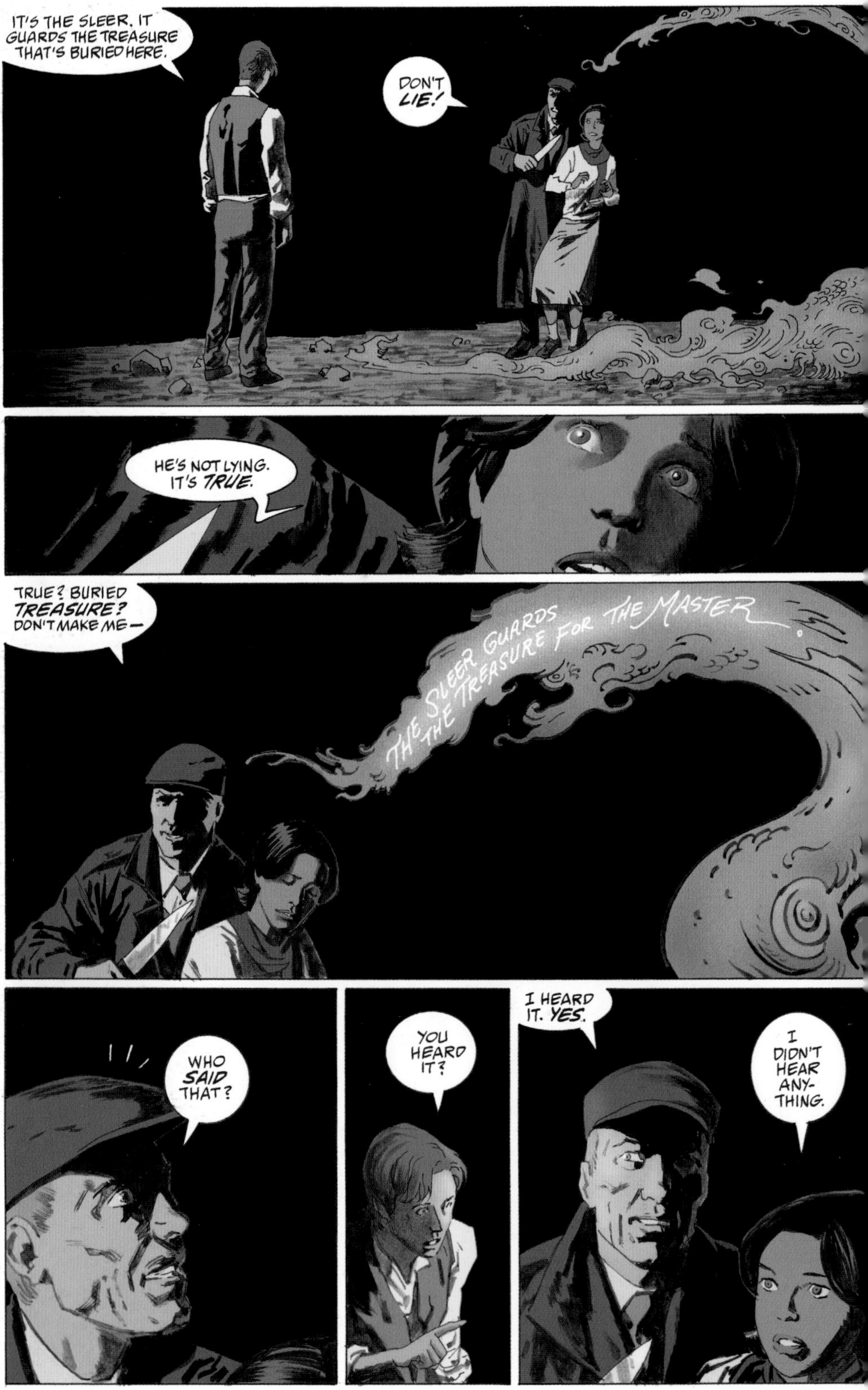
IT'S THE SLEER. IT GUARDS THE TREASURE THAT'S BURIED HERE.
DON'T LIE!
HE'S NOT LYING. IT'S TRUE.
TRUE? BURIED TREASURE? DON'T MAKE ME—
THE SLEER GUARDS THE TREASURE FOR THE MASTER.
WHO SAID THAT?
YOU HEARD IT?
I HEARD IT. YES.
I DIDN'T HEAR ANY-THING.

... 124 ...

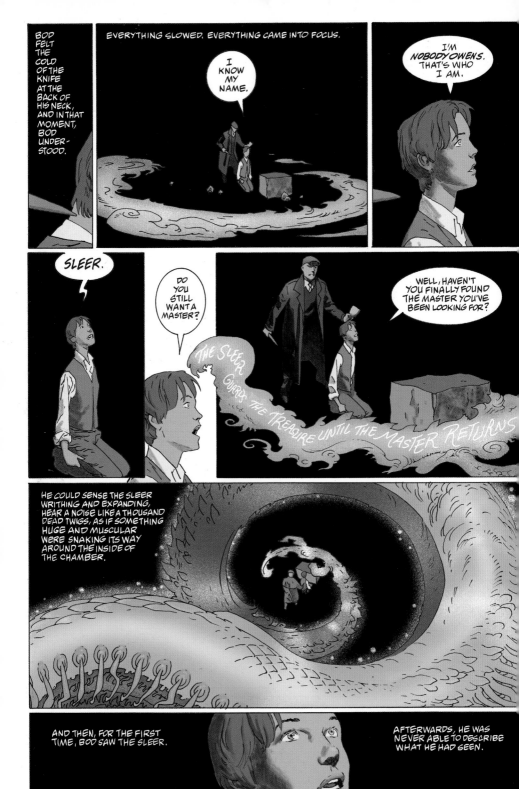

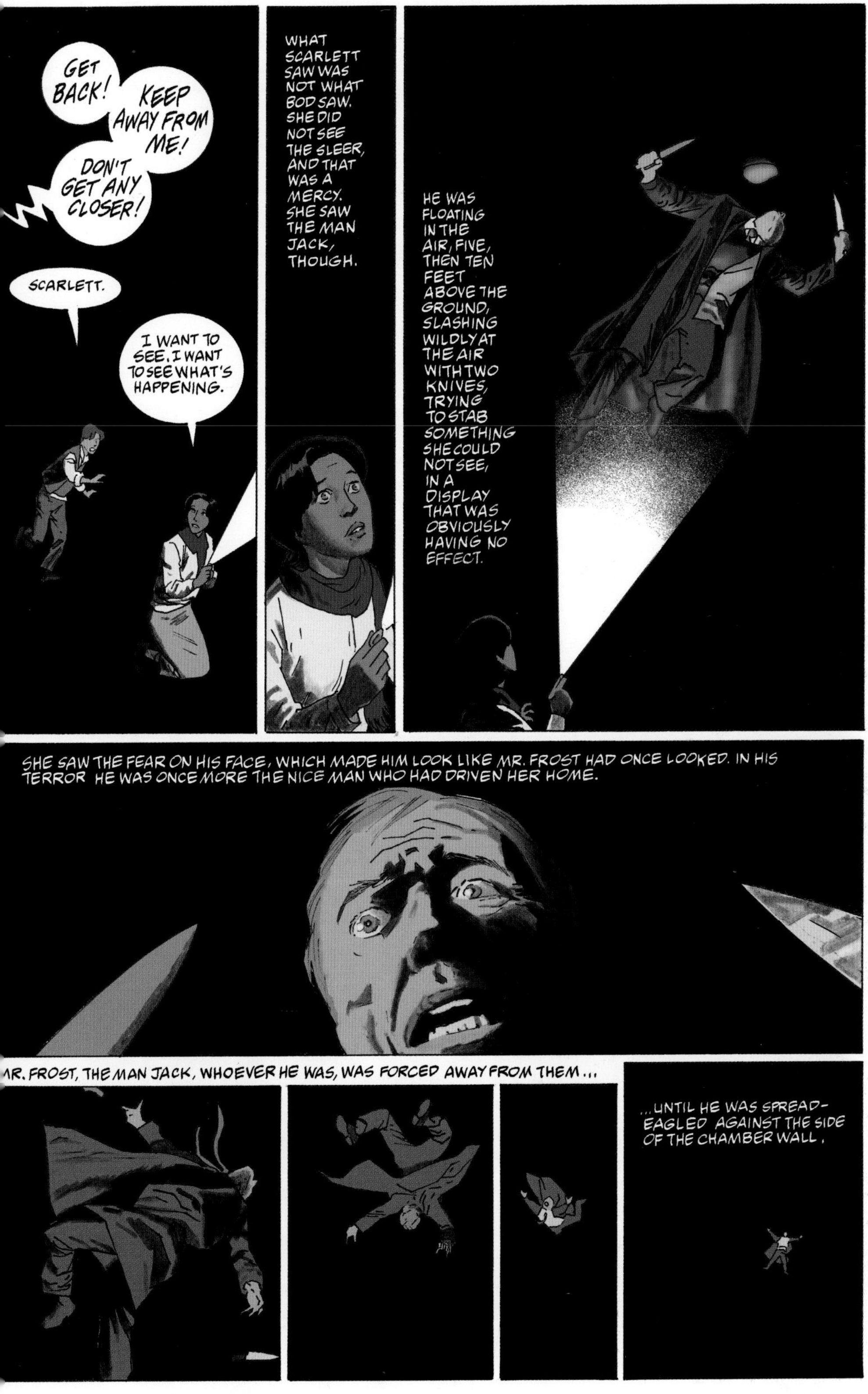
GET BACK!
KEEP AWAY FROM ME!
DON'T GET ANY CLOSER!
SCARLETT.
I WANT TO SEE. I WANT TO SEE WHAT'S HAPPENING.
WHAT SCARLETT SAW WAS NOT WHAT BOD SAW. SHE DID NOT SEE THE SLEER, AND THAT WAS A MERCY. SHE SAW THE MAN JACK, THOUGH.
HE WAS FLOATING IN THE AIR, FIVE, THEN TEN FEET ABOVE THE GROUND, SLASHING WILDLY AT THE AIR WITH TWO KNIVES, TRYING TO STAB SOMETHING SHE COULD NOT SEE, IN A DISPLAY THAT WAS OBVIOUSLY HAVING NO EFFECT.
SHE SAW THE FEAR ON HIS FACE, WHICH MADE HIM LOOK LIKE MR. FROST HAD ONCE LOOKED. IN HIS TERROR HE WAS ONCE MORE THE NICE MAN WHO HAD DRIVEN HER HOME.
MR. FROST, THE MAN JACK, WHOEVER HE WAS, WAS FORCED AWAY FROM THEM ...
... UNTIL HE WAS SPREAD-EAGLED AGAINST THE SIDE OF THE CHAMBER WALL.

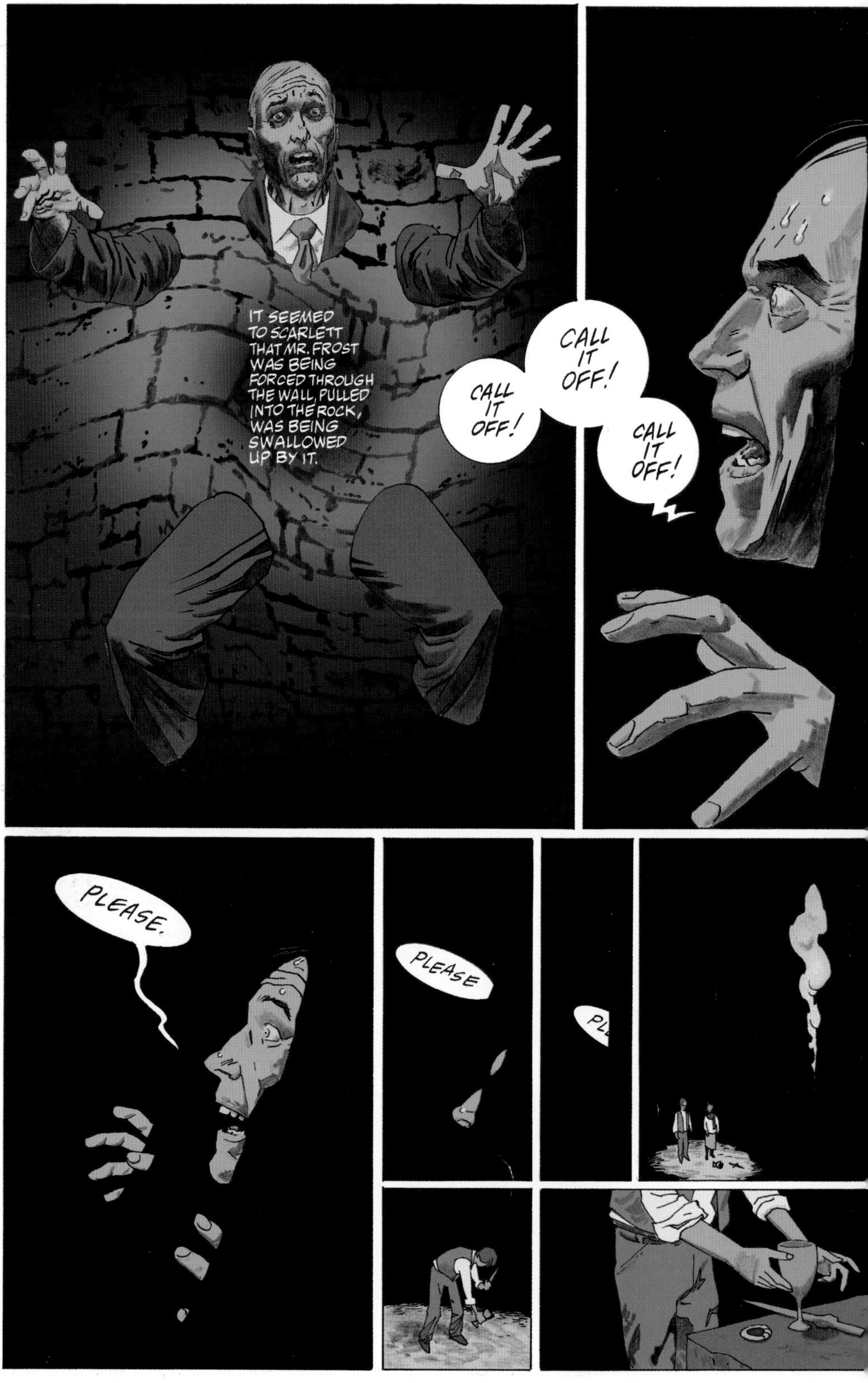
IT SEEMED TO SCARLETT THAT MR. FROST WAS BEING FORCED THROUGH THE WALL, PULLED INTO THE ROCK, WAS BEING SWALLOWED UP BY IT.
CALL IT OFF!
CALL IT OFF!
CALL IT OFF!
PLEASE.
PLEASE
PL

... 132 ...

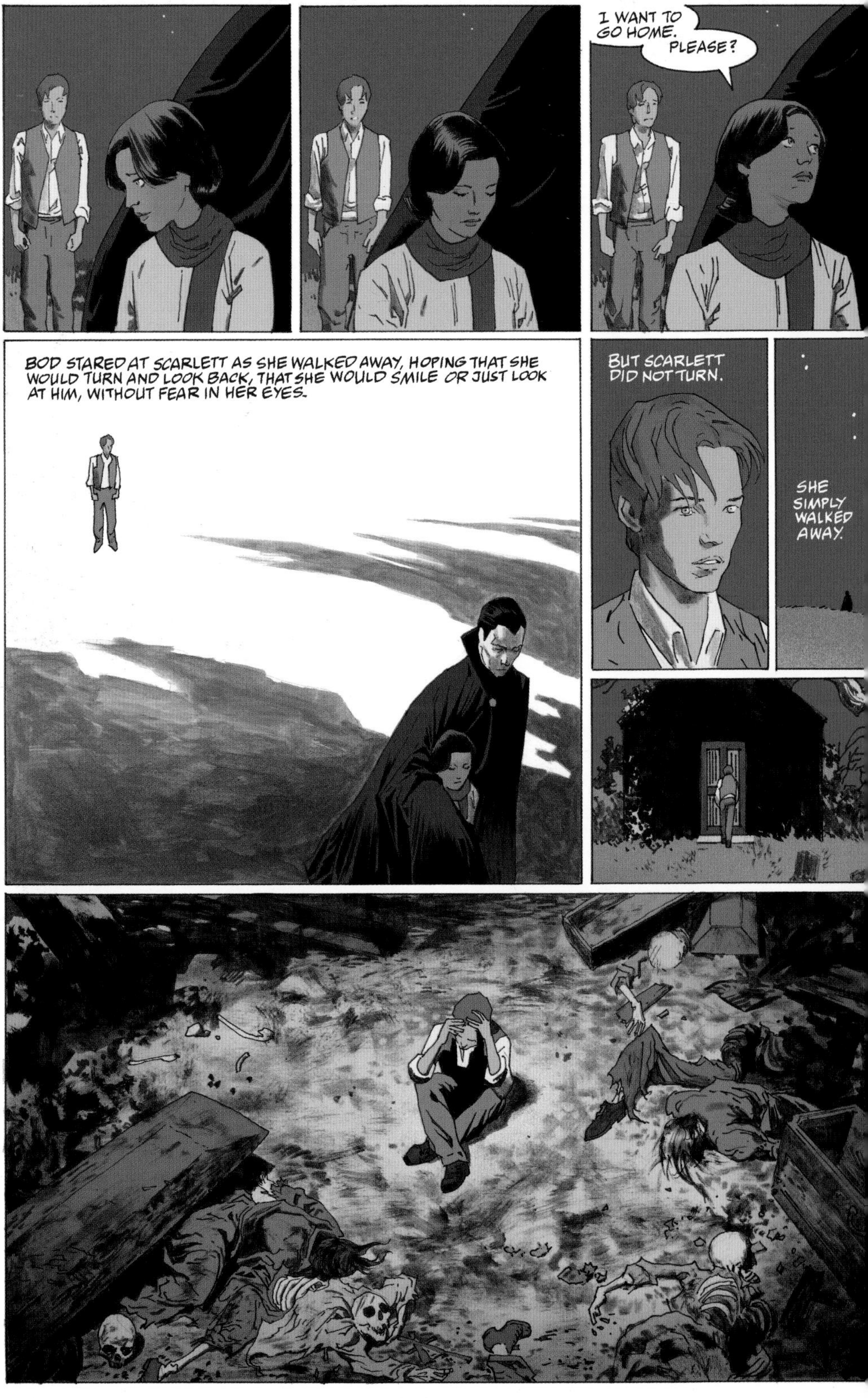

I WANT TO GO HOME. PLEASE?
BOD STARED AT SCARLETT AS SHE WALKED AWAY, HOPING THAT SHE WOULD TURN AND LOOK BACK, THAT SHE WOULD SMILE OR JUST LOOK AT HIM, WITHOUT FEAR IN HER EYES.
BUT SCARLETT DID NOT TURN.
SHE SIMPLY WALKED AWAY.

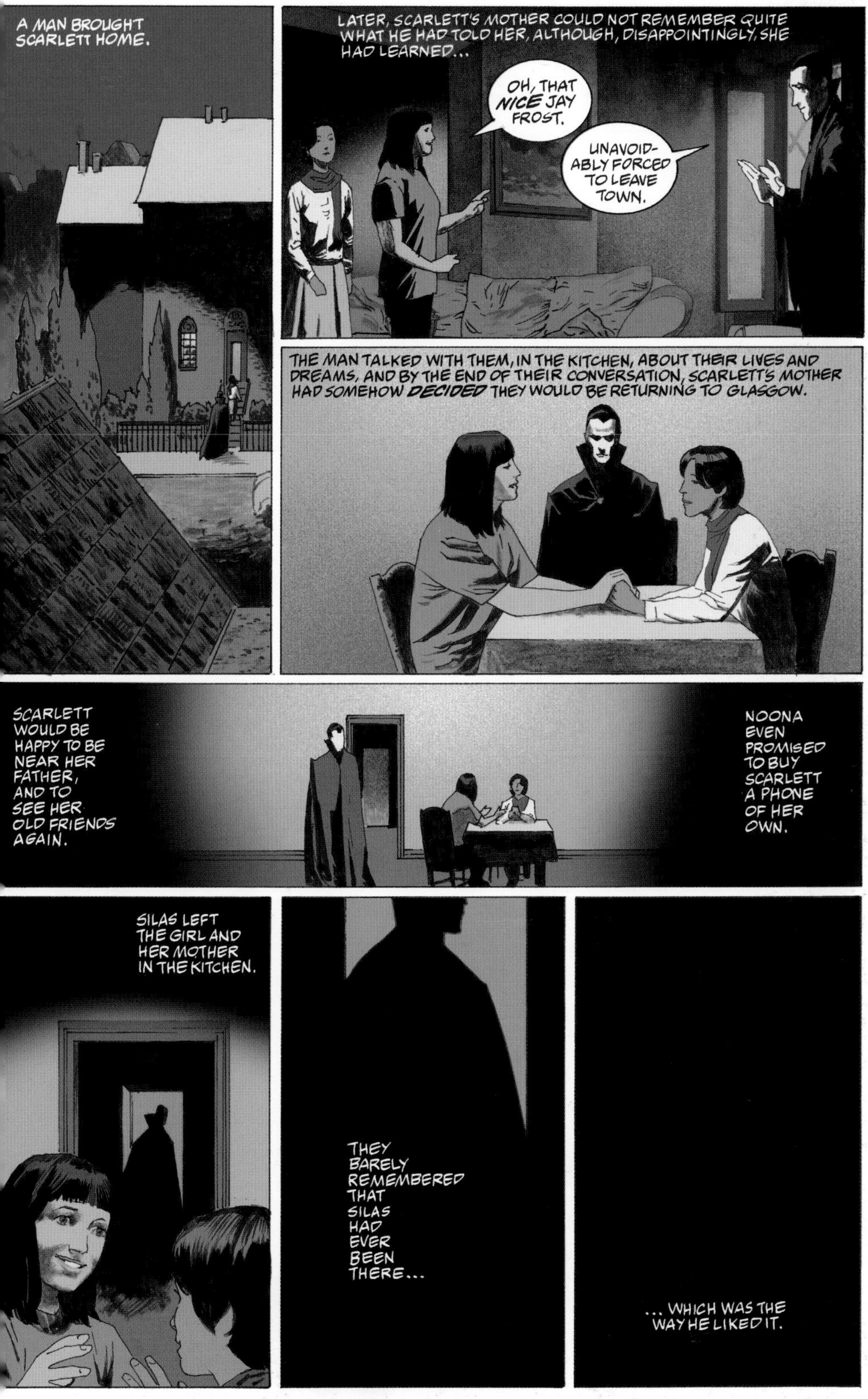
A MAN BROUGHT SCARLETT HOME.
LATER, SCARLETT'S MOTHER COULD NOT REMEMBER QUITE WHAT HE HAD TOLD HER, ALTHOUGH, DISAPPOINTINGLY, SHE HAD LEARNED...
OH, THAT NICE JAY FROST.
UNAVOIDABLY FORCED TO LEAVE TOWN.
THE MAN TALKED WITH THEM, IN THE KITCHEN, ABOUT THEIR LIVES AND DREAMS, AND BY THE END OF THEIR CONVERSATION, SCARLETT'S MOTHER HAD SOMEHOW DECIDED THEY WOULD BE RETURNING TO GLASGOW.
SCARLETT WOULD BE HAPPY TO BE NEAR HER FATHER, AND TO SEE HER OLD FRIENDS AGAIN.
NOONA EVEN PROMISED TO BUY SCARLETT A PHONE OF HER OWN.
SILAS LEFT THE GIRL AND HER MOTHER IN THE KITCHEN.
THEY BARELY REMEMBERED THAT SILAS HAD EVER BEEN THERE...
... WHICH WAS THE WAY HE LIKED IT.

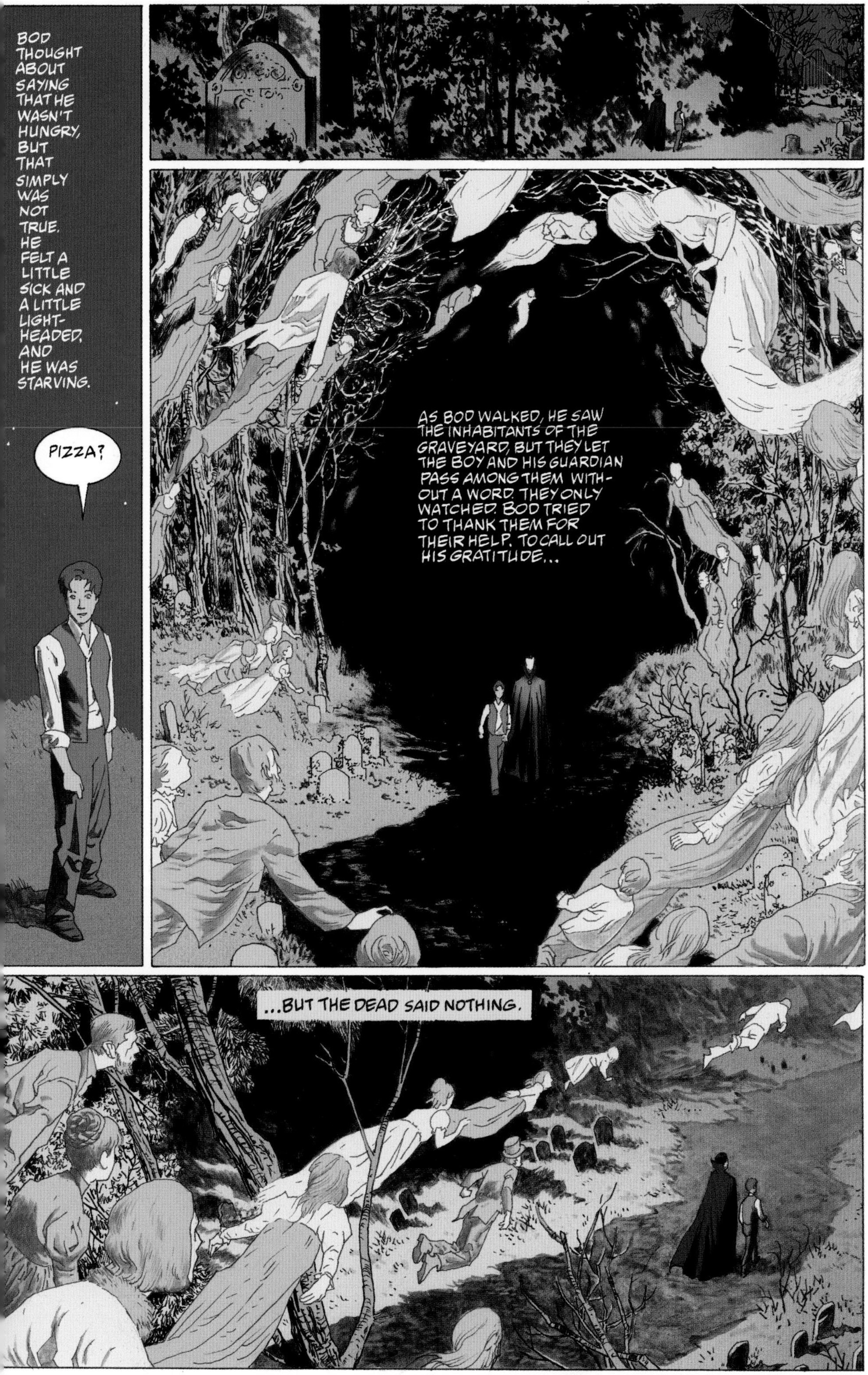
BOD THOUGHT ABOUT SAYING THAT HE WASN'T HUNGRY, BUT THAT SIMPLY WAS NOT TRUE. HE FELT A LITTLE SICK AND A LITTLE LIGHT-HEADED, AND HE WAS STARVING.
PIZZA?
AS BOD WALKED, HE SAW THE INHABITANTS OF THE GRAVEYARD, BUT THEY LET THE BOY AND HIS GUARDIAN PASS AMONG THEM WITH-OUT A WORD. THEY ONLY WATCHED. BOD TRIED TO THANK THEM FOR THEIR HELP, TO CALL OUT HIS GRATITUDE...
...BUT THE DEAD SAID NOTHING.

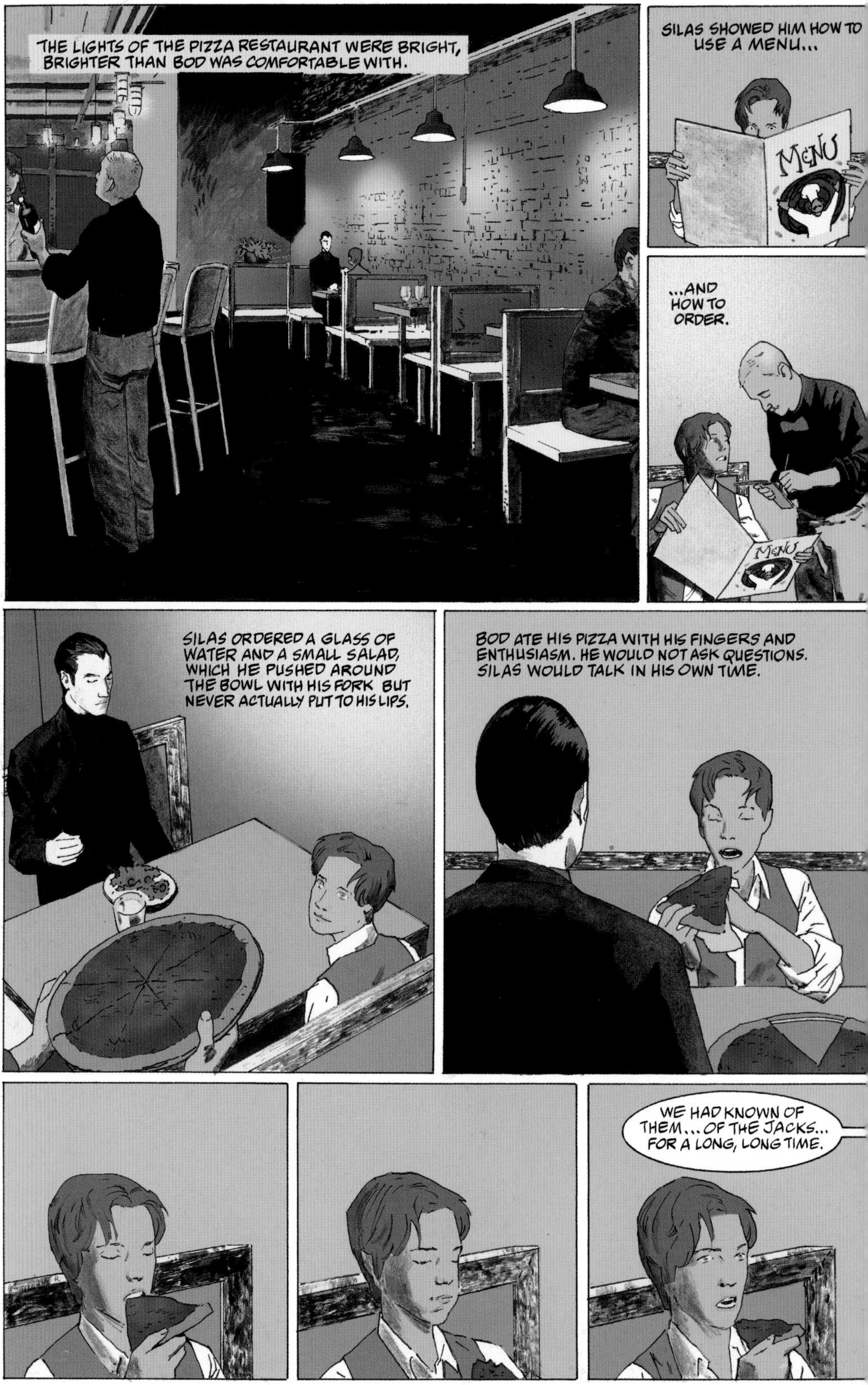
THE LIGHTS OF THE PIZZA RESTAURANT WERE BRIGHT, BRIGHTER THAN BOD WAS COMFORTABLE WITH.
SILAS SHOWED HIM HOW TO USE A MENU...
MENU
...AND HOW TO ORDER.
MENU
SILAS ORDERED A GLASS OF WATER AND A SMALL SALAD, WHICH HE PUSHED AROUND THE BOWL WITH HIS FORK BUT NEVER ACTUALLY PUT TO HIS LIPS.
BOD ATE HIS PIZZA WITH HIS FINGERS AND ENTHUSIASM. HE WOULD NOT ASK QUESTIONS. SILAS WOULD TALK IN HIS OWN TIME.
WE HAD KNOWN OF THEM... OF THE JACKS... FOR A LONG, LONG TIME.

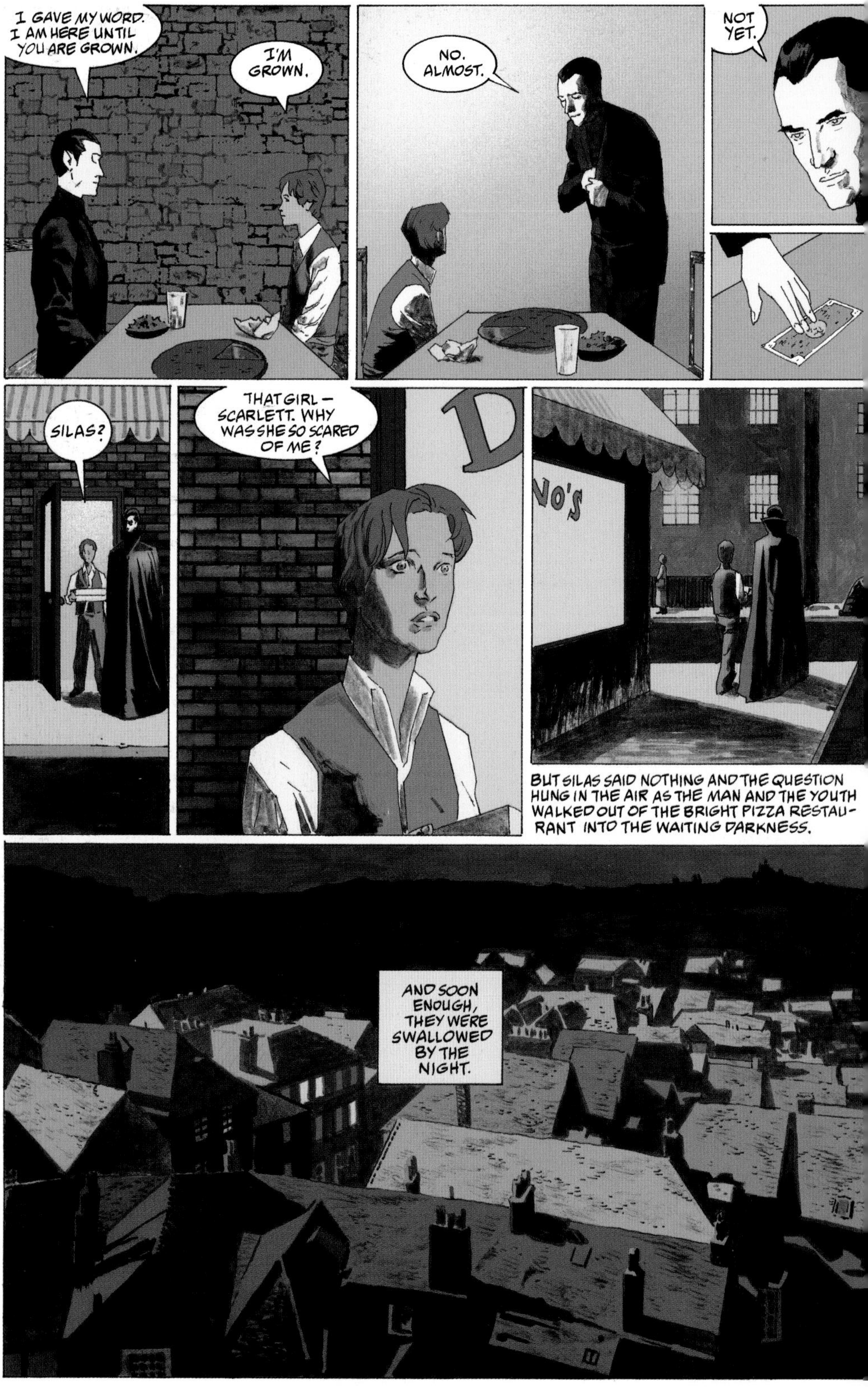
I GAVE MY WORD. I AM HERE UNTIL YOU ARE GROWN.
I'M GROWN.
NO. ALMOST.
NOT YET.
SILAS?
THAT GIRL — SCARLETT. WHY WAS SHE SO SCARED OF ME?
NO'S
BUT SILAS SAID NOTHING AND THE QUESTION HUNG IN THE AIR AS THE MAN AND THE YOUTH WALKED OUT OF THE BRIGHT PIZZA RESTAU-RANT INTO THE WAITING DARKNESS.
AND SOON ENOUGH, THEY WERE SWALLOWED BY THE NIGHT.

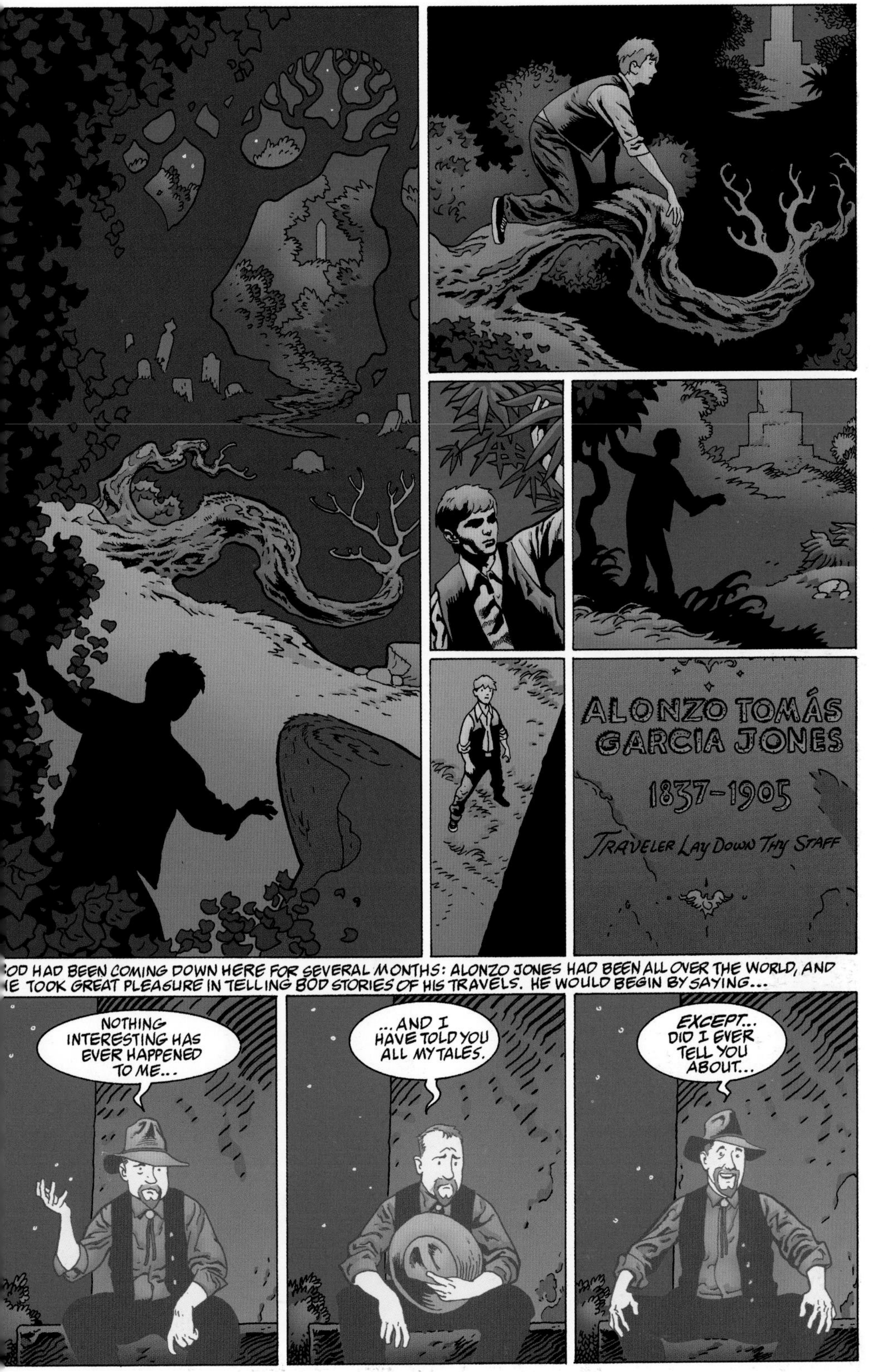
ALONZO TOMÁS GARCIA JONES
1837–1905
TRAVELER LAY DOWN THY STAFF
OD HAD BEEN COMING DOWN HERE FOR SEVERAL MONTHS: ALONZO JONES HAD BEEN ALL OVER THE WORLD, AND
E TOOK GREAT PLEASURE IN TELLING BOD STORIES OF HIS TRAVELS. HE WOULD BEGIN BY SAYING...
NOTHING INTERESTING HAS EVER HAPPENED TO ME...
...AND I HAVE TOLD YOU ALL MY TALES.
EXCEPT... DID I EVER TELL YOU ABOUT...

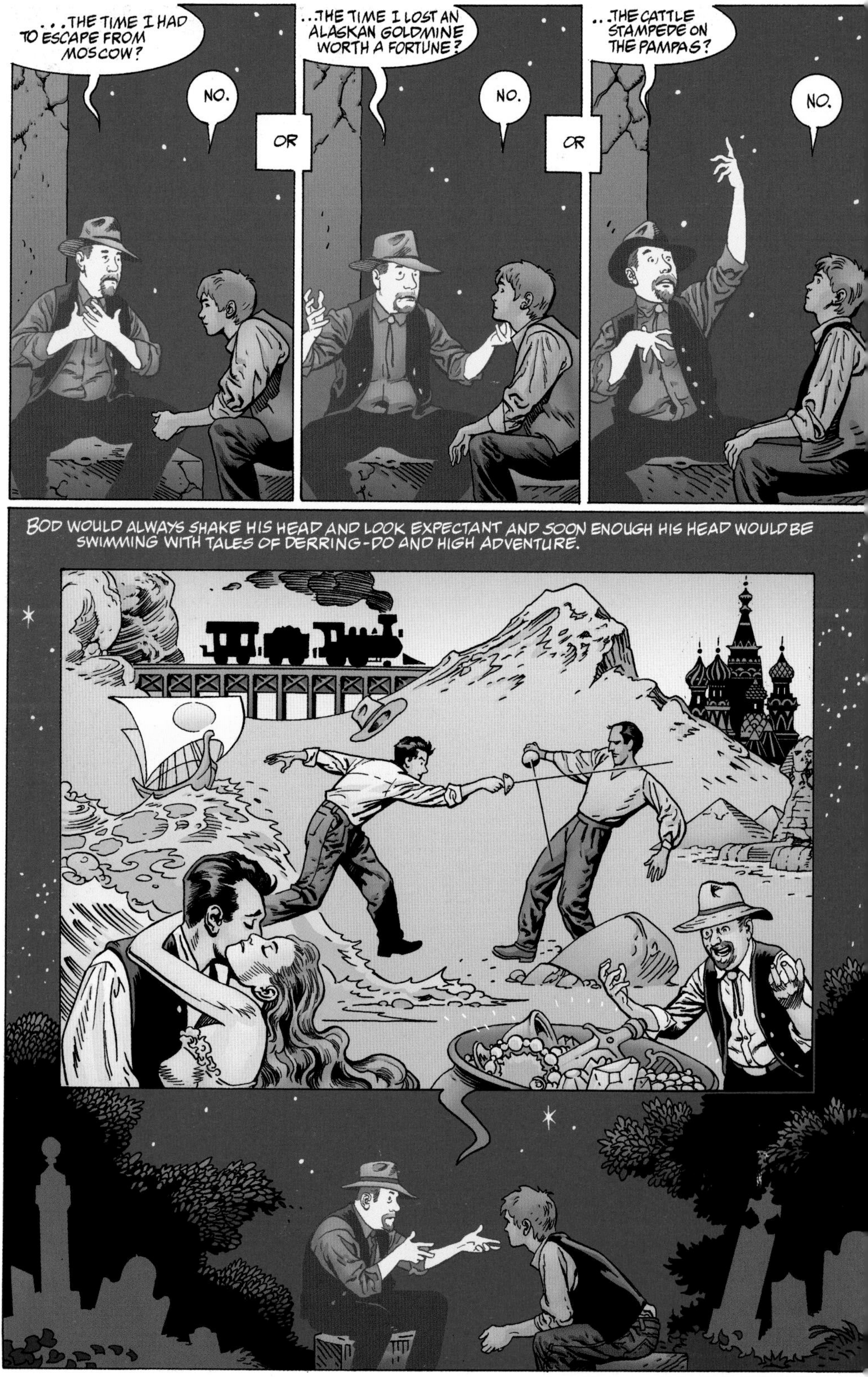
. . . THE TIME I HAD TO ESCAPE FROM MOSCOW?
NO.
OR
...THE TIME I LOST AN ALASKAN GOLDMINE WORTH A FORTUNE?
NO.
OR
. . .THE CATTLE STAMPEDE ON THE PAMPAS?
NO.
BOD WOULD ALWAYS SHAKE HIS HEAD AND LOOK EXPECTANT AND SOON ENOUGH HIS HEAD WOULD BE SWIMMING WITH TALES OF DERRING-DO AND HIGH ADVENTURE.

... 149 ...

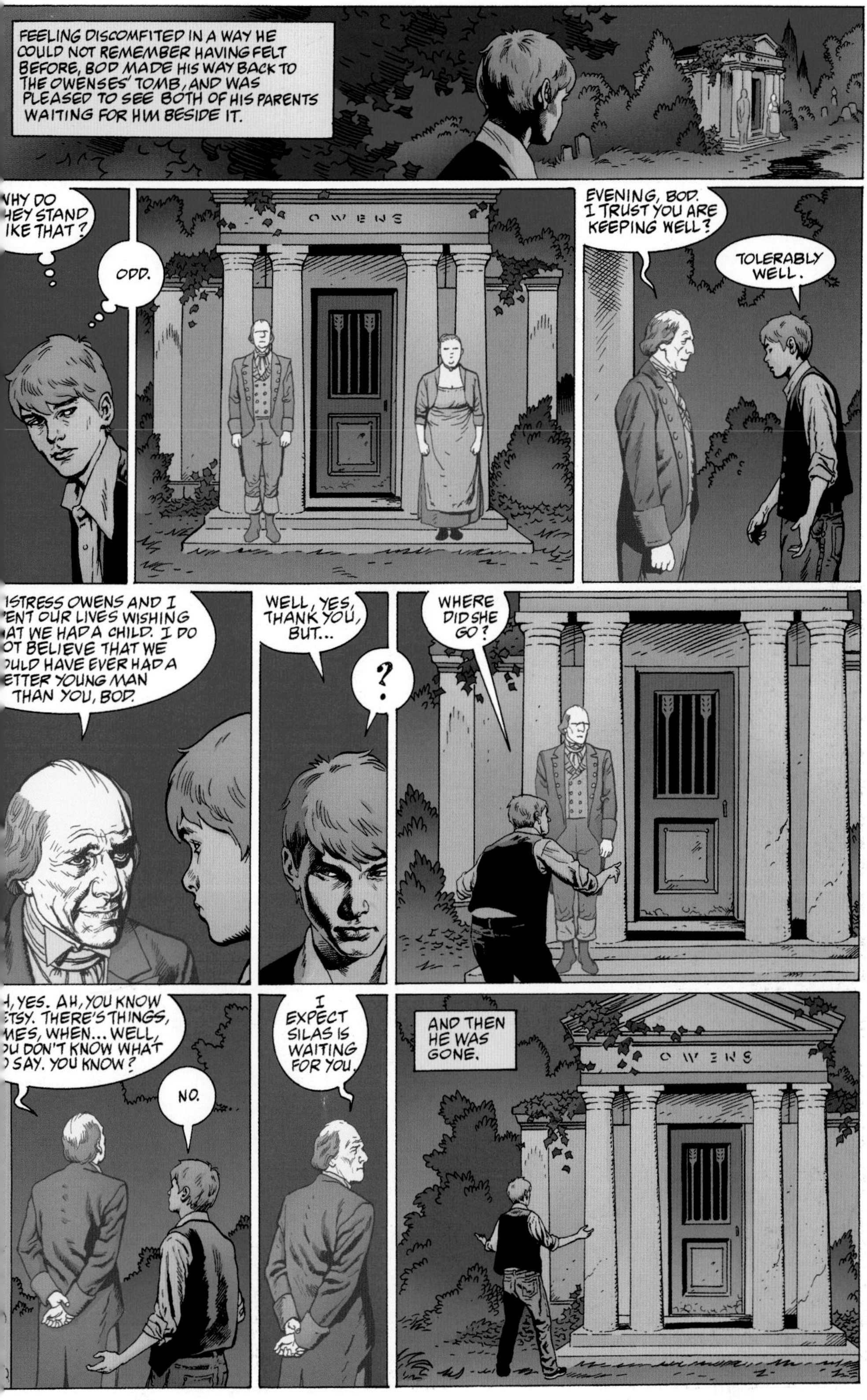
FEELING DISCOMFITED IN A WAY HE COULD NOT REMEMBER HAVING FELT BEFORE, BOD MADE HIS WAY BACK TO THE OWENSES' TOMB, AND WAS PLEASED TO SEE BOTH OF HIS PARENTS WAITING FOR HIM BESIDE IT.
VHY DO HEY STAND IKE THAT?
ODD.
OWENS
EVENING, BOD. I TRUST YOU ARE KEEPING WELL?
TOLERABLY WELL.
ISTRESS OWENS AND I PENT OUR LIVES WISHING AT WE HAD A CHILD. I DO OT BELIEVE THAT WE OULD HAVE EVER HAD A ETTER YOUNG MAN THAN YOU, BOD.
WELL, YES, THANK YOU, BUT...
?
WHERE DID SHE GO?
H, YES. AH, YOU KNOW ETSY. THERE'S THINGS, MES, WHEN... WELL, OU DON'T KNOW WHAT O SAY. YOU KNOW?
NO.
I EXPECT SILAS IS WAITING FOR YOU.
AND THEN HE WAS GONE.
OWENS

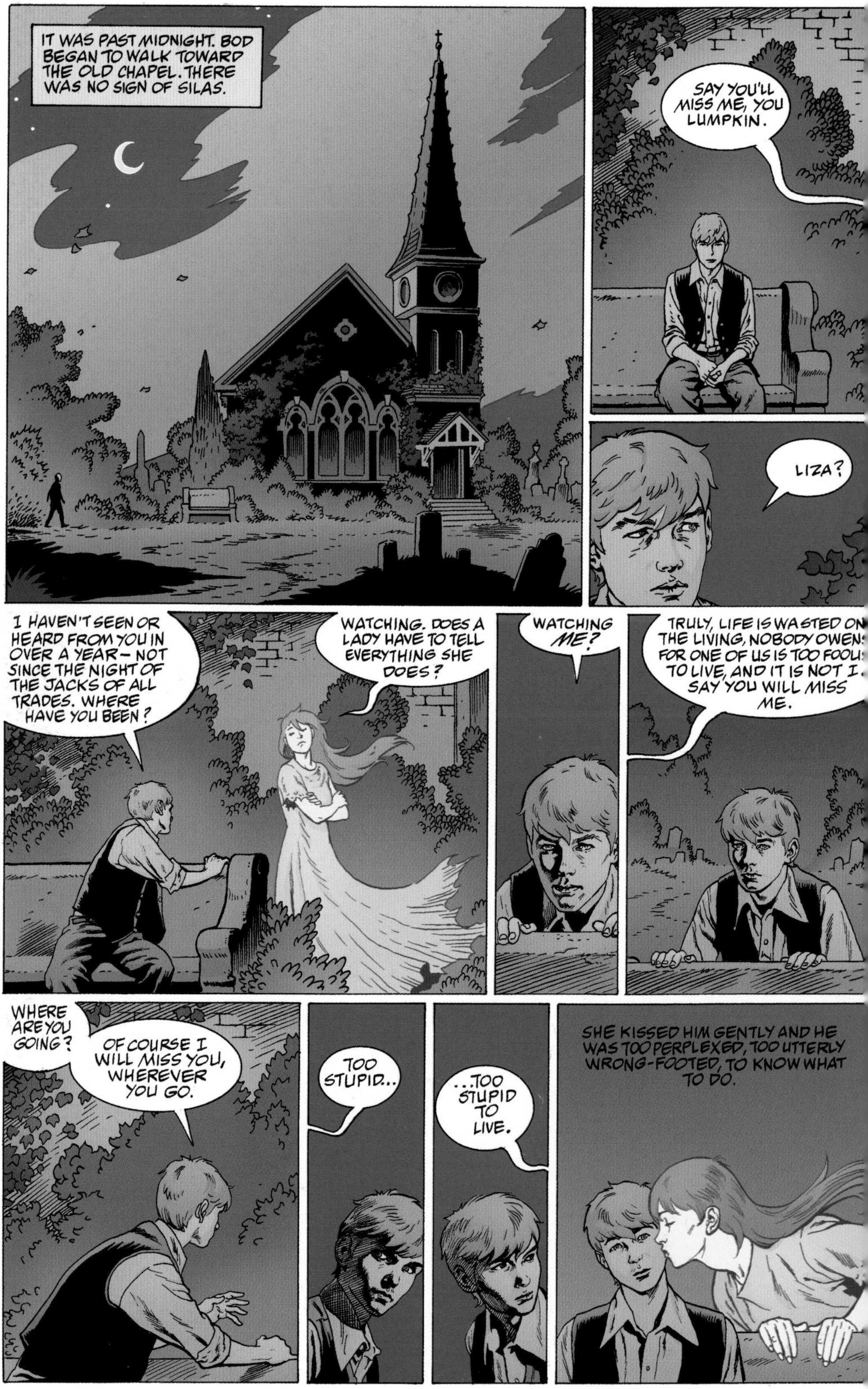
IT WAS PAST MIDNIGHT. BOD BEGAN TO WALK TOWARD THE OLD CHAPEL. THERE WAS NO SIGN OF SILAS.
SAY YOU'LL MISS ME, YOU LUMPKIN.
LIZA?
I HAVEN'T SEEN OR HEARD FROM YOU IN OVER A YEAR—NOT SINCE THE NIGHT OF THE JACKS OF ALL TRADES. WHERE HAVE YOU BEEN?
WATCHING. DOES A LADY HAVE TO TELL EVERYTHING SHE DOES?
WATCHING *ME*?
TRULY, LIFE IS WASTED ON THE LIVING, NOBODY OWENS. FOR ONE OF US IS TOO FOOLISH TO LIVE, AND IT IS NOT I. SAY YOU WILL MISS ME.
WHERE ARE YOU GOING?
OF COURSE I WILL MISS YOU, WHEREVER YOU GO.
TOO STUPID...
...TOO STUPID TO LIVE.
SHE KISSED HIM GENTLY AND HE WAS TOO PERPLEXED, TOO UTTERLY WRONG-FOOTED, TO KNOW WHAT TO DO.

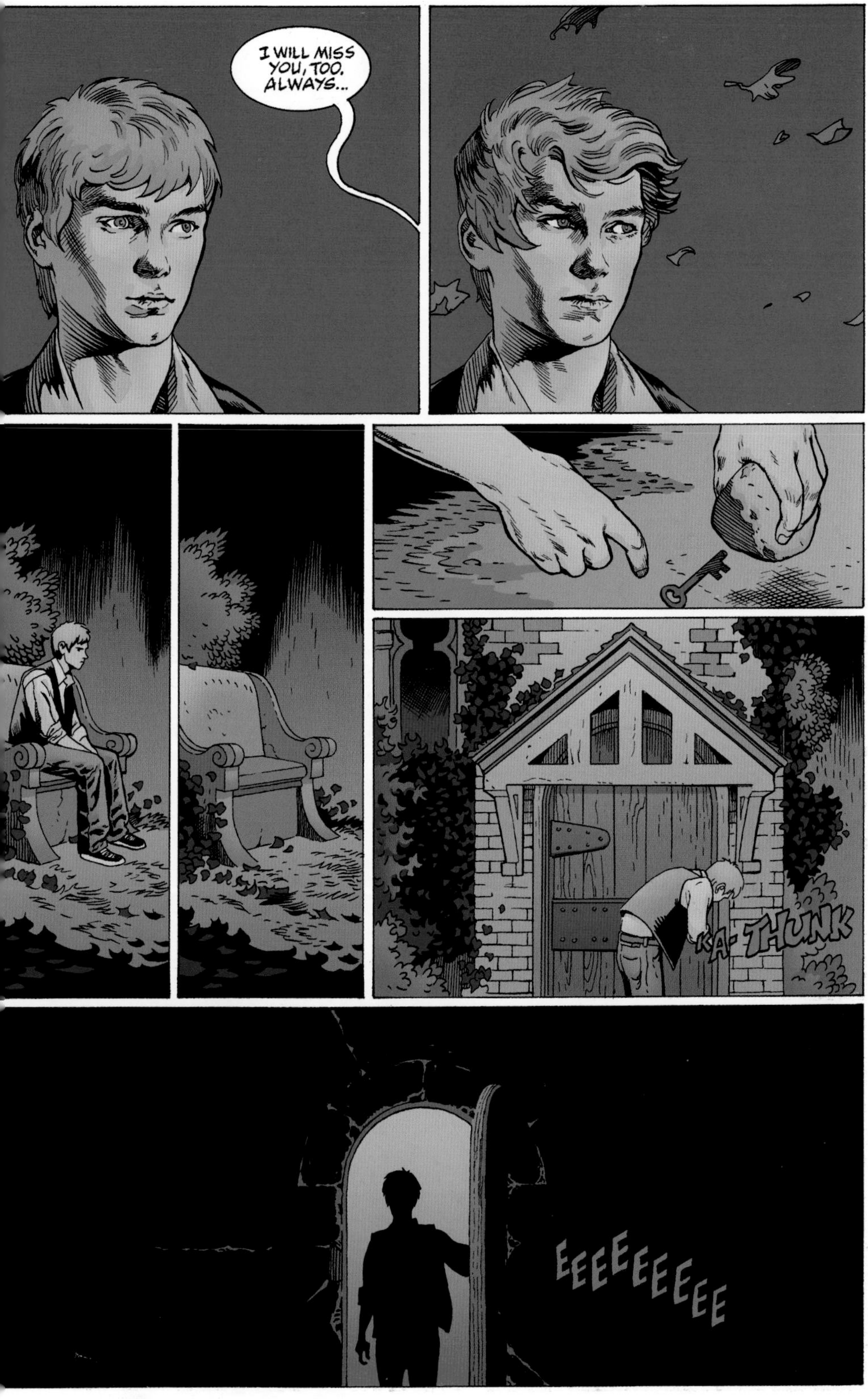
I WILL MISS YOU, TOO. ALWAYS...
KA-THUNK
EEEEEEEEE

... 154 ...

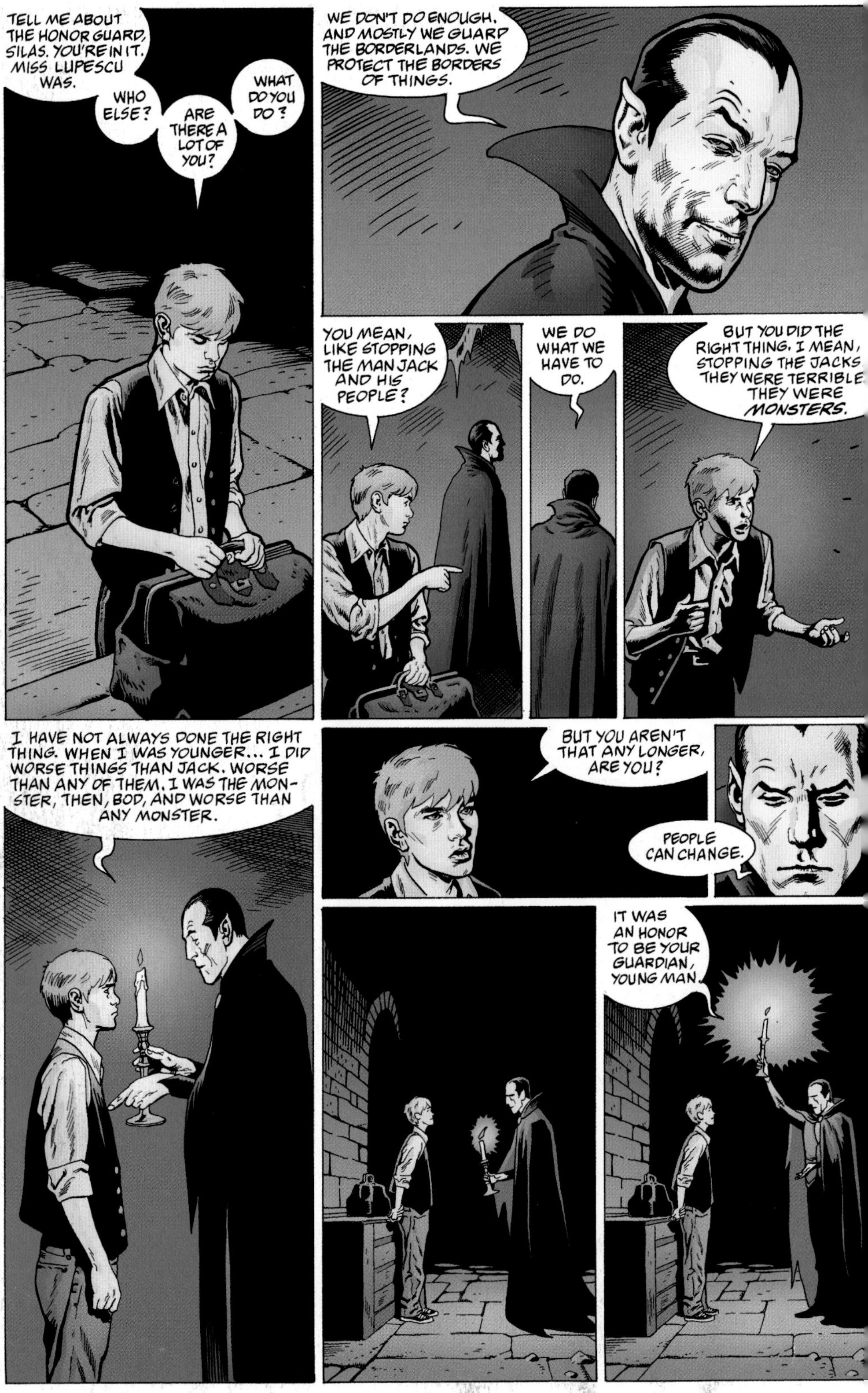
TELL ME ABOUT THE HONOR GUARD, SILAS. YOU'RE IN IT. MISS LUPESCU WAS.
WHO ELSE?
ARE THERE A LOT OF YOU?
WHAT DO YOU DO?
WE DON'T DO ENOUGH, AND MOSTLY WE GUARD THE BORDERLANDS. WE PROTECT THE BORDERS OF THINGS.
YOU MEAN, LIKE STOPPING THE MAN JACK AND HIS PEOPLE?
WE DO WHAT WE HAVE TO DO.
BUT YOU DID THE RIGHT THING. I MEAN, STOPPING THE JACKS THEY WERE TERRIBLE THEY WERE MONSTERS.
I HAVE NOT ALWAYS DONE THE RIGHT THING. WHEN I WAS YOUNGER... I DID WORSE THINGS THAN JACK. WORSE THAN ANY OF THEM. I WAS THE MONSTER, THEN, BOD, AND WORSE THAN ANY MONSTER.
BUT YOU AREN'T THAT ANY LONGER, ARE YOU?
PEOPLE CAN CHANGE.
IT WAS AN HONOR TO BE YOUR GUARDIAN, YOUNG MAN.

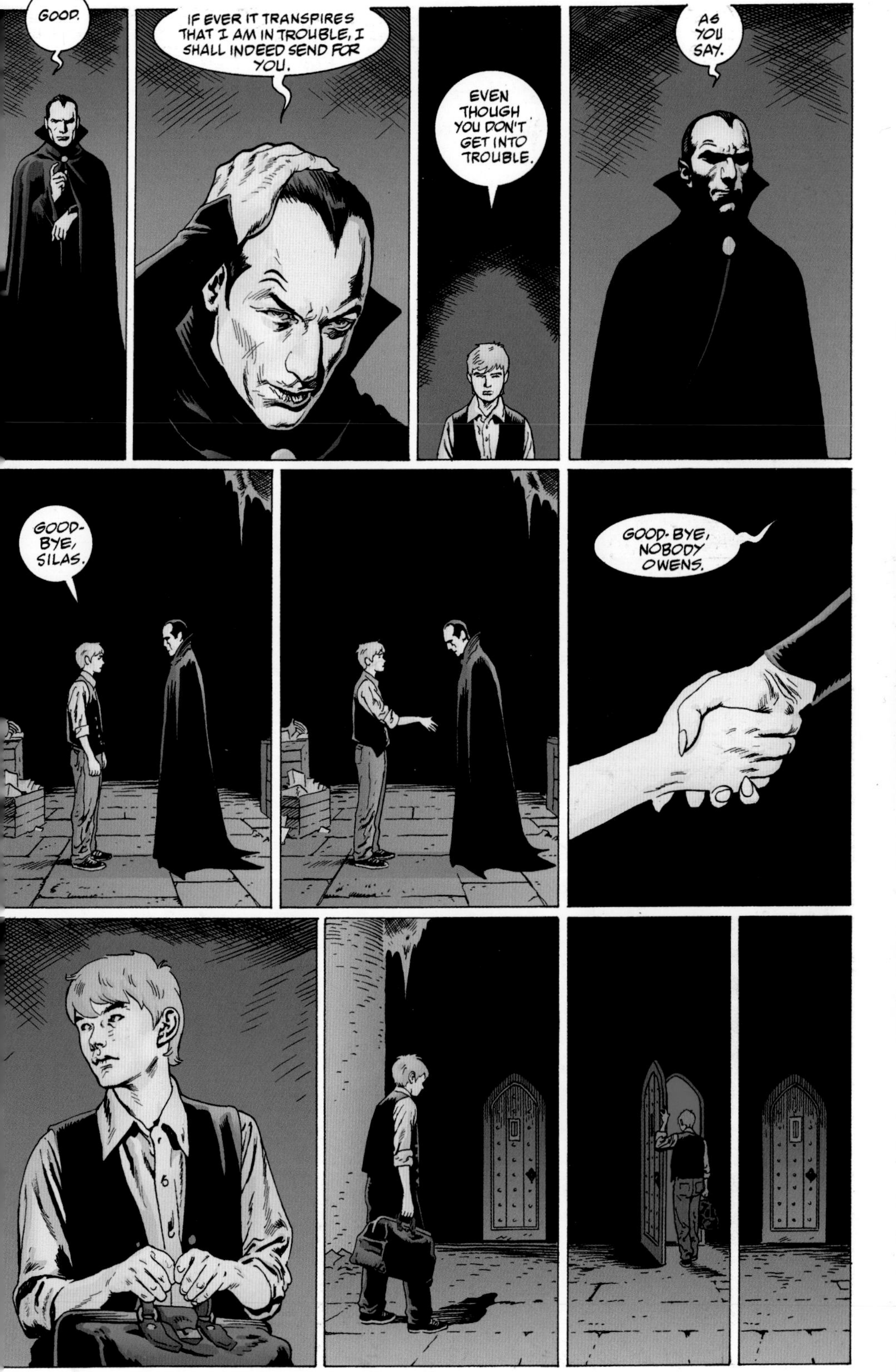
GOOD.
IF EVER IT TRANSPIRES THAT I AM IN TROUBLE, I SHALL INDEED SEND FOR YOU.
EVEN THOUGH YOU DON'T GET INTO TROUBLE.
AS YOU SAY.
GOOD-BYE, SILAS.
GOOD-BYE, NOBODY OWENS.

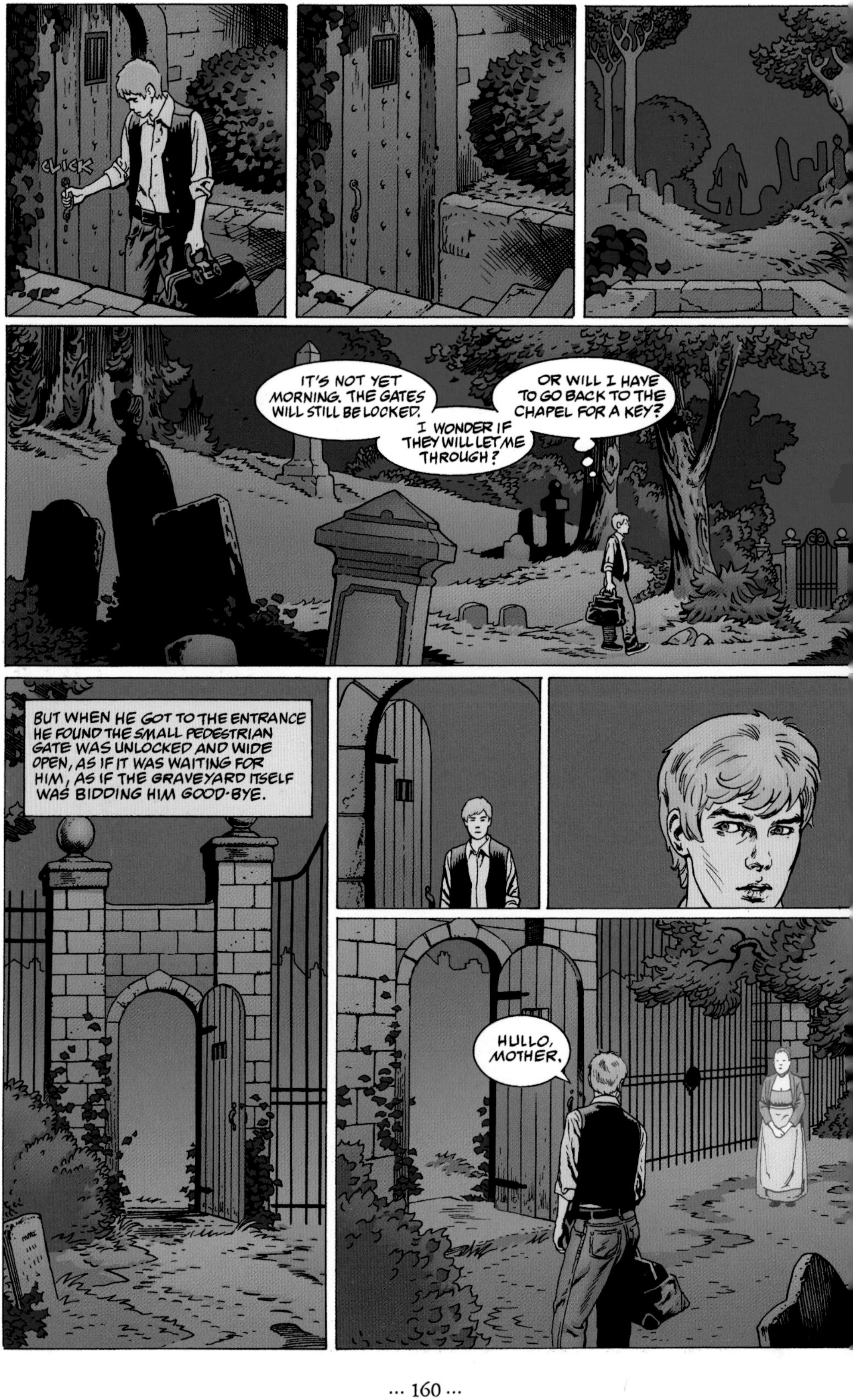
CLICK
IT'S NOT YET MORNING. THE GATES WILL STILL BE LOCKED.
I WONDER IF THEY WILL LET ME THROUGH?
OR WILL I HAVE TO GO BACK TO THE CHAPEL FOR A KEY?
BUT WHEN HE GOT TO THE ENTRANCE HE FOUND THE SMALL PEDESTRIAN GATE WAS UNLOCKED AND WIDE OPEN, AS IF IT WAS WAITING FOR HIM, AS IF THE GRAVEYARD ITSELF WAS BIDDING HIM GOOD-BYE.
HULLO, MOTHER.

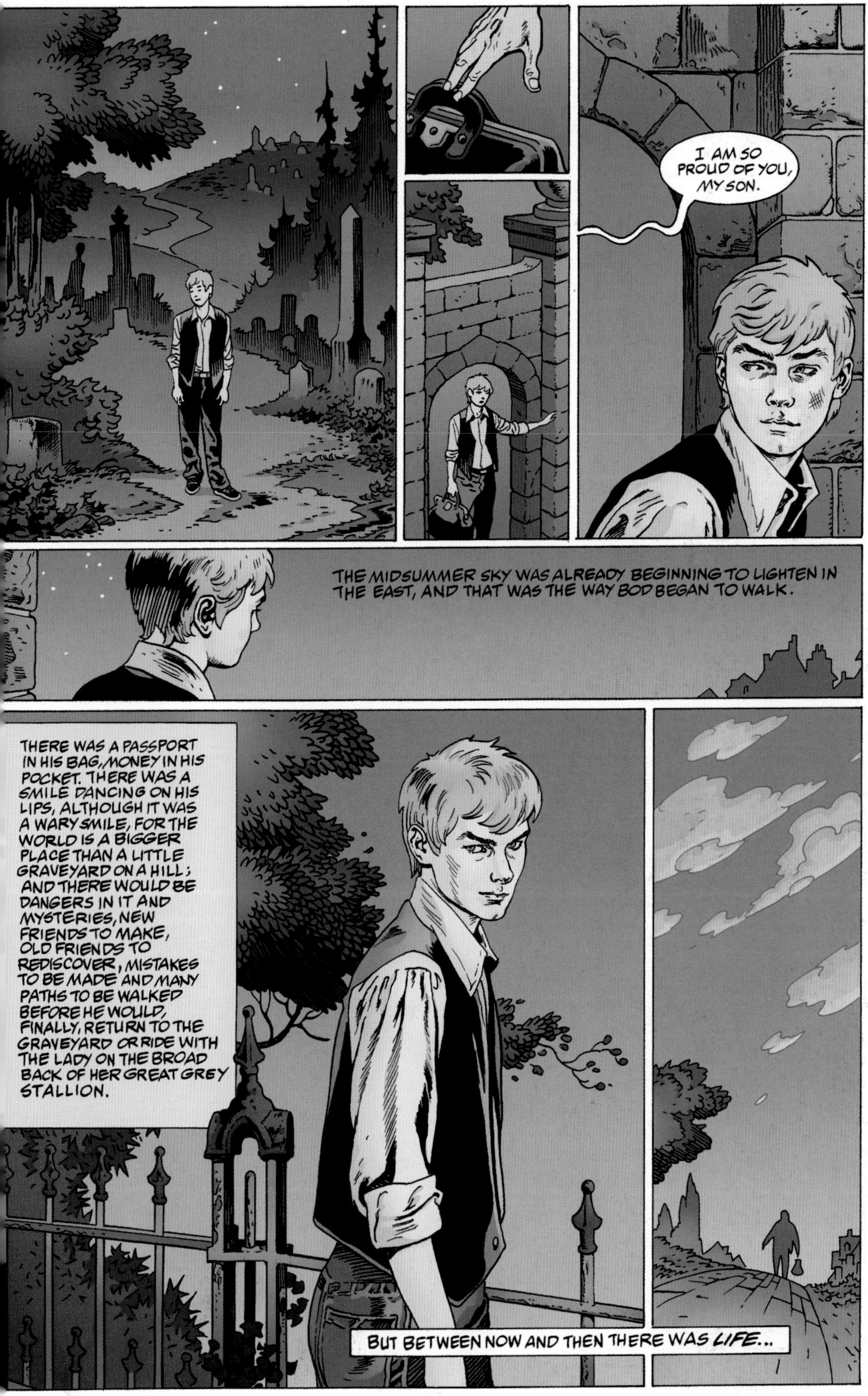
I AM SO PROUD OF YOU, MY SON.
THE MIDSUMMER SKY WAS ALREADY BEGINNING TO LIGHTEN IN THE EAST, AND THAT WAS THE WAY BOD BEGAN TO WALK.
THERE WAS A PASSPORT IN HIS BAG, MONEY IN HIS POCKET. THERE WAS A SMILE DANCING ON HIS LIPS, ALTHOUGH IT WAS A WARY SMILE, FOR THE WORLD IS A BIGGER PLACE THAN A LITTLE GRAVEYARD ON A HILL; AND THERE WOULD BE DANGERS IN IT AND MYSTERIES, NEW FRIENDS TO MAKE, OLD FRIENDS TO REDISCOVER, MISTAKES TO BE MADE AND MANY PATHS TO BE WALKED BEFORE HE WOULD, FINALLY, RETURN TO THE GRAVEYARD OR RIDE WITH THE LADY ON THE BROAD BACK OF HER GREAT GREY STALLION.
BUT BETWEEN NOW AND THEN THERE WAS *LIFE*...

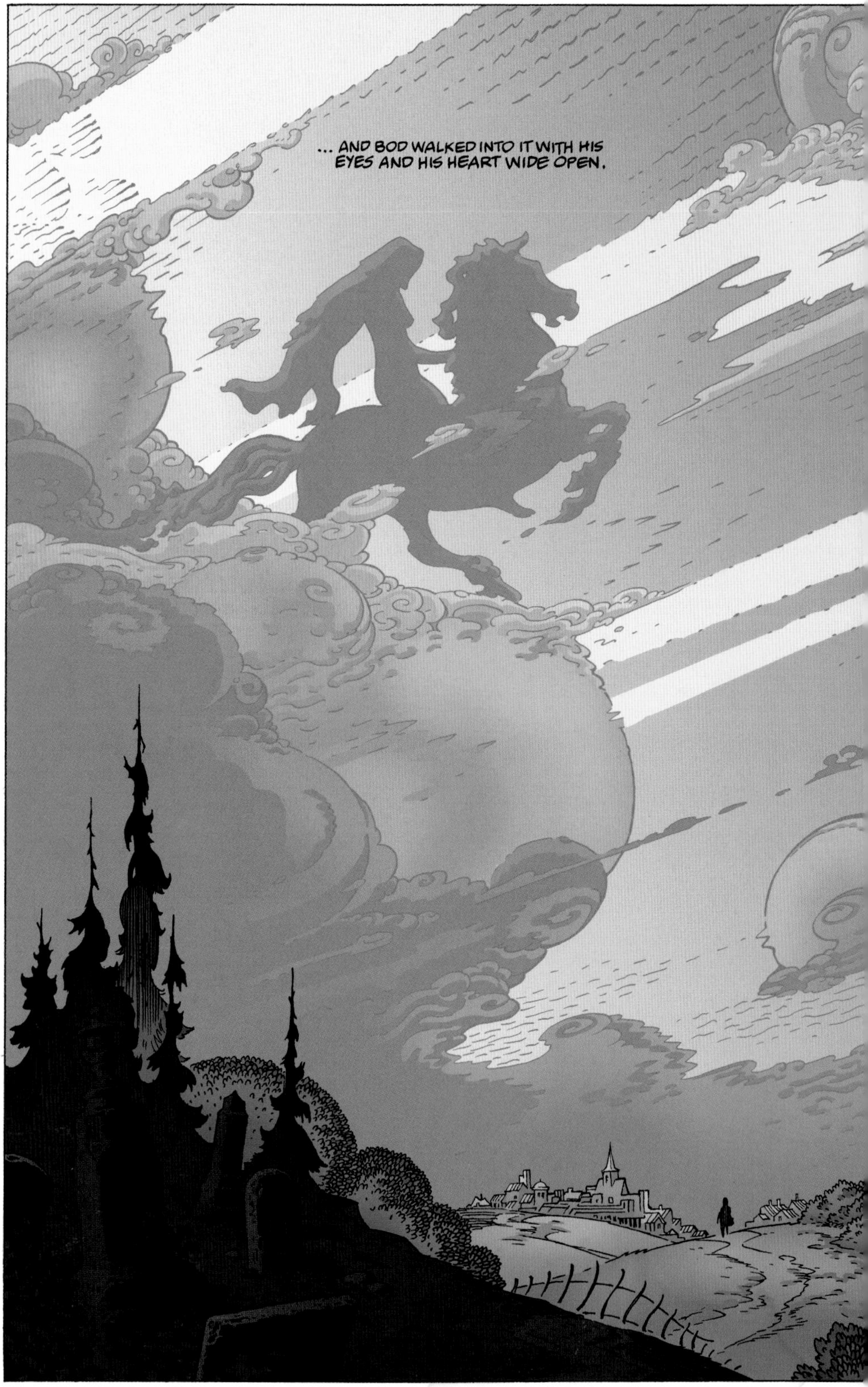
... AND BOD WALKED INTO IT WITH HIS EYES AND HIS HEART WIDE OPEN.

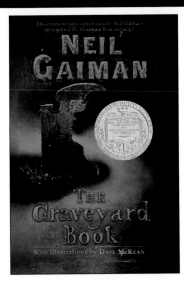
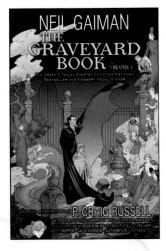
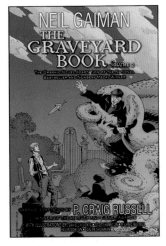

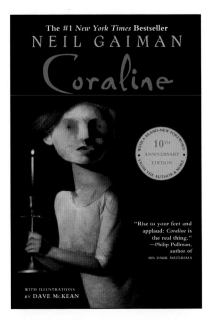
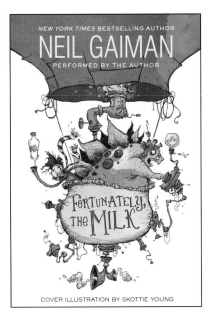
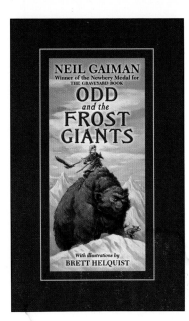